THE
STONE
MAIDEN

THE
STONE
MAIDEN

Velda Johnston

DODD, MEAD & COMPANY
New York

To Dolores Mulvihill Zebrowski

THE
STONE
MAIDEN

1

In the afternoon silence the sound of Katherine Derwith's footsteps over the cracked sidewalk echoed between the buildings. Ahead of her the street lay empty under the unusually warm November sun. Grass, still green, actually grew through the broken concrete, and what looked like a young maple tree, still holding its autumn-yellow leaves, grew from the roof of one of the empty warehouses lining the street's right-hand side.

Strange that these almost deserted streets were a part, not of some long-abandoned midwestern town, but of the borough of Manhattan. It was so strange that she wondered why curiosity did not draw more people to this now-desolate area near the Hudson River.

In her case, of course, it was far more than curiosity which had prompted her repeated visits during the past few years. These all-but-deserted streets were where her own personal history had begun.

Oh, not actually. She had no idea where she had drawn her first breaths. All she knew was that when she was about three months old, the police had found her lying in a shadowy corner of a Tenth Avenue warehouse.

On that summer night twenty-eight years ago, of course, this street could not have lain entirely silent and deserted, not even in the hours past midnight. Men's voices and the rumble of hand trucks must have sounded from at least some of the warehouses. Perhaps in that diner she had passed a minute or so ago, now a windowless ruin surrounded by weeds, longshoremen and roustabouts had sat at the long counter. At least an occasional taxi or private car must have moved along the street, perhaps some of them carrying people to passenger ships tied up at Hudson River piers.

Now, on this afternoon almost three decades later, she had reached the first of a row of boarded-up warehouses. She stopped, hands thrust into the pockets of the light denim jacket she wore over blue jeans and a navy-blue turtleneck. Was this the one? Those old newspaper accounts she had read said that the warehouse had been the property of Selman and Sons. But even ten years ago, when she first started wandering through this district every now and then, the painted signs above the doorways of many buildings had been boarded over or weathered to illegibility. Of the signs still visible, none had been that of Selman and Sons.

And anyway, she thought, weighed by a familiar sense of desolation, it did not matter which building it had been. What mattered was that she had been so little valued, perhaps so downright burdensome, that she had been abandoned.

But not entirely abandoned. There had been the man who called the police that night, a man who had a foreign accent, according to those old newspaper accounts, and who sounded young. He had cared something about her, at least enough to make a phone call. From where? That phone booth across the street, with one of its glass sides shattered and its phone torn out? Perhaps, if there had been public phone booths on the streets in this area twenty-eight years ago. She had no idea whether or not there had been.

She walked on, and then paused again before a low building sandwiched in between two warehouses. Letters of rusting metal above the door read, "DA NY'S LIQ OR ST E." Its wide front window had been smashed, revealing an interior gutted even of its shelves. One large glass fragment still stuck to the window frame, though. In it she could see, not only the dim reflection of her tall, slender self, but, at least a half mile beyond the weeds and dilapidated buildings on the street's opposite side, the Empire State Building soaring against the blue sky.

Had he been her father, that young man with the foreign accent? More than likely. Was he still alive? Who *am* I, she thought, feeling a familiar depression. What am I?

She hesitated a moment, and then moved closer to her own image in the glass fragment. Dark red hair, cut fairly short, and shaped to her head like a smooth cap. Gray eyes, aquiline nose, soft, full mouth contradicted by a firm chin. Features pleasant enough, but not remarkable, and offering no clue as to whether her ancestry had been chiefly German or Scandinavian or French or something else.

But that really did not matter, the two people who had raised her said—those two beloved people who, as long as she could remember, had lavished upon her their tenderness and care and considerable income.

The Derwiths had not always been well off. During Katherine's infancy they had lived in a house she could not remember, a modest one in Massapequa, Long Island. Ed Derwith had been employed as a chemist by a small paint manufacturing company in Brooklyn. Then he had developed a formula for a new kind of automobile paint, one of superior durability and brilliance. Even though he'd had to share the profits with the paint company, he rapidly became well-to-do. The Derwiths had moved to the pleasant Westchester town of Bellmont. Katherine had been enrolled in private schools from kindergarten on. Until her mid-teens she'd had no idea that Ed and Clara Derwith were not her natural parents.

When she was eleven something happened that might have made her guess the truth, had she been a little older. One Saturday morning an uninvited visitor, a Mrs. Mason or Miller or something like that, had rung the Derwiths' bell. As she sat in the living room the woman had said, with a bright, I'm-only-joking smile, "Since you're too high-toned these days to ever visit your old friends in Massapequa, I thought I'd come look you up."

Clara Derwith had murmured something about being awfully busy. Katherine, sitting in an armchair in the corner with a Nancy Drew mystery in her lap, sensed that her mother was not only embarrassed. She was uneasy, even frightened.

A few minutes later Mrs. Mason—or Miller—smiled at Katherine and said, "You're certainly a pretty girl, aren't you? And so lucky! Have your mother and father given you any idea of how lucky—"

"Katherine!" Clara Derwith had shot to her feet. "It's time for you to go upstairs and do your homework."

"Homework! I've got all weekend to—"

"Now, Katherine! I know how it will be. You'll leave it all until after dinner Sunday night."

Resentfully Katherine had climbed the stairs. For a moment or two she thought of slipping down again to try to learn whatever it was her mother did not want her to hear. Then she remembered that there was a good program on TV, a Saturday special about the Beatles. She switched on the small set that had been one of her Christmas presents. By the time the program was over the Massapequa woman had left. Katherine forgot all about her.

Thus the truth, when the Derwiths finally told it to her, came as a devastating shock.

It happened the day after her sixteenth birthday. Smiling, but with a terror of hurting her, even losing her, in his eyes, Ed Derwith had said, "We were so lucky to get you, Katy. As soon as it was in the papers—about the police finding a girl baby, I mean—there were lots of people wanting you."

Seated beside her husband on the living room love seat, Clara Derwith said, "Maybe the adoption people chose us because they could tell how much love we had to give you." The china blue eyes in her round face were bright with that same pleading fear. "And you do know how much we love you, don't you?"

Still too numb to feel anything much, Katherine forced herself to say, "Of course, Mother. Of course, Dad. I've always known you loved me."

"We could have taken a chance," Ed Derwith went on, "and not told you the truth. After all, your adoption papers were sealed. Perhaps you might never have known anything about it. But there was always the chance that someone might tell you, someone who knew you as a baby when we all three lived in Massapequa. And then you might feel that we had deceived you just for our own sakes, and you might—turn against us."

"So we promised each other," Clara said, "that we would tell you as soon as you were old enough, as soon as we could feel fairly sure that it—it wouldn't make a lot of difference to you. And it doesn't, does it?"

That terror in her mother's eyes. "No," Katherine said.

"Of course it doesn't!" Clara said rapidly. "You're the same Katherine Derwith you were yesterday. And we're so proud of you, aren't we, Dad? How could we help but be? You're among the best in your class, and as popular as any girl could want to be—"

Katherine said, "Is it okay if I go up to my room?" Then quickly, to take that look off their faces, "It's all right. I just want to be alone for a while."

It wasn't all right, of course. Nor was she the "same Katherine Derwith" she had been yesterday. That Katherine had been a more-or-less-average teenager with a more-or-less-average relationship—sometimes stormy, but on the whole loving and warm—with the two she believed to be her biological parents. This Katherine was an X. "Solve for X," the problems in her algebra text said, and usually she could, because there were known factors to work with. But here all the factors were Xs. The man who called the police, the Derwiths said, had hung up without giving his name. There had been no note left in the wicker basket—

She had walked across the living room and then turned in the doorway. "You're sure there wasn't anything at all to tell who I was?"

The Derwiths had given up trying to smile. "There was nothing," Ed answered in a tired voice. "There were no laundry marks on your diaper or your socks, which was all you had on, or on the blanket in the basket. And the basket itself was the kind you could buy in any hardware store."

Katherine had gone upstairs. In her room she lay down on the bed and looked at her blue-and-gold cheerleader's pompons, their crossed handles bracketed to the walls. Yes, she thought, with a strange detachment, it was true, what her mother had said about her being a high achiever—good in her classes, and at sports, and with many friends of both sexes. But now it seemed to her that being the Derwiths' fortunate daughter was just a role she played, one that she had no right to.

My real parents could have been anything, she thought. Criminals, crazy people. Certainly there must have been something terribly wrong with them, to make them practically throw me away.

And what about things like hemophilia? What if she was a carrier? In biology class she had learned that females passed along hemophilia, even though only male children suffered from the disease.

Kids, she thought. She would never dare to have kids.

Clenching her hands until her nails bit into her palms, she tried to fight off a black despair. Why, maybe she wouldn't even want kids. And anyway, perhaps in a few years they'd find a way to check a person out, so they'd know ahead of time whether you were apt to have hemophilic kids, or schizophrenics, or anything like that.

She became aware that under her shock and disorientation she felt a bitterness toward those two gentle people she had loved for as long as she could remember. After a moment she identified the reason for it. She wished they hadn't told her, so that she could have gone on being the same Katherine Millicent Derwith.

But that was both unjust and unreasonable. Always there *had* been a chance that she would learn about her adoption from someone else, someone who, like that Mrs. Mason or Miller who had shown up five years before, did not wish the Derwiths well. Thinking of the Massapequa woman, Katherine realized the suspense in which her parents must have lived all these years, waiting for the time when, in their judgment, she would be able to withstand the shock of learning the truth. Well, she owed it to them to make them feel that their judgment had been correct. She would go down to them now, and tell them how glad she was that it was they who had raised her rather than any other couple, even whatever pair it was who had been her natural parents.

For the next two years she had tried to make the Derwiths feel that there had been no change in her. She continued to make good grades, and to date some of the "smoothest" boys at St. Alban's, the co-educational preparatory school she attended. She swam and played tennis at the country club which the Derwiths, sponsored by the parents of Katherine's best friend, recently had joined. But almost as soon as she moved to Manhattan to share a room with two other freshmen girls in a Barnard College dorm, she had gone down to the *Daily News* and looked through its microfilmed back files.

The newspaper account, when she found it, told her no more than the Derwiths had. The police on that long-ago July night, alerted by an anonymous phone call, had gone to Selman and Sons warehouse and found a female infant of about three months. Neither her clothing nor the wicker basket in which she lay offered any clue to her identity.

A follow-up story the next day said that the child had been taken to the Gotham Foundling Home. It also stated that the police had received "scores" of calls about the child from would-be adoptive parents. After that, apparently, the story no longer had been considered news, because later editions of the paper had made no mention of it.

Katherine had been enrolled at Barnard only a week when, on

Saturday morning, she had gone for the first time down to the warehouse district mentioned in the old newspaper story. Even then the area had been deteriorating, with many of the warehouses closed. Mingled with the workmen who moved along the sidewalks were derelicts of both sexes and last-of-the-flower-children types from old tenements on the side streets—bearded young men, and girls with long straight hair, ankle-length skirts, and dirty feet in flat-soled sandals. Even though Katherine had dressed as inconspicuously as she could, in a raincoat and with a scarf tied beneath her chin, it seemed to her that people looked at her curiously, as if wondering what she was doing in this neighborhood. But that, she realized, was probably just her imagination, stimulated by her own consciousness of what had brought her here.

She had walked for several blocks, scrutinizing the façades of boarded-up warehouses, and looking through wide doorways into the shadowy interior of those still in use. At last she had stopped at a corner stand and ordered a soft drink.

"Do you know where Selman and Sons Warehouse is?"

"Selman, Selman." The man behind the counter shook his bald head. "No, I never heard of that one. Maybe it's one of those that've been boarded up these past few years. I wouldn't know. I've worked here only eight months."

Over the next few years Katherine every now and then visited the warehouse area, finding it each time emptier and more decayed. Those were the years during which she had a few not-too-important love affairs, and finished college, and went to work, first as a manuscript reader for a series of magazines, and then as a sort of woman-of-all-work for *The Eastside Courier,* one of New York's many neighborhood weeklies.

She liked the newspaper job better than any she had ever had. Busy with work, and men and women friends, and frequent visits home to Westchester, she for a period no longer felt a need to wander through that area close to the Hudson River. In fact, days and even weeks might pass without her giving a thought to that child in the wicker basket. True, she often woke with a confused memory of a dream in which she hurried along a dark street in pursuit of a couple who were very important to her, a couple who would not turn around in answer to her calls, and who, whenever she got close to them, would vanish around a corner or inside a doorway. But always by the time she brewed her morning coffee the details of that shadowy pursuit had grown dim, and by the time she had been at work an hour or so the vague sense of depression the dream always left had slipped from her.

For the past few months, though, no matter how occupied her mind had been with work or pleasure, she had always been aware of that painful question just below the surface of her thoughts: who am I? Because she was in love now, really in love. In love with a man who, by whatever standard you might mention—intelligence, looks, family background, or achievement—was definitely a superior person. And although Gil Motthill seemed willing to run whatever risks their marriage might entail, she herself did not have that much courage, or recklessness.

And so for the first time in almost a year she had come down here today, drawn by a completely illogical feeling that this time it might be different. This time she might find something to help her trace those two who had begotten her, those faceless two she had pursued down the dark streets of her dreams.

Now, looking at her dim reflection in the fragment of the empty liquor store's shattered window, she raised her hand and smoothed her dark red hair. Then she turned and walked on. In the next block she passed two men, evidently longshoremen employed on the few active docks left in this area, with cargo hooks slung over their shoulders. A few seconds later she passed a wino who, seated on the curb with a paper-bag-swathed bottle in his hand, grinned at her toothlessly and called, "Hiya, Red." As often before in this neighborhood she felt a momentary uneasiness. But for some reason —probably because the empty warehouses still held valuable equipment—police cars patrolled this area. One had passed her only minutes ago. These streets were probably safe enough, at least in broad daylight. And anyway, in her mind the need that brought her here outweighed any risk she might be running.

She turned at the next corner, passed several boarded-up buildings, and then stopped at the edge of the old Penn Central Railroad yard. Obviously it was little used now. The rails were rusty, and weeds grew tall beside the tracks. She knew that soon even the rails and the ties, with their smell of sun-warmed creosote, would be covered over. This was the spot upon which New York's new convention center would be erected. And once the center rose, this whole area of abandoned and decaying warehouses and stores and tenements would give way to new apartment houses and office buildings.

The thought oppressed her. She knew it was irrational, but she had a feeling that the bulldozers and wrecking balls would obliterate, not only the old buildings she had passed, but whatever small chance she'd had of learning who she was.

Movement out there in the weeds. A woman stood up, a thin woman with a man's brown overcoat buttoned to her chin, and on her tangled, shoulder-length gray hair a hat that a silent movie star might have worn, a wide-brimmed black satin one ornamented with a big yellow rose. Her hands were wringing some sort of wet material. Golden in the late afternoon light, drops of water showered down onto the weeds.

A shopping bag lady, Katherine thought. One of those independent spirits who, scorning society's offer of shelter at least somewhat more suitable to their sex and years, roam the city's streets, carrying their possessions with them, and bedding down in bus stations, doorways, and empty buildings.

On impulse, Katherine waded through the weeds toward her. The woman, who had been christened Wanda Jean more years ago than she had been able to keep track of, watched the girl with a blend of suspicion and curiosity.

"Hello," Katherine said.

Not answering, the woman gave the garment in her hands a final twist and then, moving away from the battered bucket that stood at her feet, spread it out on the tracks to dry. It was a green-and-white checked blouse. Further along the tracks lay black cotton stockings, knee-length white knit underwear, and a pair of dark-blue sneakers. Obviously, this was the bag lady's washday.

Katherine said, "Do you live around here?" Perhaps she lived in the railroad yard. In spots the weeds were about four feet tall, high enough to conceal some sort of structure made of packing crates.

"What's it to you?" Wanda Jean said. Then, because in spite of her suspicion of strangers she wanted to keep the conversation going, she asked, "Do *you* live around here?"

"No." Without knowing she was going to, Katherine added, "But I've been down here quite often, because something happened to me here twenty-eight years ago."

Wanda Jean stared at the tall, pretty young woman. Twenty-eight years ago? Why, she didn't even look like she'd been born then. But maybe she had. "Something happened to you?"

"Yes. I suppose you don't know anything about it. I mean, you weren't—living in this neighborhood that long ago, were you?"

Had she been? Well, let's see. She'd been sticking to this neighborhood for a long, long time. She'd been forty when they let her out of that booby hatch—a state hospital, they called it—that they'd put her in after her husband left her and voices in her head had started to tell her to do funny things. After a while in that place she'd stopped paying any attention to the voices, and she'd decided that having her husband leave her was good riddance to bad rubbish. Once she was out of the hospital, though, she'd never wanted to be shut up anywhere again, not even in a room or apartment of her own.

For a while she stayed around the Battery. Then she moved up to westside-midtown, near the Hudson. Back then—oh, maybe thirty years ago—this neighborhood was a lot busier than now in the daytime, but it was pretty quiet at night. Nobody seemed to mind her sleeping in the warehouses. And unless she tried to hit them up too often, the men who worked around here in those days were willing to supply her with eating money.

Katherine said, her voice tense now, "You *have* been in this neighborhood a long time, haven't you? Maybe as long as twenty-eight years."

"What's it to you if I have?"

"Please! Maybe you remember something about it. A three-months-old baby girl was left in a warehouse down here. Do you remember anything like that happening? Do you?"

Dim recollection stirred in Wanda's mind. A young fellow, fellow with a limp, carrying something in his arms and slipping into a wide doorway. There'd been something—oh, sort of scared and sneaky in the way he acted, so after he'd come out, without whatever it was he'd been carrying, she'd slipped inside—

But she mustn't talk about that. Cops had been mixed up in it. They'd come down the street blowing their sirens only about fifteen minutes after she'd left the warehouse. She'd been several blocks away by then, sitting in a doorway, but just the same she'd skedaddled even farther. Anything cops were mixed up in was bad news. Maybe it would still be bad news for her, no matter how long ago it had happened.

The girl was leaning toward her. "You do remember something, don't you?"

"Get lost," Wanda Jean said.

"Please, it's so very important to me. If there is any way you could help me—"

"Now, listen! I'm just a poor old woman who's been in the booby hatch, but I've got my rights." She picked up the water-filled bucket and held it, poised, in both hands. "You going to leave, or am I going to throw this at you?"

Her hope of a moment before dying, Katherine said, "I'll leave." She turned away.

Wanda Jean set down the bucket. The girl had almost reached the freight yard's edge when Wanda Jean heard herself yell, "The key was no damn good to me anyway!"

Now what had made her say that? This was the reason why, even though she got lonesome sometimes, she didn't like people getting close. There was always a chance she'd blab out something she shouldn't.

The girl had turned around. "What key?"

"What's it to you?" Wanda yelled. She picked up the bucket. "Get lost!"

I've been making a fool of myself, Katherine thought. I should have realized from the first that the poor thing must be dotty.

"All right." She moved out of the railroad yard and then along the sidewalk that ran past the row of abandoned buildings. Most of the street was in shadow now. Wanda Jean watched her until she disappeared around the corner, probably headed for the bus line along Forty-second Street and then to wherever it was she'd come from.

2

Cautiously Mike Russo turned the wheel which opened the boiler's valve. The entire heating system in this building was so old and shaky that any sudden jar might break a connection. And then the tenants, coming home from work to find that they had no hot water, would start banging on the pipes, or even descending several flights of narrow stairs to his quarters. Thank God the weather was still very warm for November. So far he hadn't had to supply heat as well as hot water.

He reached up and pulled a cord, extinguishing the two-hundred-watt bulb that dangled from the ceiling. Now the only light was that of the late afternoon, struggling through dirty panes set high in the wall. He walked with his slight limp across the cement floor to an old black leather couch. Some of its stuffing protruded but still it was real leather, not this vinyl stuff. Mike wondered if years and years ago it had belonged to one of those head doctors, maybe one who'd had an office in this building when this was still a fairly good neighborhood. But of course Mike couldn't know about that. The couch had been here when he took the super's job in this building five years ago.

He stretched out. Soon he ought to go through the doorway into his two-room apartment and cook his supper. Right now he was much too weak. He could feel the sweat of weakness on his forehead and rolling down his sides from his armpits. He thought, as he often had these past few weeks, "It's come back." As yet the pain in his stomach was not bad, nor was it constant. Some nights he managed to sleep straight through. Sooner or later, he knew, he would have to go back to the hospital. But there was no reason why he shouldn't stay out as long as he could. After all, a second operation wasn't going to help. Not that the doctors had come right out and said so. But he'd guessed it from the way they'd acted. Well, so what? Some might feel that fifty-two was too young to die, but for him fifty-two years had been enough.

He clasped his hands behind his head, a thin man of medium height, with regular features, hazel eyes, and sandy hair that had turned almost entirely to gray. An old scar, slanting across his cheek, slightly drew up the left-hand corner of his mouth. Not many Americans would have guessed from his appearance that he was of Italian birth. But then many Americans didn't realize that in northern Italy people of fair complexion are almost as numerous as on the other side of the Alps, in Austria and Germany.

A complex of heating pipes ran along the dirty gray basement ceiling. When he squinted his eyes, as he was doing now, the pipes almost looked like the interlaced branches of a pine tree. Almost he might have been a teenager again, lying beneath a pine at the edge of an Alpine meadow, and hearing the bells of sheep brought up from the valley for summer pasturage.

A fierce longing twisted his heart. Lately he had missed the mountains, and the high meadows, and the village where he had been born almost more than he missed any of the people in his life. Almost more than his innkeeper parents, or Maria, or Sophia with her fuzz of dark red hair and her gray eyes like Maria's and her wide, toothless grin. Oh, for about twenty-eight years now she had been Katherine Millicent Derwith, but to him she would always be Sophia.

Strange that he could think of her so calmly. Perhaps it was in part because he knew she was having a good life. Perhaps it was partly because of the cancer, which made him feel set apart from all people with an indefinite number of years ahead of them.

Whatever the reason, he could remember that night twenty-eight years ago without reliving its terror. And yet that night his stomach had been knotted with fear as he drove along the dark street bordered by warehouses, most of them closed at that past-midnight hour. Heart pounding, aware that the men might have followed him after he left his dingy apartment house, knowing that at any moment he might see their lights in his rearview mirror, he nevertheless had forced himself to drive slowly. Otherwise he might pass up a place to hide Sophia for the necessary few minutes.

Up ahead dim light and subdued sounds spilled from a wide doorway. Perhaps a ship was loading or unloading at one of the Hudson River piers. Anyway, that warehouse was still open. What was more, he saw with a surge of triumph, a phone booth stood almost directly opposite, on his side of the street.

He stopped the car, got out, lifted the wicker basket from the floor between the front and back seats. "It's all right," he said softly as, limping, he carried the baby across the street. But by the light of a standard lamp about thirty feet away he saw that she did not need reassurance. She smiled up at him, waving her fists, evidently convinced that this was some new game her father had invented.

Inside the warehouse doorway he halted. There were lights down at the far end. Mike could hear voices and the rattle of hand trucks over cement. But this end of the warehouse was almost in darkness, illuminated only by the mingled glow of those distant loading lights and that of the street lamp outside.

He looked to his right. Packing crates lined the wall to a height of about seven feet. If he left the basket on top of that corner pile of crates—

For a moment everything within him contracted at the thought of a wheeled cargo lift rumbling to this end of the warehouse, then adding another crate to the stack in the corner.

But no. There was little chance of that happening within the next few minutes. And even if the men did start to work this end of the warehouse, they would have lights on and so would see the basket in time. Besides, anything would be better than to risk her falling into the hands of the German and the men with him, because then they could force him to do anything they wanted. He lifted the basket and set it atop the corner pile of crates.

For a few seconds he stood motionless. Then he bent and took the key from inside his right sock. Stretching, he dropped the key inside the basket, close to the small feet which, barely visible in the dim light, waved in the air. That key stunt of his had been pretty dumb. He'd never have tried it if he'd realized how much smarter and quicker the German was. But at least now there was no chance that the German would get the key. And to the police it would be just a locker key, a key that might have been designed to fit any one of tens of thousands of lockers in New York bus and railroad stations, airports, schools, factories—or, for that matter, a locker in Detroit, or Tampa, or Tumbleweed, Arizona.

Outside, swift glances toward the right and left showed him that there were no pedestrians at the moment and no cars except his own old Chevy, the one he'd bought in hopes of getting a salesman's job. He darted across the street and into the phone booth. Not enough light came from the street lamp to show him the figures and letters on the dial, or the card listing the police phone number. He'd have to risk keeping the door closed and the light on long enough to place the call.

He closed the door, dropped a coin, dialed. When a man's voice responded he opened the door, darkening the booth. In his agitation he forgot for a moment the English words for warehouse and basket. Sweating profusely, he finally made himself understood. While the cop was still trying to get his name, he hung up and left the booth.

His heart gave a physically painful leap. Their car, a heavy dark sedan, had stopped in front of his car, and the three men were moving toward him on foot. He whirled and ran.

An alleyway led to his right. He turned down it. The alley was short. He could see street-lamp glow at its end, only about a hundred feet away. Should he go on, even though, silhouetted against the light at the alley's end, he would make an easy target if they wanted to bring him down with a bullet in his leg? Or would it be best to hide among those dim objects—barrels? trash cans?—only a few feet ahead against the alley's right-hand wall?

He darted in between two of the cylindrical objects and crouched. They were trash cans, to judge by the metal his hand had brushed and by the ripe smell seeping out from under their lids.

The sound of running feet. The men passed him and continued on down the alley. After a few seconds the sounds ceased. Then he heard them coming back and knew what a fool his panic had made of him. Of course when they reached the next street, and saw no sign of him, they'd conclude he must still be in here.

Running feet very close now. Clatter of overturning metal cans. Hands hauling him upright. A fist looping upward against his chin.

When he came to he was still in the alley, spreadeagled on his back. They'd ripped open the short-sleeved yellow sports shirt which was all he wore above the waist, and taken off his shoes. He must have groaned or made some other sound, because one of them said, in an accented voice he recognized as the German's, "Make him talk."

A hand grabbed his hair and jerked him to a sitting position. Someone else's hand seized his left arm and twisted it behind his back. "Where is it?" the German asked. "Have you got it on you?"

He said nothing.

The pressure on his arm increased. He clenched his teeth to keep from crying out. He could see the dull gleam of the gun one of them held by the barrel, and he knew that if he started to scream that gun butt would crash down on his skull. But if he could just hold out—

"Where is it?"

That hand gave his arm another twist. Nausea in the pit of his stomach now. If he didn't speak that hand twisting his arm would soon dislocate his shoulder. But he had to keep silent.

"Are you going to tell us, Russo?"

Bathed in sweat, head hanging, he said nothing. The hand twisted once more. He felt agonizing pain, and tasted a rush of sourness in his mouth.

The hand relaxed. Half unconscious, and with a merciful mist closing in, he crumpled sideways. The German-accented voice sounded disgusted. "All right. Finish searching him."

Hands fumbled at his belt buckle. Then he heard the wail of a police siren, blocks away but drawing closer. One of them, not the German, said, "God! The guinea bastard must have been calling the cops."

The sound of their running feet dwindled away. He waited until he heard their car start up, drive off. Then he managed to drag himself between the overturned trash cans to the alley wall. The black mist hovering around him seemed to affect his hearing as well as his vision, for the sirens sounded near one second and far away the next. Then their shrieking ceased. He heard slamming car doors back there on the street, and voices. With an effort he turned his head. From somewhere near the alley entrance came the refracted, pulsing glow of a police car's ceiling light.

Propped up against the wall, he kept slipping in and out of pain, in and out of consciousness, sometimes aware for a minute or so of voices and that pulsing glow near the alley entrance, other times aware of nothing at all. When he came out of his last blackout the flashing light was gone and the night silent.

He thrust his right hand into his trouser pocket. Empty. But perhaps they hadn't taken his wallet and car keys, just dropped them and gone on searching for that other, more important key. Gritting his teeth against pain he felt around him on the alley floor. He found his car keys and then his wallet, unfolded but still thick enough that he felt his money must be there. Get to the car, he thought. Get out of here. Now that the cops were gone, those others might be back soon.

Left hand gripping his shirt front for as much support as he could give to his dislocated shoulder, teeth set against the nauseating pain, he struggled to his feet, stood swaying for a moment, and then limped back along the alley.

His car was still there. No doubt the police had taken down the license number and would find out where he lived, but with any luck he would be well out of town in a few hours.

Moving as fast as he could, he crossed the street. The warehouse workmen no doubt had been drawn to the Tenth Avenue end of the building by the arrival of the police, but now, apparently, they had returned to their tasks. As he hesitated in the doorway he could hear their distant voices and see the glow of cargo lights.

He took a step inside the entrance. He looked to his right. The basket was gone.

Still clutching his shirt front he recrossed the street and got into his car. His left arm brushed against the steering wheel. For a moment he feared he would faint, but he managed to fight back the mist and the sense of spiraling down into darkness.

What should he do? Not go back to his apartment, that cold water flat where he had lived alone with Sophia since he had brought her home from the hospital. Those three would show up there even before the police did. Besides, he had to get his shoulder fixed.

Go to an emergency hospital? No, they'd ask questions, and in his shocked and weakened state he might tell them too much.

Suddenly he knew what he should do. He started the car and drove, fighting off nausea and imminent blackout at each unevenness in the pavement, toward West Fourteenth Street. At this hour in the morning, past three by the dashboard clock, New York was as near sleeping as it ever is. He saw only a few vehicles, mostly cabs and trucks and small delivery vans, and only one pedestrian, a man walking a pair of boxer dogs. There was a parking space not far from the brownstone where Dr. Kincaid maintained his professional apartment. Bathed in cold sweat, right hand supporting his left arm, Mike climbed the brownstone's steps. In the dimly lighted foyer he pressed Dr. Kincaid's bell, waited a second, then pressed it again and again.

A man's angry voice, hoarse with sleepiness, came over the intercom. "Who are you? What do you want?"

"Mike Russo. My shoulder's out of joint."

John Kincaid was a kind man. Mike would never forget the distress in the doc's face when he told him, in the hospital waiting room, that his newborn daughter was fine but that they'd been unable to save Maria. Even the kindest man, though, is apt to be irate if awakened past midnight, especially if he's sixty-two-years old, and has to start his hospital rounds at eight in the morning.

"Damn it, why didn't you go to an emergency hospital?"

"I didn't think of it." The doc would think he was what people called a dumb guinea, but that didn't matter. "Please, Doc. It hurts."

"Of course it hurts," Dr. Kincaid snapped. "All right. Come in." A buzzer sounded as he released the catch on the front door.

In his first floor apartment he led Mike through his office and into a fluorescent-lighted examining room. Easing off his patient's yellow sports shirt he asked, "How did this happen?"

"I fell down the stairs at my apartment house."

From the way the doc's eyes narrowed Mike could see that he doubted that. But all he said was, "Lie down on your stomach on that table and hold tight to the table's edge with your right hand. And try not to yell too loud. If my wife's been able to get back to sleep I don't want her waked up. She's had a bout of summer flu."

Mike didn't yell at all, but by the time his shoulder snapped back into place he was groaning, and could taste his own sweat, running from his temples to the corners of his mouth. Dr. Kincaid fashioned a sling from a square of white cloth he took from a cabinet drawer.

"I'm sure it'll be okay, Mike. Just the same, it might be well to have it x-rayed within the next forty-eight hours. Don't have the x-rays sent to me," he added. "After all, I'm an obstetrician, not a G.P."

He opened a glass-fronted cabinet and took down a bottle of

pink capsules. "Take one of these every four hours, starting right now. They'll help kill the pain."

As Mike downed one of the capsules with water from a paper cup, the doctor asked, "How's your baby girl?"

"She's fine."

Something in his manner must have aroused the doc's suspicion, because he demanded, "Where is she? My God, man. You didn't leave her alone in your apartment, did you?"

"No, she's with Mrs. Scarpi."

Mrs. Scarpi had the apartment across the hall from Mike's. Ever since he had brought Sophia home from the hospital, Mrs. Scarpi had taken care of her during the day.

"Well, you won't be able to work for a few weeks. Pushing a hand truck through the garment district is no job for a man with a bad shoulder. Or have you been able to find that salesman's job you hoped to get?"

"No, not yet." And wanting to be a salesman had been a dumb idea. Salesmen had to be smart about people and able to guess what they might do. He knew now he was no good at that sort of thing.

He thanked the doctor and left. The sky had begun to lighten in the east. With his pain lulled by medication, he headed toward the Lincoln Tunnel and all that vast American landscape beyond which he knew only from magazines and movies.

Now, staring up at the basement's interlaced pipes, he told himself for the hundredth time that he'd been pretty stupid that night. As soon as he realized the danger, he should have tried to take Sophia to the police. But he'd still been quite young in those days. And scared. Scared of being deported as an illegal alien. Even more scared that the American authorities would find out that he had once been a witness—almost certainly the only witness—to a hideous war crime on an Alpine mountainside, and had never reported it.

Stopping only at gas stations to wash down the pink capsules with water from washbasin taps, he had driven across New Jersey and into Pennsylvania. Near sunset, on a stretch of highway beyond Reading, he spotted a row of dismal small frame structures. A wooden sign with faded black letters said, "Tourist Cabins. Vacancy."

The afternoon before he had drawn his two weeks wages from

the paymaster of a Seventh Avenue dress manufacturer. With over-time it had come to ninety-two dollars, of which he had eighty-four left in his wallet. The tourist cabins' proprietor, an unshaven man smelling of booze, told him that the rate was two dollars a night. Mike figured he had enough money to hole up there until his shoulder was well.

Two days after he moved into one of the cabins, he drove back to Reading and stopped at a stand which advertised out-of-town newspapers. He bought a New York *Daily News*. The story, plainly a follow-up of one published the day before, said that "Baby Jane Doe" had been placed in the Gotham Foundling Home. With min-gled relief and pain and longing he looked at a photograph of a smiling Sophia cradled in a burly cop's arms, with two other cops smiling down at her.

Twice during the next week he drove back to the Reading news-stand, but the New York papers carried no more stories about his daughter. With anguish he realized that sooner or later some cou-ple would adopt her. That night he had left her in the warehouse he'd had a hope that, if he remained free, he would somehow get her back. But now, with his own life so thoroughly messed up, he faced the fact that she would be better off without him.

In a small town near the tourist cabins he bought the cheapest food available, rice and beans and potatoes and chuck stewing beef, and cooked his meals over the two-burner gas plate in his cabin. To supplement his diet, he drove through the hot summer darkness down a side road and raided a truck-farmer's garden for corn, green peppers, and tomatoes.

In three weeks' time he judged that his shoulder, although stiff, had healed sufficiently for him to move on and even to look for work. He drove back to Reading, sold his car, and bought a bus ticket to Denver. He had been fascinated by the thought of Colo-rado ever since, as a small boy, he had visited relatives in Bolzano with his parents, and had seen an Italian-dubbed movie called "Man of the Rockies." Besides, ever since he had left Italy he had longed for the sight of tall pines, and the scent of mountain air, blowing cold and tangy from snow-covered slopes.

He had been in Denver only two days when, in response to a newspaper ad, he had hitched a ride to a cattle ranch up near the Continental Divide and been hired as cook. The food he turned out, mostly stews, Bisquick biscuits, Aunt Jemima pancakes, and fried eggs, would have taken no prizes, but evidently it was not too much worse than what the ranch hands were used to. Besides, they seemed to like him, even though they mocked his accent and told jokes in his presence about the alleged inadequacies of Italian soldiers. After a few months there he learned to ride and asked to be hired as a wrangler, even though it paid less than his job as cook. He never learned to rope. However, he was useful enough as a fence rider and a wielder of branding irons to stay in the ranch's employ. The pay was low, but since there was nothing to spend it on except an occasional visit with the other hands to the bars and brothels in a town about twenty miles away, he managed to save a sizable sum over the next nine years.

Even though a bucking horse, throwing him against a corral post, had left him with a scarred cheek to go with his gimpy leg, he'd felt that ranch life wasn't bad. Always, though, just below the surface of his thoughts, he was haunted by his need to know what had become of the baby he had left in the warehouse that night. Surely now it would be safe to go back to New York. The German had not trailed him to Colorado. Perhaps he had found some other means of getting his hands on whatever it was that lay buried within that worked-out Alpine mine. Or perhaps he had just given up. Perhaps he was no longer even in this country. Anyway, the risk in Mike's returning to New York was very small. With his appearance altered by nine years, and sun-weathered skin, and that scar on his cheek, it was doubtful that the German or anyone would recognize him. He wouldn't even have to change his name. New York was full of Russos, many of them named Mike.

The day after he arrived in New York he went to the West Forty-third Street offices of a private investigator whose name he had picked out of the Yellow Pages. A detective, he figured, might be able to find out who had adopted Sophia, even though such records were supposed to be closed. But the typist-receptionist in the detective's waiting room, a middle-aged brunette, had a cold, hard look which made him think she was an ex-hooker. And when she took some papers into the inner office he caught a glimpse of a sly-faced man behind a desk. The thought of blackmail flitted through Mike's mind. He'd heard of unscrupulous detectives who ferreted out information about their clients in order to shake them down.

Better to try to get a job at the Gotham Foundling Home and find out on his own.

Getting the job was no trick. In the prosperous Sixties, few people wanted to wash dishes or mop floors or perform any of the dull, low-paid tasks. After pushing brooms and mops and a waxer along the Foundling Home floors for a few days, he learned which room held the records of all the children who, however briefly, had been in the Home's care. It was the office of a Mrs. Aldrich, a pleasant-faced blond woman. Less than a week later he managed to slip into her office and take from a desk drawer a bunch of keys, including one tagged "office key" and another tagged "master file key." On his lunch hour he had duplicates made of both keys. That afternoon he spent a nervous hour and a half, slowly pushing a floor polisher back and forth in the hall, until Mrs. Aldrich emerged from her office and walked away toward the restroom. He slipped inside the office and returned the original keys.

That night, in work clothes, he returned to the Home, ready to say if challenged that he was looking for a watch he had lost in the building that day. No one did challenge him. Apparently if nurses and other staff members noticed him at all, they concluded that he had been transferred to the night shift. In Mrs. Aldrich's office with the door locked, and with only a pocket flashlight for illumination, he soon found that it was just as he had hoped. In one of the files the children were listed by the dates they had been brought to the Home. The card he knew must be Sophia's listed "baby girl approx. 3 mos." It also stated that four months later the child had been adopted by a Mr. and Mrs. Edward Derwith, and given the name Katherine Millicent. Evidently the Home kept track of adoptive parents for a certain period of time, because another entry on the card stated that on a date less than a year after the child's adoption the Derwiths had moved to a certain address in the town of Bellmont, Westchester County.

Mike quit his job the next day. Early in the morning the day after that he drove in the secondhand Dodge he had acquired up to Bellmont. For half an hour he waited, parked at the curb on a pleasant street of large houses and of wide lawns set with beds of daffodils and tulips and with blossoming ornamental trees. Then a station wagon bus with the words "Morton Day School" on its yellow side drew up in front of the Derwith house. The door between the colonial's white pillars opened and a child came down the walk, dark red hair, the same shade Maria's had been, shining in the sunlight, blue denim book bag dangling from her wrist. She looked healthy and happy. And she gave promise of being even lovelier than her mother had been.

Longing tightened like a vise around his heart, but he did not get out of his car to go to her, and he did not follow the school bus when it moved on. She was well off, maybe even better off than she would have been with him and Maria if Maria had lived, and if the German had never found him, although he didn't like to think that. He made a U-turn in the quiet street and drove back to New York.

For a while, looking for work, he lived off his savings in a Times Square residential hotel. Finally he took the job of super in a walk-up apartment house off West End Avenue. There was lots he liked about the job—the free apartment, and the tips at Christmas times and for making small repairs for tenants. Besides, he didn't have the stamina any longer to work as hard as he had on the ranch.

All through the years since, while he worked as super in various walk-up apartment houses, he had managed to keep track of his daughter. By subscribing to Bellmont's weekly newspaper, he had learned when the Morton Day School's eighth-grade class, with Katherine Millicent Derwith as a member, had been graduated. By the same means he knew when she had been graduated from her private high school and accepted by Barnard College. Her picture had been in the paper that week.

He had a job farther uptown then, only a few blocks from the Columbia University–Barnard College campus. Several times he saw her, a girl inches taller than Maria had been, almost as tall as himself, but looking so much like Maria that he would have been sure, even if he had seen her under other circumstances, that she was Maria's daughter.

Shortly before she was to be graduated, a virus he had contracted turned into pneumonia, and he was in the hospital for almost three weeks. By the time of his release he was in a panic at the thought that he might have lost track of her. He phoned the records office at Barnard, but they had no information except the home address she had given when she entered college. Leaving his Puerto Rican assistant to take care of the tenants, he drove up to Bellmont three days in a row and waited near the Derwith house, but saw no sign of his daughter.

As he drove back to New York he made up his mind that he would phone the Derwiths the next day, after making up some story which, if he were lucky, would extract information from them. But when he reached his super's quarters he found the new phone book outside his apartment door. If Katherine had rented a place in Manhattan, he suddenly realized, doubtless she'd had a phone installed. Even though her number wouldn't be in the book, not this soon, he could call Information.

Yes, Information told him a few minutes later, they had installed a phone for a Katherine M. Derwith. She gave him the number and the address, which was in the Eighties near the East River. Despite his relief at knowing where Katherine was, he would have liked to shake her. Didn't she realize she should have listed herself as K.M. Derwith? Hadn't she heard that there were weirdos in New York who liked to call up women they didn't know?

Two mornings later he went to her apartment house, an old but well-cared-for brick structure, and waited across the street until he saw her leave the building, chic and slender in her blue-and-white checked pantsuit, and with a brisk, bound-for-work air.

A fortyish man of obviously Italian extraction was shining the apartment house's brass door handles. Mike crossed the street. Even though he and the other man, a swarthy Sicilian, could scarcely consider themselves *paesanos*, they did share the same language. After a certain amount of casual conversation, Mike learned that the young lady who had left the apartment house some minutes before worked for a magazine. About a quarter of an hour after that Mike invited the Sicilian, whose name was Salvatore, to join him at the corner bar for a glass of wine.

They became friends. Every now and then Mike would go over to the East Side to invite Salvatore, a bachelor, to have a drink, or to have supper with him in his basement apartment. Thus he sooner or later learned whenever Katherine changed magazine jobs, and when she had gone to work for that neighborhood newspaper.

Mike was enormously proud of her. He read each issue of the *Eastside Courier*, and clipped out articles with her byline. Even while he was in the hospital for his cancer operation, one of the nurses, a homely little sweetheart with freckles and carroty hair, had saved every issue of the *Courier*, without once asking why he wanted the papers.

Yes, he was proud. But why was his daughter, at the age of twenty-eight, still unmarried? She was lovely, bright, well educated. Through Salvatore he knew that she'd had "lotsa fellas" hanging around, although lately there'd been only one, a Mr. Motthill who, Salvatore thought, was a lawyer, and who drove a Porsche, and sometimes wore a blue blazer with the emblem of some "ippsy-pippsy" athletic club on the pocket.

So why wasn't she married?

He would have liked to have a grandchild, even though the kid would never know who his real grandpapa was.

The German, he thought. It was because of the German that he had lost all rights to his Sophia, and to any children she might have.

Since Mike's return to New York, several times over the years he had seen a man on the street or in the subway who he was pretty sure was the German, each time looking older and fatter, but still recognizable. The thought of his being in New York didn't worry Mike, though. The German was no longer a threat, either to him or his daughter. Plainly he had not recognized Mike. And he had no way, at least no way that Mike could imagine, of learning that the baby girl left in the warehouse that night was now Katherine Millicent Derwith.

There had been a dull pain in his stomach for about twenty minutes now. Bland food sometimes helped that. Even though he wasn't hungry yet, he got up from the old leather couch, went through the doorway into his kitchenette, and fixed himself a supper of canned celery soup diluted with milk.

3

The telephone had been ringing even before Katherine put her key in the lock. She entered the apartment as quickly as she could and picked up the phone from the end table in the living room. "Hello."

"So at last." It was Gil's voice, sounding both relieved and exasperated. "Where the hell have you been?"

"It was such a nice day that I went for a long walk." Not exactly a lie, but not the whole truth, either. He wouldn't have liked to hear that she'd gone to that warehouse district again. "And anyway, our date isn't until seven."

"Yes, but I thought you might like to go to Bridge Inn. And if you do, I'd better make a reservation right now."

Bridge Inn, built partly over a rushing stream, was a highly popular restaurant about twenty miles up the Hudson.

He called for her half an hour later, a man only two or three inches taller than herself, but with the easy grace of someone whose body since childhood has been conditioned by horseback riding and tennis and swimming and sailing. At thirty-three his medium brown hair had grown a little thin, but a blow dryer in the hands of a Madison Avenue barber kept it looking as thick as it ever had. His handsome and thoroughly masculine features, handed down to him by eight generations of American Motthills and, before them, many more generations of their English predecessors, had a certain arrogance of which he was almost entirely unconscious.

In the Porsche they drove north to the George Washington Bridge, its lights gleaming like a diamond necklace flung across the black river. On the Hudson's western bank they took a series of tree-bordered roads to Bridge Inn.

The candlelit dining room, even at this time of the year, was fragrant with fresh flowers. The food—they both ordered broiled trout —was excellent, and the service smooth and unobtrusive. Through the soft piano music and the chatter of the other diners, Katherine sometimes could hear the rushing of the swift stream below the dining room windows. She tried to concentrate on the delicious food and on the case Gil was talking about, a law suit against the Port Authority in which Gil's firm was acting for the plaintiff. But again and again she kept seeing the old woman who had yelled, as she stood in waist-high weeds, "The key was no damn good to me, anyway."

By the time they left the restaurant, the last of the unseasonable warmth had given way to a cold front. In the east, a brilliant Dog Star followed Orion the Hunter up a dark sky swarming with lesser points of light. How beautiful, Katherine thought. And how lucky I am. I'm healthy, and have wonderful parents, and a job I like. I'm riding home from a fine restaurant in a thirty-thousand-dollar car with an attractive man who wants to marry me. Why can't I just accept my good fortune? What's wrong with me?

"What the hell's wrong with you?" Gil asked about half an hour later, rolling the bowl of a brandy glass between his hands. She had been reluctant to agree to his suggestion that they have a nightcap in her apartment because she knew it was really love-making he had in mind, and she feared that tonight her response might be inadequate. But she also knew that refusing to let him in to her apartment, after her abstracted air at dinner, would give him a real grievance.

She said, trying to smile, "What do you mean?"

"You've been miles away all evening. What happened today? Where did you take that long walk?"

Might as well tell him the truth. She sensed that he had guessed it anyway. Besides, deceiving Gil make her feel uncomfortable. "I went down to those old warehouses on the West Side."

With a short expletive he seldom used in her presence, he set his brandy glass down on the marble-topped coffee table. "Didn't you promise you wouldn't go down there again?"

"No! I didn't promise. I just said that maybe you were right in feeling that it was morbid of me to want to go there. But I can't help it, darling. I keep feeling that maybe I'll find out who I am—"

"For God's sake, Katy! How could you, just by wandering around down there nearly thirty years later? And anyway, you already know who *you* are. What you mean is, you don't know who your parents were. And what difference does that make?"

"It does make a difference! Be honest, Gil. It makes a difference to you, too."

He was silent. Of course that was true. It did make a difference. How he wished that she belonged to a family who had known his family for at least a couple of generations. How much easier that would have been. He'd had thoughts of that sort about her even when he believed she was the Derwiths' natural born daughter. After all, Ed Derwith's father had been a railroad conductor, and Mrs. Derwith's father a head gardener on a Long Island estate. The Derwiths never would have been admitted to the Bellmont Country Club if it had not been for Katherine. Ironically, it was Gil's parents who had sponsored the Derwiths for membership, partly because Gil's young sister Susan had become Katherine's best friend at the school they attended, and partly because the elder Motthills themselves could not resist the red-haired girl's charm.

It was at the club that Gil had first seen Katherine, dressed in tennis whites, gripping her racket with both hands as she returned Susan Motthill's serve. He had been aware of her loveliness, of course, but she had been a mere child, sixteen to his twenty-one.

He had spent the next three summers touring Europe with two Princeton friends. After he had his law degree and joined a Manhattan firm, he worked so hard that he seldom visited his family's rambling stone house in Bellmont. Then, a year ago, he had looked across a crowded living room at an East Sixty-second Street cocktail party and seen a tall girl chatting with two men. He thought, "Why, there's Maggie Smith!" Then he saw that she was even lovelier than the English actress, and perhaps younger, and that her hair was a much darker shade. He also realized that he knew her from somewhere. Suddenly he had it. A Westchester tennis court, and his sister Susan, now Lady Pontsby of Kent, England, serving a red-haired youngster who clutched her racket with both hands.

He crossed the room, introduced himself, and took over the conversation so aggressively—talking of Bellmont, and the country club, and his sister Susan—that the other two men soon wandered off.

On their third date she had told him that she had no idea who her parents were.

The revelation had been a stunning blow. Already he was in love with her. Already, too, he'd known that he would be in for a bad few hours when he told his parents that he wanted to marry, not one of the debs, or post-debs, or post-post-debs they had sought to interest him in all these years, but the Derwiths' daughter. Still, he had been confident that they would find the adult Katherine as appealing as the teenage one.

Now, though, when he would have to tell them that she wasn't even the Derwiths' daughter—

But he would not tell them, he resolved swiftly. So far only four people knew that she had been an abandoned infant—the Derwiths, Katherine, and himself. They would keep it that way.

One good thing about her telling him, he had reflected. It meant that she knew he was falling in love, and felt that in fairness to him she must tell the truth. And if she worried about being fair to him, perhaps it meant that she was falling in love too.

He did not ask her right then to marry him. He waited more than three months, until a night when they sat in a dimly lit corner of a cocktail room on the thirtieth story of a building overlooking the East River.

To his bewilderment she shook her head and said, "No, Gil. Thank you, my darling, but I can't."

"Why?"

"You know why. Wouldn't you want to know who your children's maternal grandparents were?"

He tried to keep his voice even. "Of course I would prefer to know. But I've had all that out with myself. You're more important to me than any children we might or might not have."

Again she shook her head. "I can't look at it like that. Maybe we had best stop seeing each other."

His hand reached across the table and grasped hers. "Don't say that. Maybe in time you'll come around to my way of thinking. In the meantime, we'll keep on as we are."

The months since had not been easy for him. Repeatedly he wished that he would meet someone who would enable him to turn away from her. Sometimes in dreams he hurled wild, vague charges at her and told her he was through. But only in dreams. In waking life he was haunted by the fear of losing her. She was so attractive to men, so much more so than she seemed to realize. Any day she might meet some man who would be able to persuade her, as he had not been able, that her origins did not matter.

Now, seated with her on the sofa in her living room, he reached out for her. "Come here, Kate," he said, and gathered her into his arms. He began a familiar ritual, running his hand up under her cashmere sweater to stroke the silky skin of her back, kissing her eyelids and her lips and that spot at the corner of her mouth where a dimple, flashing whenever she smiled, could give her sweetly grave face a mischievous look. For a few moments she did not respond. Then her arms tightened around his neck.

Half an hour later, as they lay side by side in the bedroom, he said, "Don't do that again."

"Do what?"

"Fake it. Don't you realize I can tell when you're faking?"

"I'm sorry." She added, trying to speak lightly, "Don't you want me to have good bed manners? Faking an orgasm, after all, is a woman's form of chivalry."

That did not amuse him. "Chivalry, hell. I don't want chivalry, in bed or anywhere else. I want you to want me as much as I want you."

When she didn't answer he burst out angrily, "You're going to let that obsession of yours make you frigid." He paused. "You were thinking about your afternoon down there on the West Side, weren't you?"

"Yes." For a few silent moments she looked up at the fan of light cast by the partly opened living room door onto the bedroom ceiling. Then she said, her voice weighted with misery, "Gil, as I've told you, this isn't fair to you. Don't you think we'd better call it—"

"No! We won't talk about it anymore tonight."

A few minutes later he dressed, leaned over her for a final kiss, and left the apartment.

For a long time after the apartment door closed she lay staring up at the ceiling. She loved Gil, and didn't want to lose him. No, even though she knew that he loved her, so to speak, only in spite of himself. But she would have to face a break with him unless she could discover her heritage, unless she could learn that her birth was not, as she feared in her most depressed moments, the result of incest, or of criminal rape.

Those organizations that helped the adopted find their natural parents would be of no use to her. They could help only if the identity of at least one of the natural parents was on record somewhere. In her case, apparently, neither the police nor the adoption agency or anyone else had such a record.

There was one course open to her. She could advertise, seeking contact with anyone who might have information about her origins.

It was an idea that had occurred to her often these past months. She had not carried it out because she knew it would anger Gil, filling him with the fear of the sort of publicity he most wanted to avoid. But she and Gil could not go on like this anyway. Even if she did nothing, they would sooner or later drift apart. And so what did she have to lose?

She got out of bed, catching a glimpse of her slender nakedness in the dressing table mirror across the room, opened the closet door, and put on a navy blue flannel robe. In the living room, heart beating fast, she sat down at the fake but pretty little Queen Anne desk. Like other articles of furniture in the room—the Victorian sofa and matching love seat upholstered in oyster-colored silk, and the piecrust end tables—the desk had been a present from the Derwiths. She drew a pad of scratch paper toward her.

The advertisement, she realized, must not give too many of the circumstances of her abandonment, lest any number of people be able to pretend knowledge of it. Best not to state the location, or the exact date, or even the baby's sex. After a few moments she picked up a ballpoint pen and, after several tries, composed a brief advertisement, soliciting contact with anyone who had information about an infant abandoned in New York City twenty-eight years ago. Should she add her phone number? Of course not. All sorts of cranks would call up, including some who would imitate a wailing infant. On Monday she would go down to the *Times* and *News* and ask them to assign box numbers to her advertisement.

Too tired now to even think of how she would justify her actions to Gil, she switched off the desk lamp and went back to the bedroom.

4

Four days later, calling at the *New York Times* office on her lunch hour, she found no replies to her advertisement. But over at the *Daily News* two envelopes awaited her. Too eager to wait until she was back in her office, she opened them in the *News* building's crowded lobby. The first letter was written in a ladylike backhand on pale blue notepaper. It read:

> Dear Sir or Madam,
>   If you will telephone me at Marymont 8-3321, I shall be happy to tell you anything you wish to know about the child referred to in your advertisement.
>
> > Very sincerely,
> > Martha Hartsdale

The second letter, equally brief, was typed inexpertly on dime-store paper:

> Box 710:
>   If you want more info, call me Up at Battery 6-4789. I8ll give you all the info I have.
>
> > Yrs. truly,
> > Joseph Renaldi

Her own office at the *Courier* was just a six-foot-square space, separated from the one next to it by a head-high partition. Her co-worker on the other side of it could hear all her phone conversations, just as she could hear his. Consequently while still at work she contented herself with looking up Martha Hartsdale and Joseph Renaldi in the phone book. The phone number of a Mrs. Lucien Hartsdale, at an address in the East Seventies, corresponded to that in her note. But none of the Joseph Renaldis in the book had the number he had given.

That evening in her apartment, heart beating fast, she sat down beside the phone. Which of these people should she call first? To judge by their letters, Martha Hartsdale was far more the sort of person she would like to feel was involved in some way with the first few weeks of her own life, and therefore with her parents. On the other hand, this Joseph Renaldi almost certainly was of Italian descent. That long-ago July night a man with a "foreign accent" had called the police. The accent might have been Italian.

In fact, more than once at the Metropolitan Museum, looking at Italian Renaissance paintings of women with dark red hair and high-bridged noses, she had wondered if her ancestry might be Italian.

She hesitated for a moment more. Then she lifted the phone and dialed the Marymont number. "Mrs. Hartsdale's residence," a woman's voice said.

"May I speak to Mrs. Hartsdale?"

"Who is calling, please?"

"My name is Katherine Derwith. I put an advertisement in the *News*, and Mrs. Hartsdale answered it."

"Just one moment, please."

Mrs. Hartsdale came on the line. Like her note, her voice conveyed an impression of refinement. "My dear, I'm so very glad I saw your advertisement. Now when shall we meet?"

"This evening?"

"Oh, dear! I'm afraid I retire very early these days. Doctor's orders, you know. But could you come to my apartment for tea tomorrow?"

"It would have to be rather late. You see, I have a job."

"Would five-thirty be late enough?"

"That would be fine."

"Splendid. You have my address?"

"Yes, from the phone book."

"Then I'll see you tomorrow at five-thirty."

Katherine thanked her and hung up. Strangely reluctant to call the other number, she sat motionless for a moment, hand still on the phone. Then she lifted the instrument and dialed the Battery number.

After several rings a voice said, "Joe Renaldi here." It was the sort of voice that conjured up an image of a man with cold, watchful eyes standing outside a Times Square bar.

"Hello, Mr. Renaldi. I'm calling about your answer to my advertisement."

"What about it?"

"I was wondering when I might see you."

"Anytime. Anytime at all."

"Perhaps we could meet someplace—"

"No can do. I've had an eye operation, see? I'm not supposed to go out for a couple of weeks, not even with dark glasses. So why don't you come to my place, say—oh, about eight tonight?"

She sat tongue-tied, not wanting to offend him lest he deny her any information he might have, and yet reluctant to go to this stranger's apartment. At last she said, "Mr. Renaldi, wouldn't you please give me a little information right now, just enough so that I'll know that—" She broke off.

"That I'm on the up and up? Why, sure. Your ad didn't say so, but I know the infant it mentioned was a girl. It was you, in fact."

Accurate, certainly. But also easy to guess. The advertisement had concerned a baby abandoned twenty-eight years ago. Probably her voice had told him, not just that she was female, but that she was in her twenties or thirties.

She said, "Could you—could you tell me something more?"

His reply was prompt. "No way. I'm not giving out any more info over the phone. For all you know, I was sticking my neck way out to even answer that ad. Right? So the least you can do is to accommodate me by coming here. Otherwise, just forget the whole thing."

She said, after a long moment, "Where's here? You're not listed in the phone book."

He gave her an address in the East Nineties. "I'm one flight up, apartment Two-B. How about around eight tonight?"

No, she thought, not tonight. Perhaps tomorrow, after seeing that pleasant Mrs. Hartsdale, she would have no need for further dealings with this man.

"I can't tonight. How about tomorrow night?" If, as she hoped, she found it unnecessary to see him, she would call up and break the appointment.

"Okay. See you tomorrow night at eight." He hung up without saying goodbye.

A few minutes after she finished her solitary dinner, Gil telephoned. It was the first time she had heard from him since his rather cool leave-taking of her the previous Saturday night. "Gil, darling! How good to hear your voice. Have you been busy?"

"In spades. But I have to fly out to Los Angeles next Thursday. A guy out there is being coy about giving us the deposition we need for the Port Authority case. I may be gone for several days, and so I didn't want to leave town without seeing you first. How about dinner tomorrow night?"

She was silent for several seconds. Then: "Gil, I can't."

"What do you mean, you can't?"

"I just can't. Please don't be angry. Later on I'll tell—"

"What do you mean, don't be angry?" His voice was grim. "I ask you to dinner, and you turn me down, and don't want me to even ask why—"

"Please! Please don't get any silly idea, such as—such as that I'm dating another man. I love you, Gil. You know I do. Please trust me, darling."

There was a long silence. Then he said, in a carefully controlled voice, "I guess I'll have to. All right, Katy. I'll phone you from the Coast."

A minute or so before five-thirty the next afternoon an elderly doorman admitted Katherine to the lobby of Mrs. Hartsdale's apartment house. Katherine had a sense of stepping backward in time to an era she had never known, an elegant era when even doormen guarding small, sidestreet apartment houses wore white gloves, and the flowers gracing lobbies were real, not plastic. There was even a uniformed operator, a young Hispanic, standing to the left of a pair of elevators.

One of the elevators, paneled in pale, satiny wood, let her out on the fifth floor into a little square hallway, carpeted in thick green plush, with a gilded mirror hung above a wall shelf that held white chrysanthemums in a glazed yellow bowl. Evidently Mrs. Hartsdale's was the only apartment on the fifth floor serviced by that elevator, because the door opposite it was the only one visible. Katherine's heartbeats, already swift with the hope she had felt ever since she opened that pale blue envelope, became even faster. Perhaps they were entirely groundless, those fears that her origins had been sordid. Perhaps instead, even though she might be illegitimate, she was related in some way to the woman who lived in this quietly elegant place. She crossed the little hall and pressed the pearl button set in the door frame.

After a moment or two a woman of about fifty, wearing a maid's uniform, opened the door. She was tall and quite stout. Gray-blond braids wound around her head made her appear German or Scandinavian. She said, "Good afternoon, miss."

"Good afternoon. My name is Katherine Derwith. I have an appointment with Mrs. Hartsdale."

"Yes, she is expecting you." The maid stepped back. "Come in, please."

Katherine followed the woman across a parquet-floored foyer to a wide doorway. "Miss Derwith is here, Mrs. Hartsdale," she said, and turned and walked away.

Across the big living room, its parquet floor partially covered by a floral carpet with a cream-colored background, a slender woman rose from beside a marble-manteled fireplace and advanced to meet her. "My dear," Mrs. Hartsdale cried, "you look exactly as I knew you would."

Heartbeats suffocatingly fast now, Katherine managed to murmur a greeting and to take the thin, dry-skinned hand extended to her. Could it be that this woman was— No, it was unlikely that this woman was her mother. With her snowy white hair, her fine-featured face with skin as delicately wrinkled as that of a fine kid glove, Mrs. Hartsdale must be at least in her late seventies. But perhaps a grandmother, or great-aunt, or other relative?

"Come sit by the fire," Mrs. Hartsdale said. They moved across the luxuriously deep carpet to the fire flickering in the grate. Like the rest of the furniture in the room, the two bergère chairs, upholstered in yellow satin, which flanked the fireplace appeared to be French.

When they were seated Mrs. Hartsdale said, with an oddly mischievous smile, "I'll bet you wonder how it is that I was reading the *Daily News*."

Katherine felt puzzled. True, she had wondered briefly why the writer of that gracious note had responded to her ad in the racy

News rather than the dignified *Times.* But it had been a question of unimportance compared to the others thronging her mind.

"As a matter of fact," Martha Hartsdale went on, "I never read the *News* or any newspaper. They never tell you anything of importance. I read the *Psychic Review* each month. For the rest, the TV news is sufficient. Don't you agree?"

Completely at sea now, Katherine said, "I'm afraid I don't—I mean, if you don't read the *News,* how—"

"Gretchen, my housekeeper, subscribes to it. Gretchen is the one who answered the door. She saw your ad and showed it to me."

"Why?" Katherine's voice was taut. "Why did she show it to you?"

Mrs. Hartsdale looked surprised. "Why? Because she knows me, and what interests me." Smiling, she looked past Katherine's shoulder. "Bring the cart over here, please, Gretchen."

Turning, Katherine saw that a door in the wall behind her had opened, and the stout housekeeper was wheeling a tea cart toward the fireplace.

When the housekeeper was gone, Katherine said, "Please! How is it that she knew you would be interested in my ad?"

"Oh, my dear! Let's have some tea before we get down to serious matters. I do hope you like this kind. It's blended for me specially by a shop on Third Avenue."

With an effort Katherine kept her voice even. "I'm sure I shall."

She sipped the tea. In her agitation it seemed to her that the hot liquid had no taste at all. She ate two cucumber sandwiches. And all the time Mrs. Hartsdale spoke of how her late husband would not drink anything but Earl Grey, and how he insisted on hot scones for afternoon tea, even in the warmest weather. Nerves screaming, Katherine made sounds of appreciative interest as long as she could. Then she set down her cup and said, "Mrs. Hartsdale, you were about to tell me how your housekeeper knew you would be interested in my advertisement."

"Oh, yes. Well, she's been with me for twenty years. She came to us while my husband was still alive."

Katherine's throat felt tight. "And so?"

"And so she's aware that whenever I can I like to help people find out what they need to know."

After a long moment Katherine said, "I see." She had a bleak premonition that soon she would learn that it was a will-o'-the-wisp which had brought her to this elegant apartment. "Now you said in your note that you would tell me all I wanted to know about— about the child. Just what is it you can tell me?"

Snowy head on one side, Mrs. Hartsdale gave that mischievous smile. "First of all, I know that the person who placed the ad had been the baby who was abandoned twenty-eight years ago. Am I right?"

Joseph Renaldi had made the same guess, one too simple to even be called lucky. "Yes."

"What's more, after I read your ad I closed my eyes, and I could see exactly how you looked. I told you that as soon as you walked into this apartment.

"And I also know," she went on triumphantly, "that you are try- ing to find out who your parents were."

In spite of herself, Katherine felt a faint stir of hope. "And you know?"

"Of course I know! It's just as I've told the police again and again. I close my eyes and *see* where the kidnapped people are, or the stolen money is hidden. But although they're always polite to me, I'm sure they never follow up the leads I give them."

Katherine's voice was dull with disappointment. "You say you know who my parents were?"

"Not their names. Their names haven't come to me. But then, you don't really want to find them, do you, my dear? Surely a lovely little baby such as you must have been was adopted, and surely you were happy with the couple who raised you. What you want to know is what sort of people your parents were." Again she gave that roguish smile. "Isn't that true?"

Katherine managed to nod.

Mrs. Hartsdale said promptly, "Your mother was a lovely young girl, of good family. The boy—the boy who was your father, I mean —was of good family too. They weren't wicked young people, just inexperienced and—well, rather neglected. The girl's parents espe- cially traveled a lot, and left her with relatives or just with servants. In fact, her parents were in Europe when you were born. Perhaps if they had been here they wouldn't have allowed her to abandon you. But, you see, they never knew anything about it."

Despite her utter disillusionment, Katherine asked, "*Where* did she abandon me?"

For a moment her hostess looked disconcerted. "You were never told?"

To test her, Katherine lied evenly, "No, I wasn't."

Mrs. Hartsdale's smile flashed. "Then let's find out, shall we?"

She closed her eyes. After a moment she began slowly, "I see the lobby of an apartment house. A young girl walks in. She is carrying something, a kind of bag. Yes, it's a large knitting bag. She places it behind a high-backed chair, and then hurries out to the sidewalk."

She opened her eyes. "There! You see?"

You old fraud, Katherine thought bitterly. But no, that wasn't fair. The woman was not fraudulent, merely self-deluded.

Katherine asked, in a dry voice, "Was the apartment house where she left me on the East Side or the West Side?"

"Oh, my dear! I'm sure it was the East Side."

Katherine got to her feet. "Thank you, Mrs. Hartsdale. I must go now."

"Must you?" She too stood up. "I'm sorry. I wish we could have chatted longer. But at least it is good to know that now you are easier in your mind."

"Yes," Katherine said. Then, as she saw her hostess reach toward the bell rope beside the mantel: "Please don't. I can let myself out. Goodbye, Mrs. Hartsdale."

Down on the sidewalk she turned to her right and walked through the early November dark toward her apartment. In her disappointment she felt more reluctant than ever to see the stranger with the unpleasant voice and the Italian name. But she would see him. If he could tell her anything about herself she wanted to hear it, no matter what it was. She would go home, and try to eat some sort of dinner, and then go to his apartment.

5

The East Nineties, Katherine knew, was a fringe neighborhood, a melange of new high-rise apartments, of shabby but still livable brownstone walkups, and of buildings obviously headed for abandonment, their façades graffiti-covered, and some of their windows, apparently broken ones, already boarded over. To her relief, when her taxi stopped at the address Joe Renaldi had given her, she saw that his brownstone apartment house, although rundown-looking, was not the sinister slum she had feared.

In the foyer with its floor of soiled gray and white tiles she looked along the row of buttons on the wall and then pushed the one for apartment 2-B. A metallic, squawking sound issued from the intercom grille above the row of buttons, and then a man's voice asked, "Yeah? Who is it?"

She almost said, "Katherine Derwith," but some instinct stopped her. "I'm the one who advertised—"

"Come on up."

A buzzing sound told her that he had released the lock on the heavy glass doors. She went into the lobby. A musty smell. Dim overhead light bulb revealing a worn brown carpet over a hall stretching back into the shadows, and the same brown carpet on narrow stairs leading upward. But at least there were no broken bottles or other trash, no reek of unemptied garbage pails, no sounds of family fights. In fact, there were no sounds at all. She climbed one flight, walked back through the dimness to a door labeled 2-B, and rang the bell.

Immediately the door opened. The man who stood there, dressed in brown trousers and white turtleneck, face partially obscured by dark glasses, appeared to be about forty. He was of medium height, and trim-figured. She guessed that he wore the turtleneck to show off the trimness.

He said, "Come in, come in," and opened the door wide.

She stepped past him into a room dimly illuminated by lamplight filtering through brown parchment shades. Worn-looking wall-to-wall carpeting and an equally worn red sofa contrasted with a new recliner chair, upholstered in a tweedy brown fabric, drawn up before a twenty-six-inch TV set. On a table against the far wall, where it would catch the immediate attention of anyone entering the apartment, was what its owner obviously thought of as the high point of the room's decor. In a white plastic basin shaped like a scallop shell, and illuminated by red and blue lights concealed below the basin's rim, stood a nude female figure, also of white plastic, about two feet high. She held a bucket, tilted forward, on one shoulder. Evidently the figure had a concealed recirculator, because water poured in a small but continuous stream from the bucket into the scallop shell.

He had followed the direction of her gaze. "Nice, huh? It's the one thing in here that's mine. You see, this apartment belongs to a friend and I'm just subletting, sort of. That's why the phone's not in my name. But I bought the fountain. Saw it in a store window in Queens, and snapped it right up." Without waiting for her reply, he extended his hand and said, "Let me hang up your coat."

"No need for that." If it became necessary, she wanted to be able to leave quickly, without rummaging through a clothes closet for her coat. She slipped out of it, a wool wraparound of Campbell plaid. "I'll just leave it here."

She turned toward a straight chair. On its seat was a copy of a magazine. The cover showed a fat woman, posed in an attitude so ugly, so degrading, that Katherine felt first a sick tightening in her stomach, and then a flare of rage against those who produced such cruel obscenity, and those who bought it. She draped the coat over the chair's back, with its skirt hiding the magazine, and then turned to her host. Apparently he did not realize she had seen the magazine or, if he did, was not aware of her reaction to it.

"Sit down, sit down," he said, and waved her toward the sofa.

She sat down in one corner and he in the other. Black glasses reflecting the dim light, he smiled at her. His teeth were very white in his olive-skinned face. Probably, she thought, he was as proud of his teeth as his waistline.

He asked, "What did you say your name was?"

"I didn't say." She paused, and then added, "But it's Doris Hartley."

"Nice name." He bounded to his feet. "Well, Dorie, how about a drink?"

"No, thank you."

As if she hadn't spoken, he crossed to a battered liquor cabinet against the far wall and raised the two halves of its top. Several bottles and glasses rose into view. "What'll it be?"

"Please! I don't want any."

He poured a couple of fingers of amber liquid into each of two glasses. "Now, Dorie! When people won't drink with me I get sore. And when I'm sore I don't talk." He was smiling, but his voice held an edge.

Tight-lipped, she looked back at him for a moment and then said, "All right. Soda, please, and not too much ice."

A glass in each hand, he came back across the room and handed her drink to her. He sat down on the sofa, not in the corner now, but in the middle. "Well, here's to new friends," he said, and took a swallow. "Okay, Dorie. Let's talk."

Even though she thought she had come here prepared for whatever he might say, she felt a sudden panic at the prospect of learning that this man's life was somehow intertwined with her own. She took a sip of her drink—it was bourbon, she discovered—and then said, "What do you do, Mr. Renaldi?"

"Joe. Call me Joe. I'm a promoter, sort of."

"What do you promote?"

"Oh, this and that. For a while I was promoting this comic basketball team. Sort of like the Harlem Globetrotters, only they were white. I arranged for them to put on shows for Elks clubs or other outfits that wanted to raise money, and then I'd take a percentage of the gate. But the team hired themselves a shyster lawyer and managed to break the contract I had with them. Since then I've not been doing anything much." He paused. "I guess Hartley's the name of the people who adopted you, huh?"

She had forgotten the name she had given him. For a confused moment she didn't know what he was talking about. Then she asked, "How did you know I was adopted?"

"*Hon*-ey! It figures. You already admitted you were the abandoned kid in your ad. Abandoned kids don't have names pinned to them, at least not usually. But abandoned kids do get adopted, especially pretty little white kids like the one you must of been, and then they get the name of whoever adopted them."

He took another long swallow of his drink. She saw his gaze travel from her Gucci handbag of polished brown calf, sitting on the coffee table, to her matching shoes with their medium heels and their straps across the instep. The handbag and shoes had been her parents' present to her the previous Christmas.

He said, "These Hartleys well-fixed?"

Was that why he had answered her ad? Was he hoping, this currently idle "promoter," that there might somehow be money in it for him?

She said, "No, the Hartleys are in very modest circumstances."

"Then you got a rich husband or boy friend? What I mean is, Dorie, the way you're dressed don't spell modest circumstances to me."

She said in a cool voice, "Strange. I took you for a New Yorker."

"What do you mean, took me for? Why I was born right here in Manhattan, on West Eighteenth Street."

"And yet apparently you never heard of resale shops."

"You mean thrift shops? Sure, I heard."

"No, resale shops. Rich women sell their furs, and designer dresses, and imported shoes and handbags. And the shop resells them for only a fraction of what the rich women originally paid for them."

"I get it," he said, with a falling inflection. Then, smiling: "But one thing's for sure. Those clothes look better on you than whatever Mrs. Gotrocks once owned them. Anybody ever tell you you're one gorgeous gal?"

"I gather you have, right now." She took a deep breath. Then, placing her drink on the cigarette-scarred walnut coffee table, she said, "All right. Please tell me what you know about me."

While she waited, heart thudding, he turned his glass in his hand and smiled at her. Finally he said, "For starters, I know you were left in a laundry basket in a warehouse on the West Side, midtown. The date was in July."

She felt an odd mixture of emotion, gladness that at last she was to learn something about her origins, and dismay that it was a man like Joe Renaldi who possessed the information.

Then suddenly she realized that perhaps he had not possessed it, not until after he read her ad. Just as she had done, he could have gone to one of the metropolitan newspapers, looked through the index of stories it had carried twenty-eight years ago, and then turned to the account of a girl baby abandoned in July of that year—

She said, trying to keep her voice matter of fact, "What else do you know?" She paused. "Who was my mother?"

"Your mother? To tell you the truth, I can't remember her name. I was only a kid around twelve, thirteen, in those days. But she was a friend of my oldest sister, so I knew her to say hello to. She was not exactly a tramp, you understand. Maybe a little free and easy, but no tramp. She knew that the police would be looking for whoever put the kid in the warehouse, so she split. For Florida, I think. Yeah, Florida. Later there was a story going around the neighborhood that she'd been killed in an auto accident in Tampa."

After a while Katherine managed to ask, "And my father? Do you know who he was?"

"Seems to me I heard people say he was a married man, older than her, and that he made book. But that's all I can remember."

"You have no idea where he is now?"

He shook his head. "Dead, maybe. As I said, the story was that he was older than her, with grown children of his own."

She looked at the gleaming dark glasses. Had the two people he spoke of—the married bookie and the girl who was "not exactly a tramp"—had they actually existed? Or could it be that they were no more real than the pair Mrs. Hartsdale had conjured up, the very young boy and girl "of good family?"

Suddenly she had the feeling, so strong that it was almost a certainty, that he had lied. She did not know why he had answered her ad and summoned her here, only to lie to her. Perhaps hope of some sort of gain was his motive. Perhaps he was someone with at least a slight sexual twist, someone who hoped that she would prove to be attractive, and grateful for the "information" he gave her, and therefore malleable.

She stood up. "Thank you. I must go now."

"Hey!" He got to his feet. "You can't go yet. You haven't even finished your drink."

"Sorry, but I have an appointment."

His hand shot out and caught her left wrist. "Now listen here." His voice was suddenly cold. "You can't just—"

"Let go of me!"

Instead, he reached for her other wrist. Frightened now, she evaded his hand and struck him across the cheek. The dark glasses flew to the carpet. His eyes, brown and cold and furious, almost on a level with her own, showed no sign of a recent operation.

She cried, "Liar! Everything you told me has been a lie, hasn't it?"

His voice was still cold, and perfectly even. "What if it has? No broad slaps me across the face and gets away with it."

Frantically she tugged at her imprisoned wrist. His grasp only tightened. "I went to a lot of trouble on account of you, lady. I wrote that letter. And even though I had a chance to see a guy about a deal tonight, I waited for you. And so you're going to pay off, one way or another."

He released her wrist and then, swiftly, grasped her shoulders. She found herself propelled backward to the wall. He fastened his lips upon hers, his tongue trying to thrust itself into her mouth. She felt his hand tug at the neckline of her blouse, heard a ripping sound. Twisting in his grasp, she managed to raise her hands and push him slightly away from her. Then she brought her knee up. He collapsed onto the rug, clutching at his groin and cursing her.

She snatched up her coat, whirled. He had not reversed the lock on the door. Struggling into her coat, she ran out into the hall and plunged down the stairs. Thank God, she thought, that she'd had sense enough not to tell him her right name. Even if he tried to track her down, he'd have a hard time doing it.

At the foot of the brownstone's steps she turned left down the sloping street toward Second Avenue. Now a new fear assailed her. It must be almost ten now, and this was far from a safe neighborhood. In fact, when she came to Renaldi's apartment she had intended to phone for a cab to take her home, rather than risk standing out front to flag one down. Now she saw that at the moment no taxis, no cars at all, moved down this block. Long stretches of shadow lay between the street lights. Near the corner was a construction site. The sidewalk in front of it had been roofed over, forming a long tunnel where anyone might lurk.

Cross to the other side, she told herself, before you get to the tunnel. But hurry. On Second Avenue, with its pedestrians, its bars and restaurants, its north-to-south traffic, she would be safe. Almost running, the click of her heels distinct in the stillness, she moved down the sidewalk.

Two tall male figures emerged from the tunnel in front of the construction site.

She stopped short. Then, heart leaping with terror, she managed to squeeze between two cars parked almost bumper to bumper at the curb. Not taking time to dart to the opposite sidewalk, she turned and ran down the middle of the street toward Second Avenue.

Seconds later she realized that probably there had been no need for fear. If they had chosen to, those two could have pursued her and almost certainly caught her. But with the panic-induced adrenalin coursing through her she kept running for several more seconds until she had passed the construction site. Then, with the stream of traffic along the avenue only a few feet away, she moved across the vacant space between two parked cars to the curb.

On the corner of Second Avenue an open fruit stand poured light over its colorful wares and out onto the sidewalk. Several people, most of them women, waited at the bus stop. Hoping that the quickness of her breathing was not noticeable, Katherine stopped beside them.

One of the women stared at her legs. Katherine looked down. Obviously, without her even feeling it, she had scraped her leg when, in fear of those advancing figures, she had squeezed her way between the bumpers of the two parked cars. Her right stocking was not only torn, but stained red.

Thank God a taxi was coming. She stepped off the curb and hailed it.

6

As soon as the cab turned off Second Avenue onto her block, she saw Gil's red Porsche, parked a few feet short of the entrance to her apartment house. His face turned toward hers as the cab passed him.

The cab angled to the curb. She was fumbling in her handbag for her change purse when Gil appeared on the sidewalk beside the driver's window. He knocked on the glass. The cabbie rolled the window part way down, and Gil thrust a banknote through the opening. "This cover it?"

"Yes, *sir*."

Gil opened the rear door. As soon as Katherine had stepped to the curb, the cab moved away. By the yellow glow of a nearby street lamp, Katherine saw that Gil's face was grim. She knew that her own face must look both distressed and guilty, because he said, "All right! Out with it. Where the hell have you been? What happened to you?"

"Please! Please just let me go upstairs, Gil. I told you I couldn't see you tonight—"

"And I decided I'd damn well better find out why."

"Gil, not here on the street! Let me—"

"All right, we'll go up to your apartment."

His tone told her that there would be no making him leave, not until she gave him some sort of explanation. Perhaps she could think of some story that would make him go. Certainly unless she had to, she didn't want him to know, at least not yet, even about her newspaper ad, let alone that frightening and humiliating episode in Joe Renaldi's apartment.

Silently she reached into her handbag for her keys and then turned toward the apartment house. In its foyer he took the bunch of keys from her hand and unlocked the front door. Neither of them spoke as they rose in the automatic elevator. Afraid he might see her ripped blouse, she clutched the edges of her coat together at the neck. Apparently, with his frowning gaze directed straight ahead at the elevator doors, he had not yet noticed her torn and bloodied stocking. Once in her apartment, perhaps she could slip quickly into her bedroom, get another blouse and pair of pantyhose, and in the bathroom put a Band-aid over the scraped spot on her leg.

Gil unlocked the apartment door, reached in to flip the light switch, and then stood aside for her to enter. She'd gone only a few steps into the living room when he caught her upper arm and turned her about to face him. "All right, Katherine. What is all this?"

"Please! Can't you wait just a—"

"And why are you holding your coat together like that?" His gaze swept down her body. She saw his face change. "Darling! What happened to your leg?"

The concern in his voice sent shame flooding through her. Gil loved her. Even though the truth would enrage him, might even make him turn away from her, it was wrong to deceive him. And anyway, she reflected wryly, she would not be able to. Now that he had seen that torn stocking, he would keep probing until he got the whole story out of her.

She took her hand away from the collar of her coat. "No, I'm not hurt. It was only a scrape."

"But your blouse! It's torn!"

"Yes. Let me change my blouse and put something on my leg. Then I'll tell you all about it."

A few minutes later, seated beside him on the love seat, she did tell him. The advertisement in the *Times* and *News*. Mrs. Hartsdale. Joseph Renaldi.

Soon after she began to speak, Gil had turned his head away from her to stare at the opposite wall. Now his gaze, hot with anger, returned to her face. "Katherine, you fool! You should have known what sort of people would answer an ad like that. A batty old lady and a creep. You're lucky it was no worse than that. You might have come up against some outright psycho."

Before she could speak he rushed on, "And what about the risk of publicity you've been running? Don't you realize some reporter might have spotted your ad, and decided it had the makings of a story? Did you want that to happen?"

Her voice was low and miserable. "No, but better to risk that than to risk marrying you, and maybe bringing children into the world, when we have no idea what—what sort of heritage I'm passing on to them."

After a long moment he said, in a tired, flat voice, "So you're going to keep on running that ad."

"I don't know. Probably not. In four days I got only two replies. My box number is good only until Saturday, so if there are no more replies tomorrow—"

Her voice trailed off. He stood up. "I'd better leave." His voice still held that tired flatness. "I'm catching an early plane tomorrow."

She too got to her feet. "Darling, please, please try to understand."

"Oh, I understand, all right. This obsession of yours means more to you than anything I can offer you. And don't try to tell me," he went on quickly, "that your main reason for wanting to know about your parentage is that otherwise our marriage would be unfair to *me*. As I've told you again and again, I'm the best judge of what's unfair to me."

When she didn't answer, he added, "And I'll tell you what *is* unfair to me—risking publicity that would hurt and embarrass my family."

"I haven't meant to—"

"I know you haven't. But it would hurt and embarrass them. They know I want to marry you, and they've accepted you."

She remained silent. It was true that the Motthills had treated her with warm kindness. She had spent several weekends at their beautiful old fieldstone house in Larchmont, and even though no one had mentioned marriage, the Motthills unmistakably had treated her like a future daughter-in-law.

"My parents have let a lot of their friends know that they can expect an engagement announcement soon. How would they feel, having everybody know that—" He broke off, and then added,

"And it wouldn't do my professional standing any good either. The law firm I'm with is among the oldest and most conservative in New York. But then, you know all that."

She said wretchedly, after a long moment, "Then you too feel that maybe we'd better call everything off?"

"I don't know, Katherine. I honestly don't know."

"Will you telephone me from the Coast?"

"I don't know. Maybe it would be best to wait until I get back. By then I'll have had a little time to think things over."

They looked at each other unhappily for several seconds. Then he said, "Well, good night, Katherine," and walked out.

She sank down onto the love seat and wrapped her arms around her. Even though the apartment was warm, she shivered a little. Perhaps she had lost him tonight, lost him for good.

She had been sitting there about five minutes when the phone rang. Pulse racing, she picked it up. Surely it was Gil. Unhappy that they had taken leave of each other in that painful fashion, he had stopped at some bar or drugstore to phone—

"Hello."

"Hello, darling." It was Clara Derwith's voice. "I hope I'm not calling too late. I tried to get you earlier."

With an effort, Katherine made her voice cheerful. "I was out for a while, Mother. And of course you're not calling too late."

"Well, I just wanted to find out how you are."

They chatted for a while. Then Clara Derwith said, "Are you sure you're all right? You sound—odd."

For a moment Katherine had an almost overwhelming desire to tell her mother everything. Her many visits over the past ten years to that old warehouse district. Her reluctance to marry Gil. Their wretched quarrel tonight.

But she must not let her mother know how oppressed she had felt by the mystery of her origin. Certainly the least thing she could do for the Derwiths, in return for their years of tender, anxious care, was to keep them from knowing how unhappy she was.

"Mother, I'm fine, just fine. A little tired, that's all."

"Then you'd better go to bed."

"Give my love to Dad."

"I will, dear. Good night."

"Good night." Katherine hung up and walked, shoulders drooping, toward the bedroom.

In his darkened basement apartment across town, Mike Russo lay staring at the pale rectangle of the window set high in the wall. The pain-killing drug the doctor prescribed for him almost always made him feel drowsy, but tonight, somehow, he felt wide awake. As he ate his solitary supper he had, for some reason he had forgotten, started to think about the German.

Not just thinking. Worrying. And that didn't make sense. What if it was the German he'd seen several times in the past eighteen years, the last time just about a week ago, on the subway? Mike long since had convinced himself that the German would never recognize him and never connect his grownup daughter with the baby left in the warehouse that long ago July night. Besides, the chances were that the German no longer had the slightest reason to be interested in Mike. Either the German had found some other means of locating what lay buried in a mountainside four thousand miles away, or he had given up trying, and turned to other enterprises.

Then why did he have this sense that his tall, gray-eyed daughter, who didn't even know of his own existence, let alone the German's, was moving closer and closer to some sort of danger?

A dull pain in his midriff now, rapidly growing sharper. Take as few pills as you can get by with, the doctor had said. Nevertheless, Mike switched on the light on the battered stand beside his bed, poured water from what had been an orange juice bottle into a glass, and then groped in the nightstand drawer for the vial of pills.

7

On her lunch hour the next day, Katherine made her last visit to the *News* and found that there had been no more replies to her ad. Out on the sidewalk she hesitated. Since up until today she'd received no replies through the *Times*, it seemed unlikely that she would find any letters awaiting her there now. Besides, the recent spell of Indian summer weather seemed definitely at an end. The afternoon was bleak, with an overcast sky and a gusty wind that held a hint of coming rain or even snow. It definitely was not the sort of day when anyone would want to devote one's lunch hour to a probably fruitless walk through chilly streets. Nevertheless, head bent against a blast of wind, she turned toward Times Square. It would be foolish to pass up even the possibility of receiving additional replies to her advertisement.

About fifteen minutes later she discovered that she did have a reply, encased in a business-sized envelope addressed in typescript to Box 932, *New York Times*. Unable to restrain her impatience, she opened the envelope before leaving the building.

The typewritten message inside consisted of one sentence: "Please telephone me at Wexley 9-1725 at any time after five-thirty P.M." It was signed, "Yours truly, Carl Dietrich."

On the surface, this brief communication seemed less promising than the other two she had received. This Carl Dietrich didn't even say he had any information for her, although the fact that he had answered her ad indicated that he did. Somehow, though—perhaps only because he had written to the staid *Times* rather than the brash *News*—she had a feeling that, if he chose to, this man could tell her something about herself.

She had a sudden memory of how Gil had looked last night, weary and out of patience and frighteningly remote. Perhaps she should drop this letter into the wastebasket over there. Perhaps she should just give up, and take quickly, quickly what Gil offered. But no, she'd made up her mind about that. Thrusting the letter into her handbag, she went out onto the sidewalk and headed for the subway stop.

At six-thirty that night, her hand not quite steady, she dialed Carl Dietrich's number. He lived, the phone book had told her, at an address on West Twelfth Street. For several seconds she listened to a phone ring in some room—part of a walkup apartment, a private house, a floor-through in one of those lovely old Village houses?—more than two miles away. Then a man's voice said evenly, "Hello. Carl Dietrich speaking."

"My name is Katherine Derwith, Mr. Dietrich. You answered my ad in last Tuesday's *Times*."

"The one about the child abandoned twenty-eight years ago? Yes, I answered it. I suppose you were the child in question."

After a moment's hesitation, she said, "I guess that's obvious. Now what information do you have for me."

He was silent for several seconds. Then he said, "Wouldn't it be better to discuss this face to face?"

Oh, no, she thought coldly, not again. She would not for the second time go to a strange man's apartment, nor would she allow him to come to hers. "Where do you suggest that we meet face to face?"

"I'll leave that up to you. Perhaps there is some bar or restaurant convenient to where you live. Since tomorrow is Saturday, I can meet you any time that you like."

She said, after a moment, "How about Garrity's Place, on Third Avenue near Seventy-first? We could meet around four." At that hour, with the luncheon crowd gone and the cocktail crowd still to arrive, Garrity's would be a quiet place to talk.

"That would be fine. Will you excuse me for a moment?"

He left the phone. A second or two later she heard a rasping sound, like that of an oven door opening. Then he was back on the line. "I had to go into the kitchen to make sure my dinner wasn't burning up."

So apparently he did not live in a large place, not if the kitchen was that close to whatever room—foyer, living room, or bedroom—in which his phone was placed. And probably he lived alone, since he had said my dinner, rather than the dinner or our dinner.

She asked, "How will I know you?"

After a moment he answered. "I'm thirty-seven. My hair is dark blond and my eyes are gray. I'm an even six feet tall. Is that a sufficient description?"

"I think so."

"How about yourself?"

"You mean, what do I look like? Well, as you know, I'm twenty-eight. I'm five-feet-seven and my hair is red and my eyes are gray."

"Very well. Goodbye until tomorrow, Miss Derwith."

"Goodbye, Mr. Dietrich." Katherine hung up.

She prepared and ate a simple meal, a ground round steak patty and a salad. Then, even though a movie she wanted to see was showing two blocks away, she sat down before the TV set and tried to concentrate on a Channel Thirteen presentation of the New York City Ballet. She must not go out. Gil must have reached Los Angeles hours ago. Surely he would phone.

The little ormulu clock on her desk pointed to nine o'clock, nine-thirty, ten. The phone remained silent. By ten-thirty she began to feel panic. Gil was utterly fed up. Her only chance of getting him back was to give up this obsessive search. Tomorrow she would tell him that she had given it up. From his secretary she would find out where he was staying in Los Angeles, and she would phone him there. In the meantime she would call this Carl Dietrich and break her appointment with him.

She sat down on the love seat and reached for the phone standing on the end table. Dietrich's one-sentence message, giving his number, still lay beside the phone. She dialed.

That phone three miles away to the west and south rang four times, five. Well, she shouldn't have expected a bachelor to be home on Friday night. After the seventh ring she hung up.

She was glad he had been out, glad that she still had her appointment with him. It was only a momentary weakness that had made her waver in the decision she had made days ago. Unless she could find out who she was, she and Gil had no chance of any real happiness, anyway.

Still hoping for the phone's ring, she watched *Sleeping Beauty* on the TV screen until the final pageantry of Aurora and her wedding guests moving in a circle upon the wide stage. Then, unhappily sure that Gil would not phone that late, she went to bed.

Across town, in the austerely masculine bedroom of a high-rise apartment in the West Thirties, a phone rang. Lying in bed, with the sheet and blankets folded neatly across his barrel chest, the man who called himself Hans Gorman placed the paperback book he had been reading, a biography of Himmler, beside the ringing phone. Then he lifted the instrument from its cradle. "Yes?"

"Hello, Mr. Gorman." It was Johnny Wade's voice. "You want to hear the tape?"

Light blue eyes cold behind his reading glasses, Gorman asked, "Which tape?"

"His. I haven't been able to get his stepmother's yet."

"You were supposed to phone me by five this afternoon!"

Each Friday afternoon, in a delivery man's striped apron and carrying a bag of groceries, Wade was supposed to enter Carl Dietrich's walkup apartment house. If the coast was clear on the third floor—and it always had been, apparently because all the tenants on that floor had daytime jobs—he would enter Carl Dietrich's silent apartment and swiftly dismantle the phone. He would remove the miniaturized tape he had inserted the week before and put a fresh one in its place. Then he would leave.

For performing such service, Hans Gorman paid Johnny Wade very well indeed. In fact, a good part of the money Gorman made went for keeping tabs on Carl Dietrich and his stepmother, Inga. Gorman didn't mind too much. Since he never filed a report with Internal Revenue, the money he made was tax free. And the payoff from those tapes, if it ever came, would be enormous.

"Well?" he demanded. "Why didn't you phone earlier?"

"I was going to tell you. I couldn't get into Dietrich's place this afternoon because I spent all day hanging around Knickerbocker Town, waiting for his stepmother to leave her building." Knickerbocker Town was an enormous complex of apartment houses in the East Twenties. "Finally I went up to her apartment and listened outside her door. I heard her on the phone, telling somebody she had the flu. I left, but by that time it was almost time for Dietrich to get home from work, so I just went to the bar across from his place and waited until I saw him go out for the evening. I mean, I could tell by the way he was dressed that he wasn't just going out to the deli or to get a paper, so when he was out of sight I went into his apartment and got the tape." He paused. "That satisfy you, Mr. Gorman?"

There had been a note of challenge in Wade's voice. Gorman repressed his annoyance. That was the one big disadvantage of operating outside the law. You had to put yourself more or less in the hands of your associates. And although Johnny had been a docile employee so far, apparently content to pocket his money without asking any questions, all that might change if Gorman pushed him too far.

"I see. Well, get Mrs. Dietrich's tape as soon as you can."

"You want to hear his tape now?"

"Yes, please."

Gray, stubbled hair on his round head glinting in the lamplight, he leaned back against the pillow and held the phone to his ear.

The recording device hidden in Carl Dietrich's phone was active only when he was making or receiving a call. Thus there were only a few seconds of blank tape between conversations. Gorman listened patiently to the same sort of useless talk he had been hearing ever since, five years before, he had decided to bug Carl's phone as well as his stepmother's. This past week Carl twice had phoned to get the weather report, and once to get the correct time. He had telephoned a girl named Jean, and made a date to take her to the latest Neil Simon play "next Friday night." He had received calls from an encyclopedia salesman, an insurance salesman, and a colleague of his on the news desk of a local TV station.

A brief silence on the tape, a silence that might indicate a lapse of hours or even days. Then: "Hello. Carl Dietrich speaking."

"My name is Katherine Derwith. You answered my ad in the *Times*."

"The one about the child abandoned twenty-eight years ago? Yes, I answered it."

Phone still glued to his ear, Gorman sat bolt upright in bed. Twenty-eight years ago. Twenty-eight years ago! He stared at the wall, seeing in his mind's eye that alley near the Hudson River, and that smartass little wop, Mike Russo, kneeling on the ground while one of the hired musclemen twisted his arm. Gorman hadn't known then that Russo had hidden his girl baby in a warehouse. He didn't know it until more than twenty-four hours later, when he saw her picture and the story in the newspaper.

Where, he wondered fleetingly, had Russo run away to that night? Certainly he hadn't returned to his apartment house in the several weeks Gorman had hired one of the musclemen to watch the place.

Gorman had never wondered much about the baby girl. But it was only natural to expect that a pretty infant like the one in the newspaper photo would have been adopted by someone. And now, for some reason, she wanted more information about herself, and so had put an ad in the paper. It was no wonder that Gorman hadn't seen it. He seldom had any reason to look at the classifieds.

In his excitement he'd missed some of the tape. Now the girl was saying, "How about Garrity's Place on Third Avenue near Seventy-first?"

He listened intently to the rest of the conversation. It was followed only by silence. Gorman said, "Is that all?"

"Right."

"Play the tape again."

"All of it?"

"No. Start about two-thirds of the way through."

Gorman listened to the tail end of the call from Carl's colleague at the TV station. The conversation with Katherine Derwith followed.

When it ended he said, "You're not going out anyplace, are you, Johnny?"

"No. I want to catch the *Late Show*. There's an old fight movie. Kirk Douglas."

"Good. I'll call you back in a little while."

He hung up, heart pounding. So Inga Dietrich *had* lied to him all these years. Back in Berlin, after her husband's death, she had lied to him. She had lied to him when he followed her to New York.

Yes, she knew about the freight car and engine buried somewhere in the Italian Alps. Probably she even knew the exact location. And she must have told her stepson Carl at least a little about it. Otherwise why should he have answered the ad placed by Mike Russo's daughter? Russo, the only witness to what had happened to that freight car and engine, and to the poor dupes who operated it.

Perhaps, he told himself, Inga and Carl had been hoping he would die, so that they could do something about that buried loot without any interference from him. After all, they were both a lot younger than he was. Inga had been only eighteen—a blond and beautiful eighteen—when she became the second wife of former S.S. Colonel Wilhelm Dietrich. Even now she was still in her forties, and still very attractive, for that matter. As for Carl, he was about a dozen years younger than his stepmother.

But they wouldn't get the contents of that freight car, he told himself. In spite of Wilhelm Dietrich, that dead man he hated with a fierce hatred, Gorman intended to get what was rightfully his. He stared at the wall, seeing Dietrich as he had looked during the war, thin in his black S.S. uniform, black boots glistening, black cap worn at a rakish angle above his bony face.

Dietrich had promised him half, and he had earned it. Oh, not that Gorman—or S.S. Lieutenant Frederick Schweitzer, as he had been in those days—had actually helped bury the freight car. Colonel Dietrich, the sly bastard, had been careful to do that all by himself. But it was Gorman who, as a supply officer, had assembled the contents of that freight car during the last, confused days of the war. By drawing up false orders, and attaching to them the forged signatures of high-ranking officers, he had seen to it that the roof of the freight car was reinforced with steel heavy enough that, if necessary, it could withstand the impact of falling rock. And then, with the aid of forged orders, he had seen to it that the car was filled with diverted loot. A Cellini salt cellar and five old masters, two by Piero della Francesca and three by Andrea del Sarto—once destined for Hermann Goering's collection. Solid gold and silver chalices and candlesticks stripped from churches all over Italy, a country that once had been a viable German ally but, after Mussolini's fall, was just more German-occupied territory. Etruscan statues from Florence, once destined to ornament the grandiose complex of museums and other public buildings which Hitler had planned for Berlin, but which now would never be built, because Germany obviously was losing the war. Gold in the form of ingots. And several steel cases, welded shut, which Gorman had suspected held diamonds and other precious stones.

Loot worth millions, perhaps tens of millions, even then, and much more now. And because Dietrich had kept evading his promise to tell Gorman where he had buried it, probably it was still there.

He became aware that his heart was pounding at the thought of long-delayed triumph over the man who had cheated him. Relax, he warned himself. He felt that he was in fairly good physical shape, but even so he had to bear in mind that his sixtieth birthday was looming up, and that men of his physique, short and barrel-chested, seemed especially prone to cardiovascular troubles.

Taking deep breaths, he leaned back against the pillow until his heartbeats quieted. Then he began to consider what his first step should be. Well, obviously, he should try to learn more about Katherine Derwith, and about Carl Dietrich's purpose in answering her ad. He lifted the phone and dialed Johnny Wade's number.

"Johnny, I want you to go to the restaurant where they are meeting tomorrow."

"That place on Third Avenue? Sure."

"If you can, get close enough to hear what they say. But in any event, follow the girl home. See what sort of place she lives in, whether it has a doorman, and so on."

"Shall I try to get Mrs. Dietrich's tape tomorrow?"

"Only if it doesn't interfere with the other. The other is more important." He paused. "There'll be a bonus for you."

"Thanks, Mr. Gorman," Johnny said, and hung up.

8

At four the next afternoon, wearing a raincoat because of the threatening gray sky, Katherine walked into Garrity's Place. It was a long narrow room, with a bar on one side, booths on the other, and a cluster of tables at the rear. Years ago, Garrity's had been a gathering place for working-class Irishmen. Now, even though it had a smart East Side clientele—advertising executives and publishing people and airline hostesses—it strove to maintain its Irish ambiance. Red-and-white checked cloths covered the square tables, and ancient photographs of such prizefighters as John L. Sullivan and Jack Sharkey hung behind the bar.

As she had anticipated, at this hour the place was almost empty. A thirty-fivish couple, who gave an immediate impression of being married but not to each other, sat at the near end of the bar, holding hands and looking deep into each other's eyes. A few stools from the bar's other end sat a man of indeterminate age who didn't look like a Garrity customer. Dark-haired and short and wizened, he might have been a jockey. And then there was a man rising from a chair beside one of the tables against the back wall. She walked toward him.

"Mr. Dietrich?"

"Yes, Miss Derwith. Would you like to take off your coat?"

He helped her out of her raincoat and hung it beside a duffel coat on a rack near the end of the bar. Then he pulled out a chair for her. Exchanging polite, constrained smiles, they both sat down.

His face, she saw, was strongly modeled, with prominent brow ridges, high cheekbones, and a well-defined jaw. As he had told her over the phone, his eyes were gray. They had an expression—reserved, inward-looking—that seemed puzzlingly familiar to her.

The bartender, beefy and white-aproned and authentically Irish, had come from behind the bar to take their order. Carl Dietrich asked Katherine, "What will you have?"

"Campari and soda, please."

He looked up at the bartender. "And I'll have the same."

When the bartender had left, Carl Dietrich said, "I suppose this must have been a pre-Prohibition saloon at one time."

"So they say."

"Do you come here often?"

"Fairly often." Every now and then Gil liked to come to Garrity's for its famous corned beef. "The food is good here."

"It is? I'll have to remember that."

Temporarily out of conversation, they sat smiling those strained smiles. But when the bartender had set drinks before them and walked away, Katherine leaned forward. "Mr. Dietrich, what is it you know about me?"

He remained silent for a moment. Before this he hadn't known how hard it was going to be to lie to her, how hard to disappoint her. But then, before this he hadn't known she had that thin, lovely face, those gray eyes that were both intelligent and vulnerable.

At last he said, with an effort, "I don't know anything about you."

He saw the dismay in her eyes. "But then why—" She broke off, and then went on in a low, indignant voice, "Why did you answer my ad? Why did you bring me here?"

"Because maybe I can help you find out more about yourself."

"And just how can you do that?"

"Well, first of all, I work for Channel Fifteen." Thank God he didn't have to lie about that. "I'm on the news desk."

"And?"

"Part of my job is to look through the classifieds for items we might use for spot news." That too was true. Often ads he'd found in the classifieds proved to be newsworthy enough to justify the dispatch of an interviewer and a camera crew. There had been the advertisement of the Long Island couple who boarded "exotic pets," ranging from piranhas to a bathtub-sized alligator to a black widow spider kept in a bottle. There had been the ad of a psychologist seeking identical twins for an I.Q. comparison study. And there had been the Woman Power Movers, a firm with all-female crews.

"That's how I happened to see your ad."

That part was not true. It was Inga, his stepmother, who had spotted the ad and come to his office, looking concerned, to tell him about it.

Katherine's eyes were even more hostile now. "And you hoped you could make a news item out of me?"

"No, not a news item. I thought it might make the basis for a documentary style program. You see, I've done a little writing of that sort, not on my present job but earlier, for one of the networks."

That also was true. He'd written two such programs, one about crooked apartment rental agents, the other about teenage alcoholics. He added, "You would be well disguised, if that's the way you want it. I wouldn't use your real name or your address."

Her face still held that accusing expression. "But what would be the point," she asked coldly, "beyond the advancement of your own career?"

He looked at her impassively. "I thought it might help you to find out more about yourself, about who your parents were, and why you were abandoned. That's what you want, isn't it?"

She nodded, tight-lipped.

"All right. Look at it this way. Probably not more than a few thousand people read your ad." He continued, closely watching her face, "And I gather that none of them responded with anything helpful." When she didn't answer, he asked, "Did anyone at all besides me answer your ad?"

She shrugged, and then said in that same cold voice, "An old lady who thinks she's psychic, and a creep who thought answering my ad might pay off for him, one way or another."

Doubtless she was thinking of him as still another one who hoped she would "pay off." But at least he knew that in the last few days she had not gained any new knowledge about herself, or her father, or an event which had occurred in the Italian Alps when Carl himself was only two years old, and she hadn't even been born.

He went on, "A semi-documentary program of the sort I have in mind, going out all over the country, would be seen by millions. Even though the actress playing your part would not be given your name, and even though other circumstances would be disguised, anyone with any knowledge about you might decide to get in touch with the network."

She didn't answer, just sat there with that mingled disappointment and distrust in her eyes.

He said, trying to keep his voice casual, trying not to let anything in his manner betray that this was the information he had come here to get, "Maybe to start with you should tell me what you already know about how and why you were abandoned."

She hesitated. She as yet didn't know what she would decide about that proposed documentary. But surely there would be no harm in answering what he had just said.

"All I know is what my parents told me. The couple who adopted me, I mean. When I came down to New York from Westchester to enter Barnard, I looked up the stories about me in the newspaper back files. It was just as my adoptive parents had said. Someone, probably a man who later called the police, had left me in a warehouse near the West Side docks. There was nothing to indicate who I was."

He had been watching her closely, and he had no doubt she told the truth. She had never had the slightest inkling that her life was tied up with his own.

"I see." After a moment he added, "How about your life now? Do you work?"

"Yes." Her lips curved in a slight smile. "I'm in the news business too, in a small way. I work for one of those neighborhood throwaways that are mostly ads."

"Married?" She shook her head. "Ever been married?"

"No."

"Engaged?"

After a moment she said, "No."

He had noted her hesitation. So there *was* some special man in her life, someone she wanted to marry. Was that why she was trying, at this late date, to find out what her origins were?

She asked, still in that cool voice, "How about you? Are you married?"

"Divorced."

"Any children?"

"A daughter. She's eleven now."

His face had changed. Suddenly she knew why the look in his

eyes had seemed familiar to her. Sometimes, catching sight of her reflection in a mirror, she had seen that same lonely, inward-looking expression in her own eyes.

He asked, "Would you like to see her picture?" He opened his wallet, took out three snapshots, and handed them to her one by one. "That's Ellen when she was six."

As she looked down at the photograph of a child with dark straight hair cut in a Dutch bob and an engaging gap-toothed smile, she couldn't keep her own lips from curving into a smile.

"Here's the way she looks now," he said, and handed her another photograph.

A thinner, older Ellen, whose smile lacked the spontaneity of that gap-toothed grin. Was that partly because her parents had been divorced sometime between the taking of those two snapshots?

Carl Dietrich said, as if reading her mind, "My daughter developed emotional problems after the divorce. A school phobia. She seems all right now, though."

Perhaps it was no wonder that the child hadn't wanted to go to school, Katherine thought. Perhaps she had fear that, if she left her house for even a few hours, she might find that her mother as well as her father was no longer with her.

"And here's another recent one taken with her mother. They live in Rockland County. Ellen spends one weekend a month here in the city with me, and six weeks each summer."

A picture of Ellen and a dark, pretty young woman on a rustic wooden bench, with a blossoming trellised rosebush behind them.

Katherine said, "Your wife—your ex-wife, I mean—is very attractive. Is she Jewish?"

"Yes, Naomi is Jewish." Which meant, of course, that Ellen too would be considered Jewish in religious circles, since the mother's Jewishness or non-Jewishness is the determining factor.

"Not," he added, "that Naomi is in the least religious."

No, not religious. But just the same, when she learned that he was not only German by birth but the son of an officer in Hitler's S.S., she had not been able to stomach the knowledge, even though she had tried to. Within a few weeks, she had flown to Reno, taking Ellen with her.

Katherine handed the picture back to him. "You must be very proud of your daughter." How long had he been divorced? She somehow had the feeling that it had been several years. Strange that he hadn't remarried. "Well," she added, "I must go now."

"What about that semi-documentary?"

He'd never had the slightest intention of writing it. He'd merely used the idea as an excuse for seeing her, and finding out how much or little she knew. Still, it wouldn't do to let her guess it had been only a ploy.

"I'm not sure," she said, "but I think I'm against it." Certainly Gil would be. If ever such a TV film were made, he would walk away from her forever. Yes, even if she learned, as a result of the documentary, that she was descended from a long line of Lowells, Cabots, and Saltonstalls.

He paid the bartender. Then they moved to the coatrack. He said, "Well, why not at least think my proposal over? Maybe we could have dinner Monday night so that you could tell me your decision."

If her decision happened to be yes, he thought, as he helped her on with her raincoat, he would have to discourage the notion somehow, discourage it strongly enough that there would be no chance of her taking the idea to some other writer. He must not run the risk that her father was alive somewhere, and might see such a program. If he did see it, he would realize how unhappy her ignorance of her origins had made his daughter. And then, no matter what fears had kept him silent all these years—fears of deportation, or of being named an accessory-after-the-fact in a war crime?—no matter what those fears, he might come forward—

She said, "I'm not sure I'll be free for dinner." Perhaps Gil would be back in New York Monday night, or at least phone her if he was still out on the Coast. On the other hand, she thought bleakly, he might not phone her from the Coast or anywhere else.

"Why don't you phone me around six Monday evening?" she said. "My number's in the book."

He was getting into his duffel coat. "All right. I'll do that."

They walked out of Garrity's into the November twilight. Tiny snowflakes, almost as fine as salt, slanted down through the streetlamps' glow, melting as they hit the sidewalk. She said, "Thank you for the drink. I'll leave you here. It's only a few blocks to my apartment."

"All right. I hope to see you Monday night. Anyway, I'll telephone you."

They exchanged goodbyes. As she walked away he looked after her, noting the gleam of her smooth hair in the lamplight, and the squareness of her shoulders beneath the beige raincoat, and the grace of her long legs. Was it just to squelch once and for all the idea of the documentary that made him want to see her again? Or would he have wanted to meet her again anyway, this girl who'd had no idea all these years that he was even alive, even though he had known of her existence ever since he was nine?

He turned and walked south. He'd have dinner alone, he decided, at a small Japanese restaurant on East Forty-seventh Street. He'd walk there, just for the exercise. And afterward he would walk another twenty-odd blocks south to Inga's apartment, and assure her that there was nothing to worry about.

A few doors south of Seventy-ninth Street, Katherine stopped to look at a display of penny banks in an antique store window. Just as she was about to move on she glanced to her right. About thirty feet away, standing in front of another shop window, a thin, very short man looked in her direction. Quickly he turned his gaze to whatever was displayed in the window. After a moment she realized that she had seen him only minutes before, sitting on a bar stool in Garrity's Place.

Had he found her so irresistibly attractive that he had followed her? Since he was only about five-feet tall to her five-feet-seven, she found the idea amusing. She walked on across the street. Perhaps a minute later she looked back. There was no sign of him.

9

Hans Gorman, shaving in preparation for a solitary dinner at Luchow's, heard his phone ring. Wiping lather off his face with a towel, he walked into the bedroom and lifted the phone from its cradle. "Yes?"

"It's Johnny Wade, Mr. Gorman. I saw them at that Third Avenue place."

"Well? What did they talk about?"

"I don't know. I couldn't get close enough to hear, not without them knowing. If they'd taken a booth I might have slipped into the next one, but they sat at a table."

Gorman swore briefly. "You didn't find out anything?"

"Well, one thing. The coatrack was near the end of the bar. While he helped her on with her coat he asked her to have dinner with him Monday night, and she said she didn't know but he could call her around six. They went out then, and I followed her part way home."

"Part way! What was the use in—"

"Take it easy, Mr. Gorman. She spotted me, but so what? She's in the phone book. I waited about three-quarters of an hour and then went to that address to make sure she still lives there. She does. There's no doorman at night, but I suppose there is in the daytime. The elevator's automatic. I went up to her apartment. She was there. I could hear music through the door, a record player or a radio. Only one lock on her door, and it's a piece of cake."

For Johnny, nearly all locks were a piece of cake. He could open ninety percent of them with just a plastic credit card.

"One bad thing, though," Johnny went on. "There are a lot of professional apartments in that building. Doctors, two of them on her floor. That means people would be going in and out all day and maybe evenings, too. If we bug her phone, it might be tough getting the old tapes out and putting fresh ones in."

Gorman thought for a moment. "Then don't bug it. At least not yet."

"Anything else right now, Mr. Gorman?"

"No. I'll let you know when there is." He hung up and returned to the bathroom mirror.

As he drew the razor along his gray-stubbled jaw he began to think, not of Carl Dietrich, but of Carl's father, back in those first bleak years after the war, when Allied soldiers had strolled through the ruins of Berlin like the conquerors they were.

No doubt that back then Colonel Wilhelm Dietrich had figured he had plenty of time to recover the contents of that freight car. He would wait until the occupation was over, and then put into effect whatever plans he had made. In the meantime he had kept, as the Americans said nowadays, a low profile. Because he had been a civil engineer before the war, he had been assigned to drafting plans for cleaning up the rubble-strewn city, just as Gorman, once a freight despatcher, had been assigned to what was left of the railroad yards. Now and then the two men would meet in a café where, over steins of beer, Gorman would argue that he had every right to know the location of that freight car, and Dietrich would answer that he would be told "when the right time comes." Until then, Dietrich said, it was enough for Gorman to know that the car was "safe," buried in one of the scores of abandoned Italian Alpine mines from which, over the centuries, men had extracted salt or iron pyrites.

Only once, after several glasses of schnapps, had Dietrich let something slip—the name of a village, San Simone. From the rueful look that had come into Dietrich's eyes, Gorman gathered that the freight car was somewhere in the vicinity of San Simone, but how far away and in what direction in that wilderness of deep valleys and towering mountains Gorman was unable to learn, no matter how persistently he questioned.

On several occasions Dietrich had brought his young son, Carl, with him to the café, probably because he had no one to leave him with. Dietrich's wife, Carl's mother, had been killed during an air raid when the child was only a year old. Even though the boy was still very young in those years after the war, both men were careful to argue only in veiled terms when Carl was with them.

Five years after the war, ex-Colonel Wilhelm Dietrich had married again. Her name was Inga. Twice after the marriage Dietrich had brought her to a restaurant meal with Gorman. Both times a warning look in the older man's eyes had kept Gorman from mentioning his grievance. But Gorman had felt a helpless, bitter certainty that Dietrich had told his bride about the freight car. To Gorman it seemed that there could be no other reason why a dazzling young girl should have married Dietrich with his salary of only four hundred occupation marks a week, his balding head, his ill-fitting suit which had replaced his once-resplendent uniforms.

Perhaps Dietrich in time actually would have told Gorman the freight car's location, although Gorman doubted it. Anyway, a taxi wheeling around a Berlin street corner had made the question academic. Struck down, Dietrich had died on the way to the hospital.

A few days after Dietrich's death, Gorman visited the bereaved bride of three months and offered to help her retrieve the loot if she would tell him where it was. Cornflower blue eyes looking straight into his, Inga had said that she didn't know what he was talking about.

Twice more he visited her, and each time she denied that her husband had told her anything. The third time he went to her flat he found it vacant. Frau Dietrich, the janitress told him, had sold her furniture and flown to New York, taking her small stepson with her. Easy to understand, he reflected bitterly, how a girl with her looks could persuade an official to issue her a passport and visa.

Baffled and enraged, he had walked the streets for two hours, past the few remaining bombed-out buildings, and past new apartment houses and business structures standing where once there had been mountains of rubble. Now he was more sure than ever that Inga had lied to him, that in time she would return to Germany and retrieve the vast fortune that was half his. But he dared not apply for the documents he needed in order to follow her and keep an eye on her. A routine check of his war record was sure to reveal incidents that would not only keep him out of the United States but probably land him in front of the War Crimes Commission.

Then he recalled the S.S. non-commissioned officer who—asking no questions, merely pocketing Gorman's five thousand marks—had helped with all the forged documents necessary to direct those stolen riches to the freight car. The man still lived in a Berlin suburb. Gorman went to him and, a few days later, received seaman's papers made out, not to ex-Lieutenant Frederick Schweitzer, but to Hans Gorman, naturalized Italian citizen born in Vienna. Confident that the forged papers would pass muster with the port authorities in Naples, he took the train south.

After he jumped ship in New York that long-ago autumn, he had no trouble locating Inga Dietrich. It was just a matter of looking her up in the phone book. Afraid that he might cause her to run again before he had the means to follow her, he did not talk to her on the phone or approach her in any way. But over the next two years, while he worked at various obscure jobs—dishwasher, short-order cook, street vendor—he kept tabs on her. Every now and then he would telephone her apartment in the huge new complex of buildings known as Knickerbocker Town and then, when she or her young stepson answered, hang up. A few times he had sat, hat well pulled down, on a bench bordering one of the walks between the tall blocks of apartments and watched her return home, usually from some modeling assignment. He knew she had become a model, not only because of the big flat photograph case she often carried, but because once he had trailed her to a modeling agency.

He had been in New York over two years when, in a seaman's bar on West Street, he struck up an acquaintance with the purser of a Brazilian freighter-passenger ship. It led to what proved to be a lucrative opportunity for Gorman, a chance to smuggle uncut industrial diamonds from Rio de Janiero to New York. But he had best get a passport, the Brazilian said. Aware that fake passports were easier to obtain in Canada, and almost sure now that Inga would stay put for a while, he had crossed the border. When he returned to New York, the purser had arranged for Gorman to ship as his assistant aboard the Brazilian vessel.

But a week before he was to sail he had seen Michael Russo, pushing a hand truck loaded with dresses in the garment district. Even though Gorman knew him only from photographs, there was no mistaking that he was Russo, grown a few years older but still in his early twenties. Russo, who at the age of seventeen had been a witness to the burial of that freight car. Russo, the little wop who might possibly be the only person alive who knew where the freight car was.

Now, drawing the razor over sagging jowls, Gorman's hand trembled with rage. He swore, dropped the razor, fished inside the medicine cabinet for a styptic pencil, and applied it to a cut on his chin. He hated that kid Russo—no kid now; in his fifties if he was still alive—almost as much as he hated the memory of Colonel Wilhelm Dietrich.

Over the years, Gorman had never been able to decide whether or not Russo had lied to him that day in the garment district. Maybe the kid didn't have any safe deposit box. Certainly an afternoon search of that coldwater flat where he'd lived with his baby had produced no such key. And they hadn't found it on him in the alley. But then, they hadn't been able to finish searching him before they heard police sirens, and knew that somehow, earlier, the little guinea bastard had managed to call the cops.

It was about thirty-six hours later that Gorman read about the baby stashed away in that warehouse. He could still remember how, reading his newspaper in the subway, he had felt cold sweat spring out all over him. If there was a key, maybe Russo had left it in the kid's basket, or beside it, and the police had it now, and were looking for the box it belonged to. Or, just possibly, in the darkness it had been knocked to the warehouse floor and was still there.

He had been afraid to go down to the warehouse himself lest the police have the place staked out, and so he had sent one of the two goons—men recommended by the Brazilian purser—who had worked Russo over in the alley. The man had found no key of any kind.

In near panic, Gorman had gone that night to see Inga Dietrich. Over the intercom in the foyer of her apartment house he had told her he was a Western Union messenger.

He could still remember the astonished alarm in her face when, a minute or so later, she opened her apartment door and saw him standing there. Obviously she hadn't known he was in New York. Then she recovered. "Why, Herr Schweitzer," she said. Her dimples flashed. "I thought your voice sounded a little old for a messenger boy's."

"Please, Frau Dietrich! May I come in?"

"Of course."

As soon as he was in her living room with the door closed behind him he said, "I am no longer Frederick Schweitzer. I am now Hans Gorman."

"I see. Please sit down, Herr Gorman. May I offer you something? Coffee? Whiskey?"

"No, thank you. I'd prefer to get right to the point. Do you remember that in Berlin, after your husband's death, I told you that there'd been a witness to what happened in the Italian Alps just before the end of the war?"

Her voice was calm. "I remember vaguely."

"Well, he's here. At least he was here." Rapidly he told her about the safety deposit key that might or might not exist. About the episode in the alley, and the infant left in the warehouse.

She said, "I read in the paper about the baby." Impossible to tell what she was thinking behind those lovely blue eyes. "But what does all that have to do with me?"

"To do with you!" His voice rose. "Somewhere in northern Italy there's a freight car and an engine buried, along with the skeletons of a half-dozen men. And somewhere in this country there is a man who saw it all happen, and who may go to the police about it. Or even if he doesn't, the police may find out. If he really did have a safe deposit box, and it contained what he said it did—"

"I still don't understand, Herr Schweitzer—excuse me, Herr Gorman—what all this has to do with me?"

"Frau Dietrich! It was your husband who buried that loot and murdered those men."

"And so? I had nothing to do with it. The year that it happened—the last year of the war, didn't you say?—I was thirteen years old. I had no idea of what a Colonel Dietrich might have done, or even that he existed."

She went on, "And if by any chance what my husband did—with your aid, of course—comes to the attention of the American authorities, I will merely tell them that I knew nothing about this matter until *you*, Herr Gorman, told me about it in Berlin. Do you think the Americans will arrest me, or even deport me, for something that happened when I was a child of thirteen?"

Baffled, Gorman looked around the pleasant room, with its chintz-covered furniture, its potted plants on the broad sills of a row of windows facing south. Yes, Inga was in what Gorman had heard a sports announcer call the catbird seat. If Russo talked, *she* wouldn't be sent back to face long imprisonment or even the hangman. True, she would lose her chances of cashing in on any knowledge she might have about the location of that wartime loot, but that was the worst that could happen to her.

"For one last time," he said in a low, shaken voice, "I beg you to cooperate with me. I'm sure Wilhelm told you where it is. We mustn't run the risk of the authorities finding out too. If we go back to Italy right now, perhaps we can—"

"And for one last time, Herr Gorman, I tell you that Wilhelm has told me nothing."

She smiled at him, head resting against the back of the armchair in which she sat. Blood pounded in his temples. He longed to launch himself at her, close his hands around that slender throat, squeeze until he heard something snap.

But he must not do that. He needed to have her stay alive. Unless some extraordinary piece of luck came his way, she was apt to remain his one chance of gaining what was rightfully his.

He got to his feet. In his anger, he did something he had remembered not to do these past few years. He bowed, and clicked his heels together. "Goodbye, Frau Dietrich."

As he turned toward the door, he became aware of a pajama-clad figure standing across the room just beyond the entrance to a shadowy inner hallway. It was a boy of about nine, his face green-white with shock. Carl had grown during the past two years, and his hair had darkened from tow-colored to medium blond. Still, Gorman would have recognized him almost anywhere as Wilhelm Dietrich's son.

Inga accompanied Gorman to the door. Hand on the knob, he said, "If you knew nothing, why were you so afraid of my questioning that you ran away from Berlin?"

"Ran away? I didn't run, from you or anyone else. I wanted to come to New York and so I came. I'm not afraid of anything. Notice, please, that I did not change my name. *Auf Wiedersehen,* Herr Gorman."

This time he did not click his heels. "*Auf Wiedersehen,*" he said, still in that strangled voice, and left her.

For the next three days he had remained taut with fear as well as rage, but evidently the little wop hadn't talked, not yet, because no police had turned up at the crummy residential hotel which was all Gorman could afford in those days. When the Brazilian ship sailed he was aboard it. In Rio he went to the address given to him by the purser and picked up the bagful of low-grade diamonds.

Back in New York everything had gone smoothly. No customs inspector had searched him for the diamonds hidden in the false heels of his shoes. And beyond the customs shed no police had waited to arrest him for a crime committed nearly a decade before on the other side of the Atlantic.

What was more, he made sure within the first few hours after his return that Inga had stayed put. He'd been tempted, poor as he was, to pass up the Brazilian trip, lest she slip away during his absence. But she was still here, still setting out from her apartment with her modeling case, still sunning herself on Saturdays on a bench at the Knickerbocker playground's edge, while Carl, looking and sounding thoroughly American by now, played basketball with other boys his age.

It had been enough, or almost enough, to convince him that she was as ignorant as she claimed. Nevertheless, as soon as he could afford to, he had arranged for a tap on her phone. After her stepson's marriage Gorman had wanted to place a similar device on Carl's phone, but with his wife at home all day in their apartment it had seemed too risky. But when, after his divorce, he had moved to his West Twelfth Street walkup, Johnny Wade had installed the bug.

Now, just after he put his razor away, the phone in Gorman's bedroom again rang. He went to it. "Yes?"

"All set?" The voice belonged to his Brazilian associate. He meant, are you ready to sail next week?

"I can't. My doctor has ordered me to have a series of tests."

"He has?" the Brazilian said, in a tone that meant, I don't believe you. When Gorman didn't speak, the Brazilian snapped, "All right. I'll call Charlie."

Charlie was their telephone code name for an Argentinian who sometimes took Gorman's place on the trips to Rio.

The Brazilian must have been quite annoyed, because he added, "Maybe you had better get a checkup. You're carrying too much fat for a man your age. All those dinners at Luchow's."

Gorman would have liked to reply that he wasn't as old as the Brazilian, not by a couple of years, and only a few pounds fatter. But it was best to allow the other man to let off steam. The Brazilian had a right to be annoyed. In exchange for very little effort and not much risk, diamond smuggling had brought Gorman a modest affluence all these years.

But now maybe it was here, that stroke of luck he had been hoping for for more than half a lifetime. And he didn't intend to leave New York until he found out why Wilhelm Dietrich's son was in contact with Michael Russo's daughter.

He said goodbye to the Brazilian. Then he called Johnny Wade. Johnny listened for a few moments and then said, "Look, Mr. Gorman, I'm not much good at tailing people. Besides, I'm busy. I've got other clients besides you, you know."

"Surely you know someone else you can get for me?"

"Yes, I know someone, but it will cost you."

"So it will cost me. Get him," Gorman said, and hung up.

He finished dressing in the navy blue suit, white shirt, and blue-and-white striped tie which, he fancied, made him look like a banker. Then, stomach juices rumbling at the thought of sauerbraten and potato pancakes, he set out for Luchow's.

10

Around eight that evening Carl Dietrich rang the bell outside his stepmother's apartment. She opened the door for him. Flu had reddened the tip of her straight little nose but she still looked attractive in her coral velour kaftan, its skirt split to above the knees in front. Carl often marveled at how good-looking Inga was, her hair still a pale blond, although with a hairdresser's aid these days, and her figure still slender.

When he had hung his duffel coat in the guest closet near the door, she asked, "Did you see her?" Her voice was calm. But then, Inga almost always had an air of cool self-control.

"Yes. Her name is Derwith, Katherine Derwith. She doesn't know anything about her origins. She wants to find out, that's all. That's why she bought that ad you saw."

"But why is she going to so much trouble about it at this late date?"

"I got the impression it's because of a man, someone she wants to marry. But first she wants to find out who she is."

After a moment Inga nodded. "That could well be. What is she like? Attractive?"

"Very."

"Will you see her again?"

"Probably."

She nodded again, but did not comment. Instead she asked, "Have you had dinner?"

"Yes, at that Japanese place."

"Would you like a drink?"

"Do you have any Scotch?"

"Yes, I'll join you. But I don't want any Scotch. Pour me the usual, please."

He walked to the liquor cabinet. Inga sat down on the sofa and crossed the legs which, with monotonous regularity, caused people to ask if she was related to that other Dietrich, Marlene. In a gilt-framed mirror on the opposite wall she could see her lamplit reflection. At this distance the changes in her appearance which years ago had brought the end of her modeling career—the slight softening of her facial contours, the lines around her blue eyes—were invisible, and she looked almost as good as she ever had.

At the liquor cabinet Carl filled a small glass with the almond-flavored liqueur his stepmother liked and brought it to her. Then he returned to the cabinet to mix a Scotch-and-soda. Glass in hand, he stood looking out the window. From there he could see the cement court where, long ago, he had played basketball.

But this was not the same apartment in which he had grown up. That sun-flooded apartment had been on a high floor of another building in the Knickerbocker Town complex. As Inga's modeling income had dropped, her rent had soared. Besides, after Carl's marriage she had needed less room, and so she had moved to this small second-floor apartment with its northern exposure and much cheaper rent.

As often happened when he was with his stepmother, Carl's thoughts reverted to his childhood. Like most people, he could remember his earliest years only in flashes, like still pictures rather than a continuous film. He had one brief memory of sitting at a table with his grandparents—his father's parents—in what must have been their Bavarian farmhouse. But he had no memory of his father coming to get him, or of where they had lived together in Berlin. He did remember piles of rubble though, and he remembered a café where his father and a short, barrel-chested man had talked about the war Germany had lost. He remembered, too, that his father had taken him and an awesomely beautiful lady to the recently reopened Berlin zoo, and that, days or weeks or months later, he and his father and the beautiful lady, who now somehow was his mother, had moved into a flat in a building so new that you could still smell the paint and the lumber.

He did not remember being told of his father's death—perhaps shock had wiped the memory out—but he did remember standing with Inga and other grownups at a graveside. The rattle of dry leaves, wind-driven over a nearby cement walk, had mingled with the voice of a stout man in black who stood at one end of the grave.

Soon after that Carl's memories became continuous. He remembered the flight across the Atlantic and the first exciting, bewildering days in a New York hotel and, later on, that sunny apartment. Thanks to the English Inga had begun to teach him even before they left Berlin, he'd had little trouble keeping up with his first grade classmates when, in the fall, he entered school. True, some of the children snickered at his accent, but they did not provoke him too far, perhaps because he was taller than any of them.

Nevertheless, those early years had been shadowed by the fact of his German birth. He knew, of course, that Germany had lost a war against the United States, and that his father had fought in that war. He also knew, from programs on the small TV set Inga had bought, that many German soldiers were considered "bad," and that the worst wore black uniforms and belonged to something called the S.S. What weighed upon him most was the vague memory of seeing, back in that Berlin apartment, a photograph of a man in such a uniform. Could the man have been his father? Finally, unable to bear his torment alone, he had turned to Inga.

Yes, she had told him, his father had been an S.S. officer, but not all of them had done bad things. Most of them, like his father, had just been soldiers, fighting for their country. As for the photograph, yes, he probably had seen it. She opened her dressing table drawer and took a snapshot from beneath its paper lining. Carl had looked down at the picture of a tall man in shiny black boots and a handsome black uniform, with a visored cap shadowing his bony face. He only vaguely resembled the father Carl remembered, a balding man in ill-fitting civilian clothes.

He accepted Inga's comforting words. In fact, over the next two years—while his English lost all but a trace of accent, while he became a fan of the New York Yankees and Superman Comics, and learned to sink baskets from the far court—he almost forgot that he had not been born an American. But then, on a summer night, he had been awakened by raised voices, Inga's and some man's. Barefooted and pajama-clad, he had padded down the short inner hall that connected the living room with the bedrooms and bath. Then he had stopped short, transfixed by what he saw and heard.

A short, heavy-set man whose face seemed hauntingly familiar, a

man who Inga addressed as both Herr Schweitzer and Herr Gorman. A man who was telling terrible things. Things about a
"smartass young wop" who'd left a baby in a warehouse and then
been beaten up in an alley. A man who had witnessed something
even more terrible that had happened years ago. A freight car and
its engine, and the men who had operated it, all buried in a mine
shaft somewhere. Buried by Wilhelm Dietrich, Carl's father—

When Herr Schweitzer-Gorman had gone, Carl's stepmother had
turned around and seen him standing there.

For a silent interval they had both stood motionless, staring at
each other through the lamplight. Then she had told him to go to
his room. Minutes later, sitting on the edge of his bed, she told him
that they were true, the things he had heard the man say. She had
not known those things when she married Carl's father. It was only
afterward that he had told her, and even then he had not told her
where the freight car was.

"I lied to you about your father," she had said, smoothing his
hair back from his forehead, "because I didn't want to see you
looking the way you look now, your poor face green-white and the
pupils of your eyes like pinpoints. But you must realize that what
your father did had nothing to do with you. And then you must
stop thinking about it. After all, it happened years ago and in another country, while you were still learning to talk. So forget about
it, *liebchen,* forget about it."

With the resilience of childhood, he did manage to forget it most
of the time. He had gone on to junior high school and then high
school, garnering grades that had won him a scholarship to New
York University's School of Journalism. During summer vacations
he had earned enough to pay Inga for his board and room, even
though she had insisted that she did not need the money. True, by
that time the only jobs she had were occasional TV soap opera roles
calling for an attractive, thirty-plus woman with a foreign accent.
But fortunately, she told him, the investments she had made during
her palmy days as a model were still paying off.

After graduation he had taken his first job, on a now-defunct
New York newspaper. One of the copy readers had been a girl with
dark curly hair, blue eyes, and a dusty-rose complexion. Her name
was Naomi Siegel. A few months later he and Naomi were married,
and less than a year after that their daughter was born.

His hand tightened around his glass. Did he still love Naomi?

Probably. Probably he always would, in a way. It was hard to tell, under all the scar tissue left by the divorce, what he did feel.

In the window pane he could see the dim reflection of Inga, now sitting with her fabulous legs curled around her. If he chose to, he could blame Inga for the divorce. It was through Inga that Naomi had learned that Wilhelm Dietrich, her husband's father and her child's grandfather, had belonged to the S.S., that organization whose duties had included the systematic extermination of European Jewry.

But Inga had been drunk the night she gave Naomi that information. Besides, Carl knew that the main fault had been his own. He'd had no right to ask Naomi to marry him, not when he knew she had lost more than a dozen relatives—two grandparents, aunts and uncles, and several cousins—to the concentration camps. No, he'd had no right to ask her, especially when all he had told her was that his dead father had been "a German soldier during the war."

Pray God Ellen, sensitive, loving little Ellen, would never know that her grandfather had worn a uniform with a death's head symbol on its cap. In all probability she would not. During those exhausted, sad last days he and Naomi had spent together—after her furious denunciations of him, after all his responses, first abjectly pleading, then bitter—after all that, when they were able to talk quietly, they had pledged to each other that they would not tell Ellen.

As for that atrocity his father had committed in the Italian Alps, not even Naomi knew about that, and pray God she never would.

Still watching Inga's dim reflection in the window pane, he wondered as he often did if Inga really was ignorant of that stolen loot's location. Carl was not the sort of man to consider all women mysterious. His wife, for instance, had never seemed to him enigmatic, nor did that girl he had met today. True, she had seemed to him a reserved sort of person, but she had not given him the impression that, if he ever got to know her, she would prove to be three or four women rather than one.

Inga, however, did seem to him to behave in a mysterious and contradictory fashion. For instance, in many ways she had been an exemplary mother to him, especially for a woman so young. She had always fed him well, and seen to it that he had regular dental and medical checkups and made good grades. On the other hand, she had never tried to shield him from the knowledge that, in her bedroom across the hall from his own, lovers often stayed with her. Surely she must have known how disturbing such knowledge was to him, especially after he reached adolescence. What made it even more disturbing was that some of the men were quite young, only a few years older than himself.

And that was another mysterious thing. Since she seemed to be attracted so strongly to younger men, why had she married Carl's father?

Across the room, Inga rolled the stem of her liqueur glass back and forth between her fingers and kept her gaze fixed on her stepson's back. How tall and trim he looked in his chino pants and brown wool shirt.

For some years she had been aware—amused rather than shocked by the incestuous overtones—that she found Carl attractive. She had never let him guess that, of course. For one thing, he was far from being the only man she found attractive. For another, she knew that at the first hint of invitation in her manner he would put distance between them and keep it there.

But sometimes she wondered if it wasn't envy of his wife that had caused her, that night four years ago, to show Naomi that old snapshot of Wilhelm in uniform. True, Inga had gotten very drunk that night, something she seldom did. But she'd also had a very bad day, which was her reason for getting drunk. In the morning she'd learned that the pilot for a soap opera in which she was to have a small but continuing role had been turned down by the last of the networks which had considered it. In the afternoon she had gone to the Plaza's Palm Court to meet a man—a good-looking young man of whom she'd grown very fond—and learned from him that he was going to marry a girl she hadn't even known he was seeing, a girl who had been graduated from Hunter College only the week before.

Carl and Naomi, leaving Ellen with a sitter, had come to Inga's apartment for dinner that night. She recalled that, as she drank her third martini, she had observed with resentment how her stepson and his wife looked at each other. It was the look of two people who, after eight years of marriage, were still in love.

There had been wine with dinner. Inga had drunk a lot of it, just how much she couldn't have said, because by that time everything had become blurred.

She did remember sitting on the sofa with a liqueur glass in one hand and, in the other, a snapshot of Ellen which Carl—or was it Naomi?—had handed to her. Then, on her feet and swaying, with liquid from her dropped glass making a puddle on the rug, she'd heard herself say, "Feel rotten. Going to bed."

As she staggered down the inner hall she was aware of Naomi following. Then they were both in Inga's room. "You want to see another picture?" she heard herself saying. "Picture of your father-in-law?"

She did not remember taking that snapshot of Wilhelm from the dressing table drawer, or handing it to Naomi. She did remember a strangled cry, and the sight of Naomi's face, not rosy and glowing now but a muddy white. Then Carl also was in the room. Inga could remember the sound of Naomi's hand slapping his cheek, and then the sight of Naomi darting out the bedroom door with Carl running after her.

Inga remembered nothing at all after that until she awoke the next morning, stretched out fully clothed on her bed. The snapshot of S.S. Colonel Wilhelm Dietrich lay on the rug, face up.

Her bedside phone had begun to ring and had gone on ringing, each of its sounds like a knife stab in her throbbing temples. At last she'd picked up the phone and carried it with a shaking hand to her ear. She heard Carl shouting with pain and fury. She kept saying, at intervals, "I'm sorry, *liebchen*, I'm sorry. I was drunk."

After she said it for the fourth or fifth time there was a silence. Then he said, in a flat, weary voice, "I know you were. Anyway, I'm really the one to blame. I had no right to marry her, no right at all."

From then on until months after his divorce, Carl and Inga had only a few brief phone conversations. Eventually, though, the breach between them had healed. He visited her frequently, and let her know whenever he heard of a TV commercial or soap opera assignment he thought she might fill. If anything, she saw him a little more often than she had during his marriage to Naomi. Inga had not been surprised when he ceased to feel estranged from her. For one thing, he obviously was lonely, even though he dated several young women. For another, Inga was the only mother-figure in his life, or at least the only one he remembered.

Now she set down her liqueur glass beside a box of paper tissues on the end table. With one of the tissues she blew her flu-reddened nose and dropped the tissue into the wastebasket. Then, glass in hand, she again looked at Carl, standing with his back turned to her. In temperament, she reflected, Carl must be a throwback to his Lutheran grandparents, that Bavarian couple who, according to their son Wilhelm, had kept as aloof as possible from the Nazis. Certainly Carl seemed to have nothing in common with his father except high cheekbones and tallness and thinness. And by the time Inga had met him, Wilhelm had lost even the thinness. It was only the old snapshot that told her how he had once looked.

She still had the snapshot. She knew exactly the reasons why she had brought it from Germany and why she kept it still. Her first reason was simple. In that snapshot he at least gave the illusion of being an extremely attractive man. Her second reason was tied up with her feelings as a German. Not that she had any great admiration for Hitler. He had been a genius, true, but also a fool, with his obsessive hatred of Jews, a hatred that during the last months of the war had made him divert precious train space from military uses to carrying prisoners to concentration camps. Still, she could not help feeling a secret pride in the fact that Germany, after its shattering defeat in the First World War, had gained so much strength under Hitler and his S.S. that it had almost—not quite, but almost—conquered the world.

Her third reason was more tenuous. In her lifetime she had seen history take strange turnings, by which onetime national enemies became friends and vice versa, and once despised groups became respectable. Perhaps someday it would be advantageous to be known as the widow of a former S.S. officer. In short, that snapshot with its inscription on the back—"For my beautiful wife, Inga"— might prove to be what the Americans called an ace in the hole.

Just as, she thought, smiling at the phrase, Wilhelm had thought of that freight car as an ace in the hole, a quite literal hole in the mountainside. Perhaps poor old Schweitzer, or Gorman, as he called himself, still hoped to gain possession of that ace. Even though he wasn't listed in the phone book, Inga knew he still lived in New York, at least part of the time. She had caught glimpses of him over the years, most recently a few weeks ago as he emerged from an expensive Fifty-second Street steak house. Whatever the source of his income—and Inga felt sure it was illegal—he had the clothing and air of a prosperous man.

Carl turned toward her. "Another liqueur?"

"No, but you go ahead."

"Thanks. I've had enough."

He collected her empty glass and carried it with his own into the small kitchen. He rinsed the glasses in hot water at the stainless steel sink and then brought them back to the liquor cabinet. When he had stowed them away he asked, "Chess?"

"Why not?"

He took the box containing the chessmen and folded board down from the shelves which, holding ornaments and a few books and a small TV set, ran along one wall. She watched him as he drew a chair up to the other side of the coffee table and placed the chessmen on the board. She had taught him the moves back in Berlin, in the weeks after his father's death. By the time he was nine he could beat her some of the time. From his high school days onward he had won almost every game they played. Tonight, though, his mind must have been elsewhere, because after the fifteenth move his situation was hopeless, and he resigned.

She said, "I'll give you a chance to get even."

"Thanks, but I'm pretty tired." He began to replace the chessmen in their box.

"Carl, why do you want to see that Katherine Donaldson again? Just because you find her attractive?"

"Derwith. Her name's Katherine Derwith. And of course it isn't just because she's attractive. If she persists in trying to unravel the truth about herself, she might just possibly succeed. And if she does, she'll learn the truth about something else, too."

"You mean about what happened in the Italian Alps."

"Exactly. And I can't allow her to find out, because then everybody would know it, including Naomi and Ellen."

Again he thought of the sickening shock his nine-year-old self had sustained that night when he had heard Gorman talk of his goons beating up a man who had left a baby in a warehouse, a man who, years before that, had seen Carl's father bury a half-dozen men alive.

"I'd do anything to protect my daughter from knowing about that," Carl said. "Anything!"

For a moment Inga was reminded of the almost murderous fury she had seen in his face the night she had shown the snapshot to his wife. Then he turned away to restore the chess set to its shelf. After that he put on his duffel coat, kissed Inga's cheek, and left.

11

As she emerged from the elevator into the ninth-floor hall of her apartment house late Monday afternoon, Katherine heard the muffled ringing of a phone. She quickened her pace. Yes, the sound was coming from behind her door. Probably it wasn't Carl Dietrich phoning, not this early. She had asked him to call around six. Gil, then? Oh, surely, surely it was Gil. She had stayed in all day yesterday, feeling almost certain that he was back in New York, and would call her. He had not. But surely now— With unsteady fingers she inserted her key in the lock.

The phone stopped ringing.

Movements slow now, she went into her apartment, hung her coat in the bedroom closet, and returned to the living room. She sat down on the love seat and looked at the phone on the end table. Suddenly she realized that whether or not that call had been from Gil it had given her a legitimate excuse to telephone him.

Swiftly she dialed. As she listened to the phone's ringing, she pictured his East Sixty-eighth Street bachelor apartment, with its Lichtenstein prints on the living room walls, and, in the bedroom, teakwood cabinets flanking the wide bed. She heard a click, and knew that he had lifted the phone standing on one of those cabinets. "Hello."

"Gil?"

After a moment he said, "Why, hello, Katherine."

"Did you call me just now?"

"No."

She waited for him to add to that monosyllable, but he did not.

Trying not to sound dismayed or even awkward, she said, "Well, someone did. I figured that you were probably back from the Coast by now, and so it might be you calling." When he still did not speak, she floundered on, "When did you get back?"

"Late yesterday afternoon."

And he hadn't called her. She was silent for a moment, while her pride battled her need to know what he was feeling. Then she asked, in an almost toneless voice, "Didn't you intend to call me at all, Gil?"

"Katherine, I don't know. Honest to God I don't. I've thought and I've thought about it. Oh, Katy! If you could just promise me that you'd put some things out of your mind—"

His voice trailed off. After several seconds she said, "I could promise you that. But how could I keep such a promise?"

When he spoke his voice sounded tired. "I suppose you couldn't. Well, what shall we do, Katherine?"

She said quietly, "I think that's up to you."

"I suppose it is." He fell silent and then said, "I think we shouldn't see each other for several weeks, or perhaps several months."

"You mean, so that we can find out whether or not we can get along without each other?"

"I guess that's what I do mean. God knows, I don't want to get along without you—"

Again his voice trailed. She said, "All right, Gil. We'll do that." When he didn't speak she said, "Maybe we'll be seeing each other again," and gently replaced the phone in its cradle.

She sat motionless, looking into space. There was really no need for a trial period to determine whether or not they could "get along" without each other. Of course he could get along without her. Not long from now he might find himself falling in love with some other girl—undoubtedly, that next time, with a girl who knew not only who her parents were but her great-great-great-grand-parents. And she could get along without him. In fact, she would be able to get by entirely without love. Some women did.

The phone rang. She reached for it. "Hello." Even though she could be almost certain it was not Gil calling, her voice shook a little.

"Hello. This is Carl Dietrich. Did you decide whether or not to have dinner with me this evening?"

One thing about breaking with Gil, she thought bleakly. Now

there was no reason whatsoever why she shouldn't have dinner with the TV newsman. And there was no reason now why she shouldn't encourage him to write that semi-documentary.

"I'd like very much to have dinner with you."

"Good. I'll pick you up. Seven-thirty okay?"

"Seven-thirty will be fine."

Two hours later they sat over vodka-and-tonics in a small restaurant, an Italian one, on Third Avenue in the Fifties. Katherine said, "I've been thinking over your idea about a TV semi-documentary."

"Yes?" His hand tightened around his glass.

"I've decided it would be a good idea."

"I was afraid of that." His smile was wry. "You see, I've checked around. Writing such a program would be a waste of your time and mine."

"Why?" Her gray eyes looked stricken.

"One of the networks is cooking up a mini-series on the subject of adoptees looking for their biological parents. It's to be based on case histories from the files of an organization called Alma, or something like that. Anyway, it helps adoptees trace their natural parents. Of course, the whole thing may not get off the ground. As you probably know, a lot of shows are killed before they even have a chance on the tube. But as long as this mini-series is in the works, there wouldn't be a chance for a shorter program on the same subject, not written by me or anyone else."

After a long moment she said, "I see."

His hand holding the glass relaxed. She'd believed him.

Katherine asked, "But couldn't we use some other angle?"

"Perhaps. I'll keep thinking about it." He paused, and then added, "Although why you let the question distress you so much, I don't know. Obviously you're healthy, intelligent, and attractive. Doesn't that tell you enough about your ancestry?"

"You sound like someone else I know."

"A man?"

She nodded.

"A man who wants to marry you?"

"He did want to."

"But doesn't now?"

She gave a bleak little smile. "He's fed up with what he calls my obsession. This afternoon on the phone we agreed not to see each other for a while."

"Maybe it will still work out."

She shook her head. "Only if I can find out that my parents were —all right. Not criminals, or insane, or disease carriers. Which is why I'd begun to hope for so much from that TV idea of yours."

Unable to look at her face any longer, he stared down at his glass, turning it around with long fingers. He had deceived her two days ago, and disappointed her tonight, and thus made her even unhappier than she had been before she met him. But he'd had to do it.

"Katherine, there are a lot worse things in the world than not knowing who your father was."

Now what, she wondered, had made him say that? "Yes, I suppose there are."

He smiled. "Why don't you try to forget about it, at least for a few hours?"

"You mean, talk about something else? I'm willing." She paused, and then asked with forced lightness, "What do you think of the energy shortage?"

"I'm against it."

She smiled. "And Woody Allen?"

"I'm for him."

After that their talk ranged over movies, and skiing, and whether or not the East Side of New York had a delicatessen as well-stocked as Zabar's. To her surprise, Katherine found that she was beginning to have a good time.

When their meal was finished he looked at his watch and said, "Only a little past ten. We still might be able to see a movie. Or would you rather go somewhere to listen to music?"

"Thank you, but no. I have to get up too early in the morning. But there is one thing I'd like to do. Why don't we walk up Third Avenue to my place? It might be good for us after all that pasta. And it's fun looking in the shop windows."

The night was chill, and the air so clear that a few major stars were visible despite the haze of city lights. Although they walked briskly, they paused every now and then to look at windows filled with antiques or books or travel posters. When they reached the foyer of her apartment house he said, "Well, I'll say good night here."

She had expected him to accompany her to the door of her apartment and perhaps hint that he would like an invitation for a nightcap. She was relieved that he had not. At the same time she felt a bit piqued. Perhaps it was only out of politeness that he had implied he found her attractive.

He said, "May I see you again?"

"Of course." She realized that she had sounded a little more cordial than she had intended.

"Fine. I'll call you tomorrow evening. Good night."

As she rose in the elevator she again reflected that it had seemed odd to see him walk away without even an attempt at a goodnight kiss. It seemed doubly strange in light of the fact that he had mentioned seeing her again. But then, from the first she had sensed that there was something strange about Carl Dietrich—

She thrust the uneasy thought away. Thanks to Carl Dietrich, she hadn't spent the evening brooding over Gil. Instead she had actually enjoyed that dinner and the walk up Third Avenue. What was more, she wanted to see him again, that tall man with the bony face and inward-looking eyes.

After she entered her apartment she undressed in the bedroom, put on her nightgown and robe and slippers, and moved to her dressing table to cold cream her face. The box of tissues on the table's glass top was empty. She dropped the empty box into a wastepaper basket and then opened the table's right hand drawer for a fresh box.

There wasn't any. After a moment she opened the left hand drawer, saw a box of tissues, and took it out. Strange. Until now she had always placed tissue boxes in the right hand drawer.

She finished creaming her face and then started to cross the room to her bed. Through the thin sole of her right slipper she felt something hard. She stepped aside, bent to the yellow shag carpet, and picked something up. It was a small silver brooch, one she seldom wore.

Her gaze went from the brooch on the palm of her hand to the box of costume jewelry on her dressing table. How had the brooch gotten from there to the carpet?

Had someone been in this room?

She thought of herself dining with Carl Dietrich in that Third Avenue place, while someone, at his instruction, searched this apartment—

No! Even if there was something odd about Carl Dietrich, she wasn't going to let herself think things like that. Besides, what motive could he possibly have had? For that matter what motive could anyone have had for surreptitiously entering her apartment? Certainly not robbery. She had no furs or valuable jewelry. As for her small color TV set, it still stood over by the window on its rollaway stand.

She herself must have placed the tissues in the left hand drawer. As for the brooch, anytime within the last few days she could have taken the brooch out of the box while she searched for a pair of earrings, say, placed the brooch on the dressing table's edge, and then knocked it to the floor. After all, this carpet had not been vacuumed since the previous Thursday.

She replaced the brooch in her jewelry box. Then she took off her robe, laid it over a chairback, and got into bed. For several minutes she thought of Gil and of her chances for happiness with him, now perhaps lost forever. She felt sadness, but not quite the desolation she had expected to feel when she lay alone in the darkness. Gradually her thoughts blurred, and she slipped into sleep.

Lying in bed, Hans Gorman said angrily into the phone, "It's about time you answered. I called you twice before this."

"I was stuck in the subway," Johnny Wade said. "Train stopped dead between the Fifty-first Street station and Grand Central. I don't know what—"

"Well, never mind that. Did you search that girl's apartment?"

"Yes. No safety deposit key."

Gorman was only slightly disappointed. After all, he'd felt that there was little chance that the girl had the key or, if she by some remote chance did have it, that it would prove to be of any value to him at this late date. But since he believed in being thorough, he'd asked Johnny to look for such a key. "All right," he said, "what did you find?"

"Nothing."

"Nothing at all?"

"Nothing like what you said to look for. No hand-drawn map, I mean, or any kind of written directions saying go north so many miles and then south and so on. And I looked good. In her desk, and under the carpets, and behind pictures, and through all the books in her bookcase—"

"All right, all right," Gorman said impatiently. He added, "Were you careful?" meaning, careful not to leave any signs of a search.

"Sure, Mr. Gorman," Johnny said, although in fact he was by no means certain he had left no sign. Searching an apartment in the daytime, when you were sure that the person who lived there would remain at his office, was one thing. Searching at night when the occupant was out on a date was quite another. You never knew when he or she might come back, either with or without the date. Nervous every time he heard the elevator out in the hall open, Johnny had completed his search as rapidly as possible.

"How about the fellow," Gorman asked, "you hired to trail them tonight?"

"Shorty? He left here a few minutes ago. He told me he trailed them to this Italian restaurant on Third. They had a reservation so they got a table right away, but he had to stand in line to even get to the bar. By the time he got in, at least, they didn't have the look of people talking about anything heavy. He trailed them to the girl's apartment. They walked the whole way, and didn't seem to have more on their minds than window-shopping."

Just the same, Gorman thought, Carl Dietrich's seeking out Mike Russo's daughter had something to do with that freight car. It just had to.

"All right," he said. "That's all for now."

Carl Dietrich was having trouble getting to sleep. He kept wishing that the Derwith girl were not so attractive, not just good-looking, but nice too. A girl with scruples. As they walked up Third she had told him a little about this Gil. Social Register. Princeton. Headed for a partnership in one of New York's most prestigious firms. No matter what the circumstances of their own birth, most girls would grab a guy like that. But not this girl.

Before he'd left her at the door of her apartment house he had felt an almost irresistible impulse to tilt her chin with his fingers and kiss her full mouth. But he must not do that. He must not even see her too often, just often enough to make sure that she had not turned to some other—and successful—means of tracing her parentage. Because he must always be aware that no matter how attractive and sensitive and decent Katherine was, and no matter how much she needed to learn that there was nothing really wrong with those who had given her life, Ellen's interests came first. No matter what the cost to Katherine, his daughter must be protected from the spirit-shattering knowledge of her own heritage.

He punched his pillow, turned over in bed, and again tried to sleep.

12

Gil did not call Katherine during the next few weeks, but Carl Dietrich did, only every few days at first, then with increasing frequency. She found that they had many tastes in common: Szechwan food, the hotter the better. The view from the terrace at the Cloisters, with the Jersey Palisades soaring above a river which, at this time of year, was trimmed along each bank by a ragged coating of ice. The Wall Street district on Sunday, with the wind keening between solid walls of skyscrapers, and the sidewalks so deserted that they might have been exploring some city abandoned hundreds of years in the past. Either that, or some city in the future, after a neutron bomb had destroyed its inhabitants and left its buildings silent but intact.

She learned something of his past during those days. How he had been born in Germany during the war. How both his parents had died, his mother in a bombing raid when he was a year old, his father in a street accident when Carl was six. He told of coming to New York a few months later with his stepmother and, with the adaptability of a child, becoming so thoroughly American that by the time he entered junior high school he had almost forgotten he had ever been anything else. He told of how, when he was twelve, his stepmother Inga had become a citizen, and filled out the certificate which conferred citizenship upon him, too.

He talked freely of his days at NYU, and of his present job. After they had lunched together one day he took her to the TV station, introduced her to the anchorman and to reporters whose faces had long been familiar to her, and showed her his own office where he prepared portions of the newscasts. But about the causes of his divorce he kept a complete and puzzling silence.

What Katherine found even more incomprehensible was that, even after they had seen each other a dozen times, and even though every instinct told her that he desired her, he had made no attempt at love-making beyond a restrained goodnight kiss. What was more, she sometimes caught a glimpse of something hostile in his eyes, as if he resented her, or resented the attraction she held for him. Then the look would disappear, so completely that she would feel she must have imagined it.

A few days before Christmas she ran into Gil—almost literally ran into him—in the men's department at Bloomingdale's, where she had gone to buy a sweater for her adoptive father. Moving down a crowded aisle, she came face to face with Gil. At first she was aware only of him. Then she saw that he was accompanied by a girl, a slender brunette with dark blue eyes and classic features. After an awkward moment he said, "Why, hello, Katherine. Merry Christmas."

"Merry Christmas." She felt jumbled emotions. Surprise, envy of that poised and lovely girl beside him, and embarrassed wonder as to how much about the breakup of their affair Gil had told his companion.

"Katherine, this is Joan Haverland. Joan, this is Katherine Derwith."

"How do you do?" Katherine said. Then, as a woman bumped shoulders with her: "I'm afraid I'd better move on. We're blocking traffic. Nice to have met you, Miss Haverland. Goodbye, Gil."

He called her early that evening. "Since we ran into each other like that, I thought perhaps I'd better call you. About Joan, I mean."

"What about her?" She made her voice light. "You mean that it's serious?"

"I think it's going to be, Katherine. I don't know what to say, except that if it upsets you, I'm sorry."

"I don't really have a right to be upset, do I? After all, I had my chance."

He was silent for several seconds. Then he asked, "Are you seeing anyone else?"

"As a matter of fact, I am."

"And I guess you're finding him an adequate—replacement." The little laugh he gave was rueful, as if he'd realized that his voice held a jealous note.

"It's not like that. In fact, I don't know what he feels about me. I just know that I enjoy his company, and that having him around has made—has made not seeing you a lot easier for me."

Another long pause. Then: "I'm glad, Katherine. And again, Merry Christmas."

"Merry Christmas."

She hung up. Almost instantly the phone rang. It was Carl. "Would you like to cook dinner at my place tomorrow night? If so, maybe you'd better give me the shopping list now."

The stove in Katherine's apartment, which the landlord was always promising to replace but never did, had an oven door that kept falling open and no pilot light. Carl's apartment, although a walkup, boasted a brand new stove with a double oven.

With a fervor that must have surprised him, she said, "I'd love to cook dinner at your place tomorrow. I'll make out a shopping list and call you back."

She and Carl did not see each other over Christmas. He went up to Rockland County to be with his ex-wife and daughter. Katherine went to Bellmont to spend two days with Ed and Clara Derwith. As Katherine had expected, Clara was appalled to hear that Katherine was no longer seeing the highly eligible man she had been expected to marry.

"But I don't understand," Mrs. Derwith said. "What went wrong?"

Not for anything would Katherine have let the Derwiths know that the break with Gil had been caused by her tormented need to know the identity of her real parents. "Mother, we just found that we didn't care as much about each other as we'd thought we did."

After several seconds her mother asked hopefully, "But this new man you're seeing. Is that serious?"

"That's a question I can't answer. I mean, I don't know what he feels about me, except that he seems to want to see me often."

Her mother frowned. "Isn't that rather strange? Here you've been seeing him for weeks, and you don't know what he feels about you."

"Yes, it's strange. *He's* strange, but I have the feeling it's not a bad kind of strangeness." She crossed the room to kiss Clara's cheek. "Now don't worry! I can take care of myself. After all, I'm twenty-eight, not fourteen."

The night after she returned to her apartment, a Thursday, Carl Dietrich called. "I'm sorry about that concert on Saturday afternoon. I'm afraid I can't take you to it. My daughter is coming in to New York tomorrow night to spend the weekend with me."

"Oh," Katherine said, trying to keep her disappointment out of her voice. "I thought it was the weekend after next that Ellen was to spend with you."

"It was, but Naomi wants to take her to Chicago for a family reunion that weekend, so she asked if Ellen could come here this weekend."

"I see."

"I'll call you Sunday night as soon as I've put her on the train."

As she was eating her solitary lunch on Saturday Katherine realized that she didn't want to go to the concert, not alone. Instead she would go to Central Park. On this clear but sub-freezing day the park would be glorious, with the snow that had fallen before Christmas still blanketing the meadows and low hills, and ice-sheathed twigs of trees flashing like prisms in the sun.

Wearing boots and jeans and a parka, and with a white woolen cap pulled low on her forehead, she went into the park at its Eighty-fourth Street entrance and then wandered southward, past green wooden benches where snow lay like long white pillows, past a hill where kids hurtled down on sleds, skis, and metal discs the size of garbage can covers, and past a long level stretch where more kids, with dogs darting frantically back and forth between the battle lines, shelled each other with snowballs. And then she found herself at Wollman's Skating Rink.

A few of the skaters were excellent, including an elderly pair who glided, hands clasped, to the rhythm of the waltz issuing from the loudspeakers. Most of those on the rink, though, were beginners, teenagers whose ankles wobbled inward, then outward, and kindergartners on double-runner skates who took only a step or two before they went down, often taking the adults whose hands they held down with them.

A familiar voice said, "Why, hello, Katherine."

She turned. Carl stood there. Beside him stood that thin, dark-eyed child whose picture she had seen.

"Carl! I had no idea you were here." But even as she spoke she wondered if that was entirely true. Hadn't it occurred to her, at least subconsciously, that Central Park was a mecca for divorced fathers, the place where they took their visiting offspring to the zoo in summer and the skating rink in winter?

He said, "This is my daughter. Ellen, this is Miss Derwith."

"How do you do?" Ellen said politely, but her dark eyes, filled with jealousy and fear, were saying, "Go away!"

Katherine felt a stab of humiliation. Then she was able to tell herself that Ellen's reaction was only natural. What child, especially a girl child, would want to share with a strange woman her few precious hours with her father?

"Hello, Ellen. It's nice to meet you. But I'm afraid I must be getting home now. Goodbye." She turned away.

"No! Wait!"

The look on his face when she turned back to him told her that he must have seen the momentary hurt in her own eyes. "Don't go. Maybe you can help us out here."

"Help you? How?"

"Ellen wants me to skate with her. I'm no good at it, never have been, and I don't fancy making a fool of myself out there. So why don't you skate with her?"

Katherine looked down at Ellen. Still that hostility in the child's eyes. "It sounds tempting. Perhaps some other time. But right now I really must—"

"Didn't you once tell me you could do a figure eight?"

"Well, yes."

A second or two of silence. Then Ellen asked, cautious interest in her voice, "Could you teach me to do a figure eight?"

"If I can remember how to do it myself. I haven't been on skates in years."

"You should have been. My mother says that people shouldn't let their abilities atro—atro—go to rust."

"And your mother is quite right," Carl said. "So why don't you two go rent your skates?"

Katherine looked down at Ellen. No real friendliness in the small face, but no hostility either. Just that cautious interest. "Well, I—"

Ellen said, "If we're going to skate, Miss Derwith, we'd better start now. Later on it will be awfully cold on the ice."

In the concessionaire's building, Katherine and Ellen sat side by side on a bench and laced up their skate shoes. Ellen asked, "Are you Jewish?"

"No," Katherine said. "Not," she amended silently, "that I know of."

"I'm half-Jewish. But my mother isn't religious and neither am I, so it's really only ethnically speaking that I'm half-Jewish."

Katherine thought, wow! Aloud she said, "You certainly have a wonderful vocabulary."

Ellen tried to hide her pleasure but did not succeed. Dimples Katherine hadn't seen before flashed at the corners of her mouth. "I really do like long words. Do you know many long words?"

"A few."

"What, for instance?"

Katherine thought for a moment. "Propinquity."

"Oh, that's a lovely one. What does it mean?"

"Nearness in place or time."

"Propinquity, propinquity. I've got it, I think. Are you ready, Miss Derwith? Or would it be agreeable with you if I called you Katherine?"

"I'm ready, and it would be quite agreeable."

Katherine and Ellen stayed out on the ice for about half an hour, skating singly and as a pair. By the time they skated toward the rink's edge for a few minutes' rest, Ellen was able to do a wobbly figure eight.

Carl rose from a bench to greet them. "You looked wonderful out there, veritable Dorothy Hamills, both of you."

"Oh, *Daddy!*" Then: "It was rather difficult, what with the propinquity of the other skaters. A fat little boy fell down right at my feet and tripped me."

Katherine and Carl avoided each other's eyes. He said, "Are you two quitting, or are you just taking a rest?"

Katherine said, "Just resting for a few minutes. We rented our skates for a full hour."

"All right. While you two young ladies take your ease, I'll go get us some hot dogs."

He moved away toward the refreshment stand. Ellen asked, "Can you think of another long word?"

After a moment Katherine said, "Serendipity."

"Oh! That's even better. What does it mean?"

"Well, it's the knack of finding or accomplishing one thing while you're trying to find or accomplish something else. For instance, while you're looking for an old swim cap you left on the beach you find a beautiful ring."

Or, Katherine thought, serendipity is wanting to like a child so that her father will be pleased, and then finding you like her just for her own sake.

"Here we are," Carl said, coming up beside them. "Hot dogs for both my— Hot dogs for both you young ladies."

Katherine was almost certain that he had been about to say, "for both my girls." As she reached out, not looking up at him, for the hot dog in its paper napkin, she was aware of a tingling warmth spreading all through her. After a moment she recognized the feeling. She was happy.

13

During the next two weeks they saw each other often, dining together at her apartment or his and in various restaurants, and spending much of each weekend in each other's company. And still it was only by a look on his face, or a sudden constraint in his voice, that Katherine knew he desired her. She began to feel a little frantic. In fact, she might have made the first advance, except that the unhappy ending of her affair with Gil had left her feeling unsure of herself.

Sometimes she wondered if Carl's stepmother's influence had anything to do with his puzzling behavior. Finally, over dinner in a Chinese restaurant, she summoned up the courage to say, "Carl, I'd like to meet your stepmother."

An odd look, startled and wary, came into his eyes. Then he said, "As it happens, she's been asking to meet you. I'll fix it up."

Two nights later Katherine and Carl had dinner at Inga's small Knickerbocker Town apartment. Even though Carl had told her that Inga had been still in her teens when she became his stepmother, Katherine was surprised by the German woman's youthful-looking beauty. The chicken paprika was excellent and the dinner table talk pleasant. Inga talked of her hopes of winning a small role, that of a Hungarian refugee, in a soap opera, and Katherine countered with stories of her Jill-of-all-trades job—reporting, copyreading, proofreading—on the *Courier*.

After dinner Katherine offered to help with the dishes. Somewhat to her surprise, Inga accepted. In the small kitchen, as Katherine lifted a plate from the drying rack, Inga said, "Carl has told me how you two met."

"Well, I assumed he had."

"He also told me about the breakup between you and a man you almost married. I mean, he told me it was because you felt you couldn't marry until you knew who your parents were."

Katherine felt resentment. Why had Carl discussed that particular matter with Inga? She waited until after she had dried a plate, added it to a stack of similar ones in the cupboard, and taken a second from the rack. Then she said, "Yes, that was why."

Inga smiled at her. "Please don't mind my knowing this. I questioned him, of course. After all, he is my stepson." She paused and then asked, "Do you feel the same way about Carl? That your not knowing about your parents rules out marriage?"

Katherine decided to be frank. Perhaps Inga would pass her words along to Carl. "No, I don't feel the same way."

"Why not?"

"In the first place, Gil is very proud of his family pedigree. No matter what he said, sooner or later he would have minded very much that I have no pedigree of any sort. He would have minded very especially when it came to the question of having or not having children."

"And Carl?"

"Carl is not a Motthill of the Massachusetts Motthills," Katherine said dryly. "I'm sure he doesn't feel the same way about pedigrees. And as for children— Well, he already has a daughter. He would not mind so much if his wife decided she did not want to risk having children of her own."

Inga rinsed a soapy salad plate, placed it in the rack, and then turned to face Katherine. "My dear," she said gently, "don't build your hopes on Carl."

Embarrassed resentment warmed Katherine's face. "I don't know what you mean."

"Has he talked to you of marriage, or even some informal arrangement?"

Katherine said shortly, "No."

"And he won't. Oh, he likes you. But he went through so much with his divorce that I doubt he will ever marry again."

So this, Katherine thought, was the reason she wanted to meet me. She wanted to tell me this.

When Katherine remained silent, gaze fixed on the plate she was drying, Inga went on, "Of course, Carl is no monk. He sees other young ladies besides you. The accommodating kind, who don't need to feel that they are in love with a man or that he's in love with them."

With jealousy twisting her heart, Katherine realized that Carl almost never said, "I watched television last night," or "I brought work home with me Thursday night," or made any reference to evenings they did not spend together.

Inga said, "So don't count on Carl. But he's far from being the only divorced man with a child or two. There must be thousands right here in New York. And a girl as attractive as you ought to be able to interest any number of them. Believe me, I'm telling you this for your own good."

Was she? Katherine didn't think so. But then, why was Inga trying to persuade her to turn away from Carl? Was there some sort of oedipal factor, conscious or unconscious, at work here? Or did Inga have some other reason for wanting to get her, Katherine, out of Carl's life, some reason connected with the strangeness which, from the first, she had sensed in him?

Katherine felt a surge of determination. Whatever the woman's motives, she would not succeed. If Carl wanted to walk away from the relationship, all right, but Katherine herself would not do so.

She said evenly, "I'll think about what you said."

"I certainly hope you will." She lifted a cream pitcher from the sudsy water. "Isn't this pretty? It's Bavarian, and quite old. I treated myself to it out of the residuals for a coffee commercial." She placed the rinsed pitcher in the rack. "I really enjoyed making that commercial. Maybe you saw it. The set was supposed to be a coffee house in Vienna—"

She chattered on, with Katherine making an occasional polite response, until the dishes were finished. They walked into the living room. Carl, who had been watching an episode of "M A S H," switched off the set and got to his feet. For a moment Katherine had the feeling that his gaze, resting on his stepmother's face, held a question. Then he smiled, "How about some three-handed bridge?"

Around ten-thirty Carl and Katherine left. As they rode north in a nearly empty subway car, she sensed that he wanted to ask what she and Inga had talked about in the kitchen. He didn't ask, though. Nor did he, when they reached her apartment, accept her suggestion that he come in for a nightcap. Instead he said, unlocking her door and pushing it inward, "I'd better not. The station manager has called for a conference bright and early tomorrow morning."

His goodnight kiss was even more restrained than usual. As she stood inside her closed door, and heard the elevator door open, she was almost certain that he was on his way back to see his stepmother.

A little before six two evenings later she approached Carl's apartment house. She carried a bag holding a slice of Brie, a jar of Greek olives, a box of water biscuits, and a half-pound of cheese cake, all purchased from the delicatessen a block from Carl's place, and intended to enhance the dinner she was to cook for the two of them. Originally she had planned to go to her apartment and change clothes before going to Carl's. Then she decided to go straight from her office to the deli and then to his apartment. Consequently she was about a quarter of an hour earlier than she had expected to be.

Afterward she was to think of how everything would have been changed if she had stopped in the downstairs foyer to ring his apartment bell. But she did not have to stop. Just as she entered the building's outer door a middle-aged man, vaguely familiar to her from some of her previous visits here, opened the inner door. Smiling politely, he held it open for her. She thanked him and walked toward the stairs. On the third floor she turned toward Carl's apartment.

Through the door she could hear him talking to someone on the phone. Well, no need to disturb him, not if he'd left his service door unlocked, as he often did. She opened a door marked "exit" and stepped into the service hall. Ahead of her were stairs leading down to the ground floor and basement. To her right was the door to Carl's kitchen. She turned the knob. Yes, the door was unlocked.

She went inside and placed her groceries on the stainless steel table. In the apartment's foyer, Carl was still on the phone. She heard him say, "Inga, stop it! I know what I'm doing."

There was a pause. Then: "I go on seeing her for the same reason I answered her ad. I want to make sure she doesn't— No! Of course I'm not going to marry her. How could I? And I'm not going to let something slip out, as you phrase it." Another pause. "No, of course it won't go on forever. Probably it will turn out the way you told her it should. She'll meet some other divorced guy, perhaps with a couple of kids. She'll marry him, and maybe go someplace else to live, Los Angeles, say, and finally reconcile herself to never finding out—

"Inga, what do you mean, I'm kidding myself? How can you know what I feel or don't—"

Katherine must have made some sound then, because she heard him say sharply, "Hold on a minute, Inga."

Then he was in the kitchen doorway. "Oh, God!" he said, with the color draining from his face. "Please, Katherine. Wait just a second."

He turned back to the foyer and the phone. Katherine whirled, jerked the door open, ran down the service stairs. Seconds later she heard his shout, and the clatter of his pursuing footsteps, but by that time she had almost reached the door that opened onto the lobby.

She ran out to the sidewalk. To her right, a cab was moving slowly along the street, its vacancy sign glowing through the early dark. She ran to it, flung the door open, got inside.

By that time Carl had emerged from between two parked cars and was moving toward the taxi. She said to the driver, "Go straight ahead, fast. Don't let that man stop you."

"Got you, lady."

The cab leaped forward. Carl made a futile grab at the door handle. She caught a glimpse of his white face, with the cheekbones appearing more prominent than ever. Then she said, not looking back, "Eighty-first Street near Second Avenue."

"Right," the cabbie said, and then added, "Got mixed up with some kind of creep, huh?"

"Yes," Katherine said bitterly, "but I'm not sure what kind."

"Well, town's full of them, all kinds," the driver said, and then remained mercifully silent the rest of the way.

When she entered her apartment the phone was ringing. She flipped on the light and looked down at the phone for the space of three rings. Then, knowing whose voice she would hear, she lifted the instrument from its cradle. "Hello."

"Katherine, listen to me."

She said, in a thick voice, "Okay, I'm listening." Then, when he didn't speak: "Go on. Spit it out."

"Katherine, I never meant to hurt you. Will you believe that?"

"Just what did you intend to do?" When he didn't answer that, she said, "One thing's clear. You never at any time wanted to help me find out about myself. Instead, there's something you've been afraid I'd find out. What is it?"

After a while he said, "I can't answer that."

"Can't, or won't?"

"Both, I guess." He sounded desperate. "Katherine, what can I say, what can I do?"

"I'll tell you what you can do." For the first time in her life she used an expression both pungent and popular, and hung up.

She sat motionless for a moment. Then she put her hands up to her face and began to cry. She'd been a fool all the way, from their very first meeting, when she had disregarded her sense that there was something wrong about him, until now, when she'd hung up on him instead of trying to get him to talk more freely. She should have listened to him, maybe consented to see him, playing him as slyly as he had played her, waiting for him to let information slip—

But she had been in too much pain for that. How could he have done this to her? All those times she'd so enjoyed, looking at him across a dinner table, window-shopping with him on Madison Avenue or Fifty-seventh Street, he'd been a complete fraud, operating from motives she did not know and was almost afraid to guess at. Even when he walked back from the refreshment stand, with napkin-wrapped frankfurters in his hand, and she, sitting beside his daughter, had felt warmth spread all through her—even then he'd been tricking her, playing her for a fool.

She took her hands down from her face. Reaching into her coat pocket she took out a handkerchief and wiped her eyes. Her thoughts went back to the first time she'd had dinner with Carl Dietrich. She had returned to find her facial tissues in the wrong drawer and a brooch on the rug. At that time she had dismissed the thought that her apartment had been entered, but now she was sure that it had. While she and Carl were at that Italian restaurant, someone at his instruction had managed to get into her apartment. It had to be at his instruction. To think that someone totally unconnected with Carl could have decided to enter her apartment on that particular night was stretching coincidence much too far.

What was more, nothing that might have interested a thief—that silver brooch, her typewriter, her small color television set—had been taken. That meant the intruder had come to search.

Search for what?

She thought it through. It was her advertisement that had attracted Carl to her, an advertisement she had placed in an attempt to learn more about her origins. Therefore it was logical to suppose that whatever object the searcher had sought was in some way connected with those origins.

But what could the object have been? She had nothing that could offer a clue to her parentage, and never had had. Even the certificate of adoption was in Clara and Ed Derwith's possession. And it would yield no information anyway, beyond the date of her adoption and her probable age at that time.

Suddenly she recalled her last visit to that old warehouse district, two days before she had placed her ad in the *Times* and *News*. The bag lady, that old woman who might have been wandering the warehouse district that summer twenty-eight years ago. That woman who had yelled, as Katherine walked away over the weed-grown railroad yard, "The key was no damn good to me, anyway!"

Was that what the searcher had been looking for in this apartment? A key? Perhaps. But a key to what?

And the bag lady. If she'd found such a key that long-ago summer night, would she have kept it all these years? Probably not. But then people—even normal people, not just eccentrics like the bag lady—often clung to worthless objects. In her own jewel box was a tiny metal ring set with a red glass "ruby" which, as a first-grader, she had found in a box of Cracker Jacks.

Heart beating fast—with pain, with rage, and with a kind of bitter hope—she decided that tomorrow she would try to find the bag lady again.

She lifted the phone and dialed the home phone number of the Warrens, the couple who owned the *Courier*. Marian Warren answered.

"Marian, do you mind if I take tomorrow off?"

"Why, of course not. Not sick, are you?"

"No, it's just that something has come up. I'll work late day after tomorrow to make up for it."

Katherine hung up. In the kitchen she made herself a cup of tea, the only thing she had an appetite for. She kept expecting Carl to phone again. In fact, she rehearsed things she might say to him, some of them cold and vicious, some conciliatory, hiding her intention to play *him* for all the information she could get.

He did not phone. After a while she turned on the TV set and watched an old John Wayne movie, scarcely aware of when the movie gave way to the commercials or vice versa. Then she went to bed.

14

When she awoke around ten the next morning after a night of broken sleep, she saw rain streaming down her bedroom windowpanes. Rain would continue, the radio told her, until early afternoon, and would be followed by clear weather.

At two o'clock rain was still falling in sheets. She would wait until two-thirty, she told herself grimly. Then, rain or no rain, she would set out in search of the bag lady.

A few minutes after two the rain abruptly slackened, almost as if someone up there had closed a giant faucet. By the time she descended to the street the rain had become a light drizzle. She walked to Second Avenue and caught the bus. Evidently many besides herself had been waiting to go out as soon as the rain stopped, because every seat was taken and the aisle jammed with standees. At Forty-second Street she changed to an equally crowded crosstown bus. When, after its slow crawl through traffic-clogged streets, the bus reached Tenth Avenue, she got off and turned south.

Soon she was in the old warehouse district. Today, under a gray sky, the long stretches of abandoned and decaying structures—warehouses, business buildings, tenements with wide, shattered windows marking what had been ground-floor shops—seemed more forlorn than ever. In the course of two blocks she saw only three persons, an old man who walked along talking animatedly to a companion visible only to himself, and a proud-faced young woman, garishly colored gypsy blouse and skirt visible beneath her coat, who pushed a stroller holding a small boy.

As she started down the third block, some instinct caused her to look over her shoulder. A man was back there, walking along about a hundred feet away on the opposite side of the street, a tall man in a tan belted raincoat. His hat, covered with a plastic rainshield, was pulled low over his forehead. The pulse in the hollow of her throat gave a nervous jump. Carl? Impossible to tell for sure. At almost four, the gray winter daylight had begun to fade. And although Carl owned a tan raincoat, so did thousands of other men.

But she had told Carl of her visits to this area. After last night, he might have guessed that she would come down here again in search of whatever it was he did not want her to know.

She walked on at a quickened pace. Even if it was Carl back there, she need not be afraid of physical harm at his hands. Somehow she was sure of that. And anyway, she resolved grimly, she was not going to let Carl or anyone else scare her away from here until she had looked for that old woman.

Two blocks farther on, as she turned left to cross the street, she again looked back. No sign of the tall man. Either he had turned a corner, or entered some building. Katherine hurried down the side street to the edge of the railroad yard.

She had a sense of *déjà vu*. The bag lady was not only there. She was bending to spread a garment across the railway tracks, just as she had that unseasonably warm November day weeks before. Then, as she waded through the tall weeds, Katherine saw that there was no bucket standing beside the woman, so evidently this was not another washday, after all.

"Hello," Katherine said. "Remember me?"

The bag lady, who had just stretched a suit of knee-length white knit underwear across the tracks, straightened up and glared at Katherine from under the sodden brim of her black satin hat. "And if I do, what's it to you?" She added, almost immediately, "My damn roof leaks. Every stitch I own got soaked." Her gaze, brooding now, went toward the northern horizon. "Looks like it's going to pour again, too."

Katherine turned and looked north. Black clouds were boiling up toward the sky's zenith. So much for the weather forecaster's prediction of clear weather.

She looked back at the bag lady. "It's too bad about your roof. Just where is your place?"

"Ha! What's it to you?"

"Nothing," Katherine said hurriedly. "Nothing at all." Then: "Do you remember mentioning a key the last time I was down here? I got the impression it was something you'd found a long time ago. Anyway, you said it was no good to you. But did you keep it, by any chance?"

Before the bag lady could say, "What's it to you?," Katherine added, "I'd be glad to pay you fifty dollars for the key, and for any information you might have about it."

"You got fifty dollars? Let me see it."

Katherine opened her shoulder bag, took out her wallet, and selected a bill. "There."

The old woman's expression was sly now. "You'll pay me fifty for it, no matter what kind of key it is?"

"Yes!" Katherine felt a surge of triumph. "You did keep it, didn't you?"

The woman nodded. "I'll go to my place and get it. Don't you try to see where I go!" she added sharply.

"I won't."

With surprising rapidity the woman crossed the weedy stretch to the sidewalk, turned left, and soon disappeared from Katherine's sight. Evidently she lived in some abandoned store or tenement nearby. She was back within a few minutes, holding something in her tightly rolled right fist.

She said, eyes bright and sly beneath the sodden hat brim, "Now I get the money, no matter what kind of key it is."

"Yes. All you have to do is give it to me, and tell me how you got it."

With a triumphant cackle, the bag lady held out her hand and unrolled her fist. "Just an old locker key! And there was nothing in the locker. Bet you thought it was a key to the kind of box banks have, where rich people put their diamonds. All right now, here's your key. Give me my money."

Katherine handed over the bill, and then dropped the key into her shoulder bag. The old woman shoved the banknote down the front of her rusty black blouse. Katherine said, "Now tell me how you got this key."

"I don't remember."

"You do! And it was part of your bargain that you tell me."

"Cops were mixed up in it. I might get in trouble."

"After twenty-eight years? That's nonsense, and you know it. Now tell me."

After a moment the bag lady said, "Is it worth another twenty to you?"

"All right," Katherine said grimly, "but not a cent more. Now tell me."

"I'd holed up outside the entrance to a hardware store that night. It was a real hot night, so hot I couldn't get to sleep even though I knew it must be way past twelve. Then this old car drove up and parked opposite a warehouse. I saw this fella—fella with a limp—cross the street carrying a basket and go into the warehouse. Pretty soon he came out and went to a phone booth on the same side of the street as his car. I figured there might be something in the basket I could use, if I could get to it before the warehouse fellas did. I was a lot younger then, and plenty quick when I wanted to be, so I slipped in there—"

She went on, telling how in the warehouse she spotted the basket right away, atop a pile of crates. She had dragged an empty wooden box over to the crates, stepped up on it, and looked into the basket.

"There was a *baby* in there! I was pretty disappointed, but since I'd gone to all that trouble, I decided to feel around in the basket, thinking maybe he'd left some money in there."

"Money!"

"Sure. When I was a little girl in Albany a strange cat came yowling around our house. It had a ribbon around its neck and a rolled-up note tied to the ribbon with a string. Inside the note was two one dollar bills. The note said the owner couldn't keep the cat and so was leaving it on the street, and would whoever found it please keep the cat and use the two dollars to buy liver. Liver was only a few cents a pound in those days. So anyway, I thought this fella might have left money in the basket, but all I found was this metal thing that turned out to be a locker key."

She had hurried out of the warehouse. Across the street the man was still in the phone booth. As she walked down the sidewalk she saw an approaching car.

"I looked back after it passed me and saw it park in front of that other car. I figured that might mean trouble so I went on two more blocks before I picked out another doorway. Later I was glad I did, because just before I went to sleep I heard cops' sirens, and I knew there *had* been trouble."

When she woke up she saw that the metal object was a locker

key. "I skedaddled to the bus terminal right away, because sometimes I slept there and I'd seen people putting stuff in lockers and taking it out. I found the locker that had the same number as the one on the key, but the key wouldn't open it.

"While I was trying to get the locker open this lady I knew—she slept in the bus terminal most of the time—came up to me. I told her I'd found the key in the street. She said it would do me no good because there must be hundreds of thousands of lockers in New York, and even if I did finally find the right one, by that time the people who collect the money out of the locker coin boxes would have opened up the locker and taken whatever was in it. She had me pretty discouraged, but I told her to go to hell and then I went over to Penn Station and found the locker with the key's number on it and it fitted. It opened up as nice as you please."

"And?" Katherine asked in a taut voice. The black clouds had spread over two-thirds of the sky now. In the almost nighttime darkness, a wind rattled the weeds, and a large raindrop struck Katherine's cheek.

The bag lady said, "There was nothing inside."

"Nothing!"

"Just a piece of yella paper, like you might buy at a dime store, with some squiggly lines and some foreign writing on it. I knew it must have been put there by some kind of nut. You ever notice how many people there are walking around who ought to be in the booby hatch? I know they belong there, because I was there once myself."

"The paper! What did you do with it?"

"Why, I was so disgusted that I just tore it up and dropped it in a trash basket. I kept the key, though. I figured maybe when someone else put something in the locker I could get it. But when I went back to Penn Station two weeks later the key wouldn't fit. That smart-aleck lady I told you about, the one at the bus terminal, said that when the key wasn't turned in the locker people must have known it was lost, so they changed the lock. Just the same, I hung onto the key, figuring they might sooner or later change the lock back, and then I forgot about the whole thing, until you showed up here that day and started asking questions about a baby left in a warehouse."

"The paper! Can't you give me a better idea of what was on the paper?" The big raindrops were falling closer together now.

"You crazy? After forty years, or thirty, or whatever it is?"

"You said there were some lines—"

"Squiggly ones. Straight ones too, I think, and some numbers."

"And words?"

"I told you. Foreign words. Oh, maybe there were some English ones, but I remember only two of them."

"All right! What were they?"

"'Stone Maiden!' I remember that because it sounded like a statue, and there wasn't any drawing of a statue. Just lines and words and numbers."

"Are you sure?"

The bag lady lost her temper. "I told you, didn't I? Now give me my twenty bucks and then get out of here!"

Katherine handed her another bill. The bag lady stashed it down the front of her blouse and then, bending, began to gather up the garments she had spread to dry.

Katherine turned away. With the wind tearing at her she moved through the weeds back to the sidewalk. In the near darkness standard lamps had come on, shining down on the deserted streets, so that more than ever she was reminded of a Hopper painting of nighttime in some lonely midwestern town. She turned the corner. Still no one on the street, not even a derelict sitting on a curb, or a group of teenagers gathered around a stripped and abandoned car. She hurried on, head bent against rain-laden gusts of wind.

Footsteps behind her.

She started to turn her head, but already a long arm had snaked around her throat. Paralyzed with shock, she did not resist as her attacker dragged her backward. She heard his breathing, inches above the top of her head, and knew he must be the tall man she had glimpsed earlier.

Her heels bumped over a sill. Then she was in an enclosed space, musty-smelling and darker than the street. She felt his left hand strip her shoulder bag from her. Then he stood in front of her, his tall silhouette dimly visible against the doorless entrance.

His hand, shoving against her breastbone, sent her staggering backward. Something tripped her and she went down, striking the back of her head against a hard surface.

Slightly stunned, she lay there for perhaps a minute. Then, head still ringing, and still too shocked to feel real fear, she sat up. No sign, of course, of the man who had taken her shoulder bag. Preparatory to hoisting herself to her feet, she laid one palm on the floor. It felt like tile. What had this place once been? Barber shop, drug-store, restaurant? Shakily she stood up and felt in her right-hand coat pocket.

Yes, she had tokens, two of them. Thank heaven she long ago had formed the habit of carrying tokens in her pocket, so that she would not have to fumble in her purse before boarding a bus or subway train. She would be able to get home all right. Salvatore, who guarded the apartment house doorway until six each evening, would let her into her apartment. Of course, as soon as possible she would have to have the locks on her apartment door changed. But aside from that expense and inconvenience, her attacker had caused her little loss. Until her new locks were installed, she could use the second set of keys she kept in her desk. Her department store charge cards could be replaced. And, after she'd paid the bag lady, there had been only a few dollars left in her wallet.

Had he been just an ordinary purse snatcher? She was sure he had not been. Probably he had followed her to this lonely place, followed her when she got onto that packed Second Avenue bus, and changed to the equally packed Forty-second Street crosstown, and got off at Tenth Avenue.

Carl? Had it been Carl's face beneath that pulled-down hat brim? True, she had felt sure somehow that Carl would not physi-cally hurt her. But then, this man had not, really. He had shoved her backward, probably so that he would have a good head start when he whirled around and ran. But it had not been a vicious shove, and it probably would not have harmed her at all if she had not been tripped by some piece of debris on the floor.

Was it Carl, then, who had followed her here? Had he spied on her from some concealed vantage point while she received that old locker key from the bag lady?

And then fear, held at bay until now by shock, and confusion, and bitter speculation about Carl, closed in on her. No matter who her assailant had been, the fact remained that she was alone in pre-mature darkness in a ruined and almost entirely deserted area, a place where almost anything might happen to her.

Ignoring the faint throb in her head, she hurried out to the rain-wet sidewalk and turned to her right. Almost running, she moved across pools of lamplight and long stretches of darkness toward Forty-second Street.

15

Mike Russo emerged from the subway steps and hurried as fast as he could through the rain and the unusually early dark toward his apartment house. The temperature had already dropped, and it would really plunge once this rain passed. He hoped his Puerto Rican helper hadn't tried to turn up the heat. The kid couldn't be trusted with that shaky old boiler.

The trouble was that Dr. Slater, the young physician who had been treating Mike for the past two years, had fallen way behind in seeing his patients. Mike had waited more than an hour. Perhaps it was because he was overworked and rushed that the doctor, when Mike finally entered his office, was so brusque. "I've arranged for you to enter the hospital a month from now," he said. "I think by the time the month's up you'll be glad to go."

Perhaps. But just the same, Mike thought, he was going to stay out as long as he could. And as long as that cranky old bitch of a furnace was his responsibility, he'd do his best to keep her going.

A girl in a yellow vinyl poncho was moving toward him past the row of shabby old brownstones, her red head sheltered by an umbrella. Even though the girl was short and plump, her hair reminded him of his daughter.

According to Salvatore, the daytime doorman and man of all work at her apartment house, the rich guy with the Porsche didn't come around anymore. Instead she was seeing a tall guy with dark blond hair. From snatches of conversation Salvatore had overheard as they went in and out on weekend afternoons, he'd gathered that the fellow worked at a TV station. It couldn't be one of those quarter-of-a-million-a-year jobs, though, because the guy didn't drive a Porsche, or even a VW. Evidently he and Katherine used taxis and subways and buses.

Mike wondered why the rich guy had faded out of the picture. Was it because he found out Katherine was adopted? Did he feel that made her not good enough for him? The very possibility angered Mike. There was nothing wrong with her people. None of the Russos had ever been rich, but their names had been recorded in the church in their village of Falcone for the past two hundred years, first as farmers and then as innkeepers. And as for Maria's people, the Donzettis, a branch of that family who had stayed back in the old country really were rich. They owned an automobile factory in Modena.

He went down areaway steps, along a narrow hall, and into the boiler room. Ernesto, who had been watching the dials, turned a smiling face toward him. "I did not touch!"

"Good. Didn't you say you hadn't collected the trash on the fifth floor? Well, do that now."

When his helper had gone, Mike cautiously turned the valve wheel, saying in Italian, "Gently, my lady. Gently." Then, when the dial needle steadied, he went over and stretched out on the leather couch.

His thoughts returned to Katherine. What strange twists life could take. If he had not been a witness to that long-ago crime on the mountainside, he would have remained in Falcone and married there. His daughter, if he'd had one, would not be a spinster working on a newspaper. By now such a daughter would be married and the mother of at least three or four children.

But of course that part of the world, too, must have changed at least a little from the time he was growing up there between the two world wars. How he'd loved those years! He'd loved the scent of pines in the crystalline air, and music of sheep bells, and the springtime carpet of wildflowers. He liked the comfortable old inn where visitors, mostly English or French or American, came in summer to climb mountains. Almost always there was some pretty lady who would rumple his hair and ask his proud mother how much she would take for him, her only son and youngest child, the last one still at home.

The war made a big difference. Mike was eleven in 1939, the year it started. No more foreign guests now, and only a few Italian ones. Army officers, though, at first both German and Italian, and then, after Mussolini's fall, only Germans. Once Italy's allies, the Germans had become an occupation force. Michael hated them for that. He would have hated them even if all of them had been friendly and polite, which they were not. Some of them ordered his mother around as curtly as if she had been a barmaid in some low dive, rather than a respectable matron and the mother of three daughters and a son. Others broke glasses pounding them on the tables in time to the army songs they roared out and then, when Michael's father asked for payment, said that the glasses must already have been cracked.

The incident that ended Mike's service at the inn happened less than a week after his seventeenth birthday. Two of the officers he disliked most came to the inn that night. As usual, they sat apart from the others at a corner table. They were both lieutenants, although one of them, a fortyish man with a loose mouth and a tendency to snigger, seemed at least a decade too old for that rank. Late in the evening, when most of the officers were drunk, Michael hated to approach that corner table. As Michael set wine before them, the older man would call him *bello* and compliment him on his fresh complexion, gray eyes, and other attributes, while the younger man made sounds that could only be described as giggles. In stony silence Michael would walk away.

That night might have been no different than other nights if Michael's father, grudgingly courteous but watchful-eyed, had been behind the bar. That night, though, the senior Russo had been confined to his bed with a stomach upset. Or perhaps it was just that the overage lieutenant had become drunker than usual. Anyway, as Michael was placing two glasses of wine on the table, the lieutenant addressed him in his broken Italian as "pretty boy," and patted his buttocks. Michael picked up a wine glass and threw its contents in the lieutenant's face.

The lieutenant shot to his feet, mopping his face and uniform with a napkin, and shouting. Michael was aware of his mother beside him, clutching his arm, pleading with him as she tried to draw him away from the enraged man. Then the senior officer in the room, a major, had walked over to them. A small, quiet man with icy blue eyes but a courteous manner, the major was one of the few German officers Michael might have liked if he had liked any Germans. The major had barked out an order, and the lieutenant had sunk back into his chair. Then the major said to Michael's mother in fairly fluent Italian, "I am sorry, signora, but you must restrain your son. A civilian cannot be permitted to behave disrespectfully to an officer of the Third Reich." Then, to the still-fuming Michael: "Leave the room at once."

Late that night in the couple's bedroom, the Russos conferred with their son. Obviously Michael must not continue to serve in the dining room. But since they would have to hire someone to take his place—probably a spinster cousin of Michael's mother—it was equally obvious that the boy should earn money to pay the cousin's wages. They decided that in the morning Michael would go to see the Divalos at their farmhouse a few miles from the village. With both their sons killed in the war, the Divalos had trouble finding anyone to help them care for their sheep. And they especially needed help at this time of year, early September, because soon the flock must be moved to lower pasture to escape the Alpine snows.

Michael liked caring for the Divalos' sheep far more than he had liked working in the inn's dining room and kitchen. He enjoyed spending the long days out-of-doors in a valley two miles away from the village and almost a thousand feet higher. At night, after he had cooked his supper over an outdoor fire, he would go to sleep on his pallet in the dirt-floored but snugly roofed shepherd's hut, leaving Estella, a two-year-old collie, to guard the flock.

He enjoyed, too, the descent to winter pasturage, with a frenzied Estella dashing in circles around the flock to keep the bleating creatures in a compact, ever-moving mass. But after he had delivered his woolly charges to pasturage near the Divalo farmhouse, and Pietro Divalo had inspected the flock, Michael learned to his dismay that three sheep were missing, two young rams born the previous spring, and a three-year-old prize ewe. Divalo did not fly into a rage, but he was firm in his insistence that Michael go back and find the missing animals.

The next day he found the two rams, and with Estella's noisy help brought them back to Divalo. Although Divalo was pleased to have two of his sheep back, the really valuable animal was still missing. Divalo made it clear that Michael was to search again, and not return until he found the ewe, even if he was still up in the higher mountains when the first snow fell. Michael went to his parents' inn, picked up a fine pair of binoculars that an Italian officer, early in the war, had left in lieu of payment of his bar bill, and then set out with Estella to look for the ewe.

For five days, with his bedroll and knapsack of food strapped to his back and the binoculars bumping against his chest, he crossed upland meadows, threshed his way through woods choked with underbrush, and scrambled up rock-choked ravines to high points from which to survey through his binoculars the endless folds of mountains and valleys. By the fifth day he was climbing the steep wall of a valley he had never seen before. He had no fear of being lost, though. He knew that anytime he started traveling south he eventually would emerge from the high mountains to the farms and villages of the Piedmont.

He crossed the mountain's crest before sunset. Wearily he moved out onto a rocky outcrop and surveyed the valley beyond, a narrow one, and the steep rise of its far wall. He looked through the binoculars. On the skyline of the mountainside ahead, rosy in the near-sunset light, was a rock formation he recognized, even though he had never been here before. Its outline suggested a standing woman with her head thrown back. Michael had seen a photograph of it in a book an English guest had brought to the inn the last summer before the war. It had been an old book on Alpine exploration, written by some Englishman around the middle of the last century. Perhaps he had been the first to photograph, and name, that particular formation. Anyway, the caption below its photograph had identified it as the Stone Maiden.

Just as he remembered from the photograph, the Stone Maiden stood like a guardian at one side of a narrow defile in the mountain's crest. Through the defile itself, though, ran something that had not been in the photograph, the parallel tracks of a railroad line which, after descending a hundred yards or so disappeared among the pines. A little way above the point where the tracks disappeared, a short spur branched off to the right along a narrow shelf, obviously man-made. The shelf ended in the opening, partially obscured by brush, of an old mine.

An iron pyrite mine? Probably. For more than a hundred years iron pyrites and salts had been extracted from mines all over these mountains. Most of them had long since been abandoned, and the rail lines that serviced them left to rust, just as those rails across the valley were rusting.

Feeling no hope whatsoever, Michael scanned the opposite

mountainside and the valley below for a glimpse of dirty white wool. The ewe must be dead. The damned fool animal had fallen into a crevasse somewhere and broken her neck. Tomorrow he would start home, even though Divalo might hold back his wages to pay for the ewe. He couldn't go on wandering through these mountains, not with his food running low, and the temperature apt to plunge any day now. He moved back among the trees, built a small fire against the evening chill, and ate sparingly of what was left of the three loaves of bread, three long sausages, and wheel of cheese he had brought with him. Then he spread out his bedroll and went to sleep.

Not only sunlight, striking down through pine branches, awoke him. There was sound, too. After a bewildered moment he identified it as the puffing of a steam engine.

With Estella trotting beside him, he moved through the trees to where he could see across the narrow valley. Yes, there was the engine, a freight car behind it, turning off the track through the defile onto the spur. A half dozen men sat atop the freight car.

Estella lifted her head. Before she could bark, some instinct caused Michael to close his hand around the dog's muzzle. "Sh-h-h!" he said. "Sit!"

He lifted the binoculars to his eyes. The engine across the valley had come to a shuddering stop at the mine entrance. The men on top of the freight car climbed down its iron ladder. One of the men, tall and very thin and carrying a rifle, wore a black S.S. uniform. The others wore the uniforms of Italian enlisted men. Michael realized that they must be some of the few Italians who, after Mussolini's downfall, had chosen to fight on beside the Germans. One of the men pushed back the car's sliding door and began to hand out objects which, at first, Michael thought were rifles. Then he saw that they were crowbars.

The noisy engine started up, drew its car into the mine. Moments later the engineer came out into the sunrise light. A middle-aged man, to judge by his movements, he too wore an Italian uniform.

And then, to Michael's astonishment, the men began to tear up the short spur line, lifting ties and rails with their crowbars, then carrying them, two men to each tie or length of rail, into the mine at almost a dogtrot. Only the S.S. officer did not work. He stood a few feet away up the slope, rifle slung over his shoulder. Now and then he gave an order, his gestures and even the movements of his mouth visible through the binoculars.

For nearly an hour, while Michael watched, the men kept up their feverish work. Then, when there was only a bare dirt shelf where once the spur had lain, the S.S. officer walked past the exhausted Italians, now seated on the ground, into the mine. Evidently something in there—perhaps the way the ties and rails were stacked—was not to his liking, because when he came out he began to wave his arms and shout. The Italians hoisted themselves to their feet and filed into the mine.

While Michael watched, the S.S. man climbed up the steeply sloping ground to a point about fifteen feet above what had been the roadbed of the now-vanished spur. He bent over something concealed in a clump of bushes. At first, as in a silent film, Michael was aware only of dirt and smoke and clumps of earth and rock radiating from the old mine's entrance. Then the explosion's sound reached him, a roar that echoed back and forth between the valley's walls. Transfixed, binoculars glued to his eyes, Michael stared at the man across the valley who stood there calmly, waiting for the smoke and dust to settle. After a few minutes it did.

There was no mine opening now. Just a jumble of earth and rock where the entrance had been. Michael lowered the binoculars.

His movement must have caused the binocular's metal trim to send a flash of light across the valley. Too dumbfounded to move, he watched the S.S. man raise binoculars to his own eyes.

Michael's paralysis dropped away from him, and he was able to turn away. But already it was too late. He heard the whine of a rifle bullet, felt something burn through the calf of his left leg. He went down. Then, pulling himself along on his elbows, he moved a few yards deeper into the trees.

Estella was beside him now, whining, trying to lick his face. The dog would be no protection against the rifle-carrying man who, even now, must be scrambling down the mountainside to cross the valley. In fact, she would only betray Michael's presence to his pursuer. "Go home," he said, and pointed toward the west and south. "Go home!"

Like most of her breed, she was intelligent. She looked at him indecisively for a moment, plumy tail waving. Then she turned and trotted away through the trees.

Swiftly Michael removed his left climbing boot and his heavy knee-length stocking. The bullet, drilling through the fleshy part of his leg, had left small entrance and exit wounds that did not look bad at all. There wasn't even a great deal of blood. In fact, the damage would have been of little consequence if he had not been separated from home by many miles of rough terrain.

He ripped off the lower part of his shirt and used part of the cloth for a tourniquet just below his knee, the other part for bandaging his wound. He pulled himself over to a fallen cedar and, with his pocket knife, cut off a stout branch about the thickness of a man's thumb.

Leave the bedroll, he decided. With the knapsack on his back, and using the cedar branch as a crutch, he moved away as rapidly as he could.

Three nights later, a little before dawn, he stood exhausted and shivering in the yard of his parents' inn and threw pebbles against the window.

The last few days had been like an extended bad dream. As long as the light lasted he had tried to keep moving, with infrequent stops to drink from brooks or springs and to consume a few mouthfuls of food. At night, rolled into a shivering ball, he had slept on branches cut from pine trees. In one way he had been lucky. Even though he had no antiseptic, and no way of changing his bandage, his wound had not become feverish.

He had seen no sign of the tall, cadaverous man in the S.S. uniform. After a while Michael decided that the other man hadn't even tried to trail him, at least not for long. Instead, probably, he had made his way to the automobile he must have concealed somewhere along one of the few roads, little more than cart tracks, that ran through this region, and driven away.

But that did not mean Michael was in the clear. The tall man would still try to get his hands on him. Oh, he wouldn't come searching with a squad of soldiers. Obviously what Michael had witnessed on that lonely mountainside was one man's enterprise, not the German army's. But he would come searching, either he, or a confederate.

And the S.S. man would realize where the search should start. He had gotten a good look at Michael through binoculars. A few discreet inquiries in the region would provide the information that the Falcone innkeeper's blond seventeen-year-old son had gone up into the high mountains to search for a ewe.

Michael threw another pebble at the windowpane. Quietly—very quietly, because German officers occupied three of the inn's bedrooms—the windowpane slid up. "Who's there?"

Michael called softly, "I'm in trouble, Papa."

The windowpane slid down. A few moments later Michael heard the back door open. He darted inside. The elder Russo, in nightshirt and slippers, relocked the door. They moved along a passage to the inn's dining room, dimly illuminated by the banked coals in the fireplace. Michael's mother was there, graying dark hair hanging in two thick braids over the shoulders of her nightgown.

She cried softly, "Oh, my son! You're hurt."

"Sh-h-h!" her husband said. "Get hot water. And get a pallet and blankets from the cupboard."

Michael knew what cupboard his father meant, a concealed one beside the fireplace, with a knothole in its door that afforded a limited view of the dining room. Michael's great-great-grandparents, adherents of Garibaldi, had built it so that they could afford his partisans a hiding place from their enemies during the tangled wars of that period.

Swiftly Michael told his father what had happened, and then asked, "Has anyone been here looking for me?"

"Yes, yesterday afternoon. A German officer. All he would say was that you were wanted for 'a crime.' To prove to him you weren't here I showed him all over the inn. When he left he took that new photograph of yours with him."

The photograph had been made in Bolzano during the Russos' visit to their cousins a few months before. Brightly colored, it showed Michael's sandy hair and gray eyes and even the freckles across his nose. His mother had bought a gilt frame for it.

"What did the officer look like?"

"Short. Overweight even though he's quite young, still under twenty-five, I'd say. Blond hair, bulgy blue eyes. He said his name was Schweitzer, Lieutenant Schweitzer."

Not the man on the mountainside. A confederate, then.

His mother had returned with bedding, which she placed on a table. Then she went into the kitchen and came back with a basin of hot water. While she bathed his wound he repeated the story he had told his father.

She said, "We must go to the German commandant and tell him what you saw."

"Woman, are you crazy?" Michael's father said. "The best thing for people like us is to stay away from the military as much as possible. Oh, the commandant might believe us, and even have that freight car dug out. But he also might have us arrested for circulating slanders about an officer of the Third Reich burying Italian soldiers alive. As for our son, do you think that those two—the man on the mountainside and the fat one who came here—would risk letting him stay alive?"

His parents fed Michael, moved aside the heavy old chest that blocked off the concealed cupboard, and made up his bed for him on the floor. Twice the next day the Russos locked the dining room long enough to move the chest aside and hand food to their son.

That night, as usual, the dining room filled up with German officers and a few villagers. Michael's father had said that if Lieutenant Schweitzer came to the inn that evening he would try to seat him where Michael could see him. Just after he heard the tall dining room clock strike nine, Michael sat up in his narrow hiding place and looked through the knothole. At a table directly in his line of vision sat an overweight S.S. lieutenant with cropped blond hair and prominent blue eyes. As Michael watched, the senior Russo placed a glass before the lieutenant who, scowling, asked a low-voiced question. The very picture of distressed and bewildered innocence, Michael's father shrugged and shook his head. Looking sullen and baffled, Lieutenant Schweitzer sat there for perhaps another thirty minutes and then went away.

Hours later, his parents aroused Michael from a fitful sleep. There was a truck outside, backed up to the inn's rear door. For a sum already paid it would take Michael, concealed under a load of hides, to Genoa. From there, pray God, he would be able to get out of Italy entirely. By a flashlight's glow the elder Russo showed him an envelope holding a thick sheaf of ten-thousand-lira notes, with which he ought to be able to buy his way to safety.

Two days after he reached Genoa, a fishing boat took him along the northern Mediterranean coast to more-or-less neutral Spain. A week later he sailed from Barcelona on a New York-bound freighter with a captain who, in return for nearly all that remained of those bank notes, was willing to overlook Michael's lack of any sort of travel documents.

In New York he had no trouble getting a job. With victory still months away, most young American men were still fighting in

Europe and the Pacific. Michael went to work for a garment manufacturer. Because the firm's owner and many of his employees were
of Italian descent, Michael's lack of fluent English was only a small
handicap.

Frequently he wrote to his parents, but because he feared that
those S.S. officers might still track him down, he sent the letters to
one of his married sisters on a farm about seven miles from his village, so that she could deliver them by hand. Three years passed,
four. Michael—or Mike, as everybody called him here in New York
—was still pushing a hand truck in the garment district, but he
didn't mind. He liked the bustling excitement of the streets, and the
pay, because of frequent overtime, wasn't bad. And he had another
reason for contentment. He was in love with a girl named Maria, a
red-haired girl whose family ran a grocery on Mulberry Street.

During the early months of his fifth year in America, his parents
died within two weeks of each other. No one in the family wanted
to keep on running the inn, his oldest sister wrote to him. It had
few guests these days. Forty miles from Falcone the village of San
Simone, once just a cluster of stone huts, had been transformed into
a ski resort. Most people preferred to go there. His sisters would
sell the inn for whatever they could get and send him his share.

Even in his shock and grief, Mike realized one thing. His inherit-
ance would allow him to marry sooner. Maria's father had said that
he could not surrender his daughter to a man with less than five
hundred dollars in the bank.

They were married a few months later. For nearly a year, until
that bleak morning when Dr. Kincaid told him Maria was dead, he
probably was as happy as any man in New York.

He took the baby to live with him in his coldwater flat, leaving
her with Mrs. Scarpi during the day, caring for her himself at night.
He did not secretly resent his tiny daughter, as another man might
have who had lost a beloved wife in childbirth. Instead, because
she was all he had left of Maria, she was doubly precious to him.

Then, late one morning when Sophia was thirteen weeks old, he
almost bumped his hand truck into a man who had stopped short
on the sidewalk. Motionless himself now, Mike stared at the man.
He'd added several pounds and his blond crew-cut hair had some
gray in it, but he was unmistakably the S.S. lieutenant Mike had
last seen looking sullen and baffled in the inn's dining room.

Now, lying on the old couch near the clanking boiler, Mike remembered the cold shock of that moment. The street sounds had seemed to stop, and he was once more back in Italy, with a bullet wound in his leg and the terror of the hunted in his heart.

The German was the first to speak. He said, in heavily accented but fluent English, "You still look like your picture, more like a Scotsman than a wop." He reached out and grasped a cardboard tag hanging from the sleeve of a dress on the hand truck. "Diana Frocks. So that's where you work." Then, suddenly grim: "You know that Horn and Hardart's two blocks from here?"

Mesmerized, Mike nodded.

"Be there at ten after twelve. And I mean, *be* there. If you're not, a couple of friends of mine will look you up."

He walked on. After a dazed moment Mike resumed pushing the hand truck. What should he do? Go to the police? God, no. He was an illegal alien, and a witness to a war crime. At the very least, he would be deported. At worst, he would stand trial for not reporting the murder of those Italian soldiers. And in either event, what would happen to Sophia?

It was easy for Mike to guess why the stout German wanted to see him. He wanted to know where the freight car was. Apparently the S.S. colonel had never told him. Perhaps the colonel was dead. Mike hoped so. One of them was enough to deal with.

By the time he had delivered the load of dresses to the shipper and received a receipt for them, Mike had made a plan he thought might work. Heart beating fast, he walked to the Automat.

The German was already there at a corner table with a mug of coffee before him. Mike, also with a coffee mug, sat down opposite him. The older man said, "Where's that freight car?"

"I won't tell you." Mike's pulses pounded with both fear and defiance. "But I will tell you this. I've drawn a map showing where the car is. And under it I wrote just what I saw that day. I couldn't put down the colonel's name because I don't know it, but I know *your* name, Lieutenant Schweitzer, and I put it in. The paper's in a bank, in a safe deposit box. I told this lawyer I know that if anything happens to me the box is to be opened and the paper turned over to the police."

The German said, "My name isn't Schweitzer anymore." His prominent blue eyes studied Mike's face. Then he said, "Okay, I guess you win. It doesn't matter too much. I'm in a pretty good business now." He shoved back his chair and walked out.

Mike watched him go. Was it that simple, then? Could he fend off the German with just a bluff?

Perhaps it had best not remain just a bluff. Dealing with a man like that, he needed a real weapon. Leaving his coffee half finished, he went to a stationery–tobacco shop two doors away. There he bought a pad of unlined yellow paper. Back at the factory, he locked himself into a cubicle in the men's room and, after several minutes' thought, began to draw.

He drew the skyline of that mountain wall as he remembered it from that autumn evening of his seventeenth year. The Stone Maiden. The defile through which the rails ran. The spur leading to the mine entrance. He labeled the rock formation and then paused, frowning. In what other way could he indicate where the mine was? Well, it was perhaps forty miles northeast from his village of Falcone, and perhaps thirty miles northwest from San Simone, that tiny village which, according to his sister, was becoming a fashionable ski resort. At the top of the page he wrote, "Falcone, 40 mi. southwest. San Simone, 30 mi. southeast."

And now to write down, beneath the sketch, what had happened. He started off in English but found that, in his nervous excitement, he kept failing to find the right words. Switch to Italian. It could be translated easily enough.

He signed his name and folded the paper. What should he do now? Actually go to a bank and ask for a safety deposit box? He shrank from the thought. Probably banks were careful about who rented their boxes. For all he knew, they would demand some proof of his citizenship, or at least a visa. Anyway, he had better find out about that before he tried to rent a box.

In the meantime, he did not want to keep the paper on him, or even leave it in his apartment. Those "friends" the German had mentioned, if they existed, would have little trouble in trailing him to where he lived.

Suddenly he had the solution. Penn Station was only a few blocks away. He would put the paper in a public locker. If he had heard correctly, you could use the locker indefinitely if you kept depositing money in the attached coin box. Thus he'd have time to decide whether or not it would be best to try to rent a safe deposit box.

In a vast echoing room at Penn Station he paused before a vacant locker midway of a long row. He waited there for perhaps a minute, glancing to his right and left. No one appeared at either end of the row. He deposited a coin, twisted the locker key, opened the door. When he'd laid the paper on the locker shelf he closed the door, turned the key, and dropped it into his pocket. He knew that he would be late in reporting back to work, but no matter. With his good record, they would forgive him this once.

That evening he went to Mrs. Scarpi's second-floor flat to get Sophia. He carried her across the hall to his own flat, fed her and changed her, and put her to bed in the big wicker basket that served as her crib. After his solitary meal he sat in the kitchen and read the *News* and listened to the radio. Around ten-thirty he went to bed.

A whimper awoke him. He got up and crossed the room to the basket. Light from a nearby street lamp, shining through the open window, showed him that the baby still slept, one hand curled beside her cheek. Just a dream then.

He looked out the window. A dark-blue sedan stood across the street, a shiny new one, a Buick or maybe an Olds. A man sat in the back seat, and another beside the driver, his plump arm in its short-sleeved shirt crooked over the door's upper edge.

A big new car was rare in this neighborhood. Mike felt a small drum of anxiety start up inside him. Then the man in the sport shirt bent forward and, from the dashboard lighter, lit a cigarette. A dull red glow illuminated the German's face.

Heart pounding, Mike stepped back from the window. The luminous hands of the clock on the dresser pointed to twelve-thirty. How soon would they come up here? As soon as they figured everyone was asleep?

What should he do now?

Even if he wanted to, he could not call the police. He had no phone. Probably other people in this building did, but he didn't know which ones, and while he was pounding on doors to wake his neighbors those men outside might—

Sophia. What of Sophia?

He couldn't carry her across the hall to Mrs. Scarpi's. Early that evening she had told him that she was going to spend the night with her sister, who was ill, but would be back before he left for work in the morning. Just the same, he must get Sophia out of here. If those men got their hands on his baby they could force him to do anything, tell them anything. Probably after that they would kill him. And then what would become of Sophia?

Suddenly he thought of his old Chevy, parked up the block near the corner. He'd bought it a few months ago in those happy, hopeful days before Sophia's birth. Once he had a car, he thought, he might land some kind of a salesman's job. Maria's death had left him too depressed to even contemplate changing jobs. In fact, he'd tried to get rid of the car, but the dealer who had sold it to him for two hundred and fifty refused to buy it back for more than one hundred, and so the car was still his.

He thought for a moment. Then he picked up the basket by its handles and carried it out to the hall. He locked his door. As swiftly as he could, he carried Sophia up four flights. On the top floor he climbed an additional four steps and, holding the basket under one arm, unhooked the latch on the door that led to the roof.

Stepping across the low parapets, he carried the sleeping child through the hot darkness across five roofs. Then he began to try each door that he came to. The fourth one was unlocked. By the feeble glow of overhead bulbs, he descended flights of stairs to a grimy foyer and then went out to the sidewalk. His battered Chevy stood only a few feet to the right. Swiftly he glanced over his left shoulder at the big car at the other end of the block. Could they see him from this distance? Unfortunately, there was a street light right beside the Chevy—

Don't think of that. He put the basket in the rear of the car, on the floor, and got behind the wheel. The old engine, unmuffled, made a terrifyingly loud noise in the quiet street. Mike drove ahead, turned the corner.

Go to the nearest police station? Sophia would be safe there. But he might be arrested, deported, even imprisoned for having kept quiet all these years about those murders. He would never get his little daughter back.

Then the idea came to him. Hide her someplace. Call the police to come get her. She would be safe, and he himself would remain free. Free to figure out some way of reclaiming his daughter without risking arrest and deportation.

He'd go to the warehouse district.

He looked in the rearview mirror. A car back there. Had it turned the corner behind him, or merely pulled away from the curb? Driving as fast as he dared, he turned another corner, then another. Several pairs of headlights behind him now. He turned north onto Ninth Avenue and the edge of the warehouse district. This area, noisy and truck-thronged during the day, appeared almost deserted at this early morning hour. He looked in the rearview mirror. No headlights at all, and none when he looked in the mirror perhaps half a minute later. So they hadn't followed him.

But they had, they had.

Well, he thought, staring at the rain that still streamed down the narrow basement window, at least Sophia had been all right. Whenever Mike got to brooding over the way his own life had turned out, he thought of the way his daughter's had, and felt better.

If only there was some way he could see her and talk to her sometime—well, sometime within the next few weeks.

It was getting awfully dark in here. He stood up, pulled the light cord, peered in at the flaming heart of the old furnace. Then he went through the door into the kitchen to fix his supper.

16

Salvatore unlocked the door of Katherine's apartment with his pass key, reached inside to switch on the foyer light, and then stepped back. "There you are, Miss Derwith."

"Thank you, Salvatore. I'm sorry I don't have any change."

"Oh, that's all right, miss. I'm just sorry you got mugged." He turned and walked toward the elevator.

Katherine moved through the living room to the bathroom and hung up her dripping raincoat. Should she go across the hall and ask Dr. Harris to look at the back of her head? No, she decided. It didn't hurt at all now.

But as her pain had vanished her rage had grown. Rage against Carl. Rage against his stepmother, too, because it was obviously with her knowledge that he played whatever treacherous game he was playing.

She was trembling, not only with anger but chill. Better get out of her clothes, which despite her raincoat had become damp, and take a hot shower.

Fifteen minutes later, wearing a white terry cloth robe, she went into the living room and sat beside the phone. Should she call the police? There would be no point. Unless she could definitely identify her attacker as Carl Dietrich, and she could not, they would dismiss the whole thing as one of the hundreds of muggings and purse snatchings that took place on Manhattan streets every day. No, worse than that. They probably would have sarcastic things to say about a woman who, even in daylight, walked unaccompanied on lonely streets.

Her fury, though, demanded some sort of action. She lifted the phone and dialed Carl's apartment. It was almost six. He ought to be home by now. But apparently he was not. After seven rings she hung up.

She sat there a moment, nerves taut with frustrated rage. Then she reached down to the end table's shelf for the phone book. She looked up Inga Dietrich's phone number and, with an unsteady forefinger, dialed.

The soft, accented voice answered after the third ring. "Hello."

"This is Katherine Derwith." She was helplessly aware that her voice shook. "Is Carl there?"

"Why, no. What is it, Katherine? You sound upset."

"You can bet I'm upset! That stepson of yours, if he is your step-son—"

"Of course Carl is my stepson." The voice was infuriatingly calm.

"Anyway, he followed me from my apartment today down to that old warehouse district and dragged me into a building and stole my handbag."

Inga sounded both shocked and faintly amused. "Now, Katherine. You know Carl wouldn't do anything like that."

"How do I know? How do I know what either of you would do?" She was becoming incoherent. "But I think he saw me buy the locker key from that old woman, and so he—"

"Please! Speak more slowly. What kind of key?"

"Locker! Locker key! It fitted a Penn Station locker, or at least it did twenty-eight years ago. The old woman opened the locker and found just a piece of paper there and threw it away. From what she said it may have been some kind of map. Anyway, this tall man who'd followed me took my purse—"

"Katherine! Don't you know that purse snatchers come in all sizes? Unless you had a diamond bracelet in your bag, why don't you just write it off as part of the price of living in New York?"

"Don't try to humor me! Don't you think I know you're in on whatever game he's playing? I heard him talking to you over the phone early yesterday evening. From what he said it was plain that from the first he hadn't wanted to help me find out why I was abandoned in that warehouse. He wanted to *stop* me from finding out. And you knew he did."

There was a silence at the other end of the line. Then Inga said, "Didn't I warn you, my dear, that you would do well to break with my stepson? Perhaps now you will follow my advice."

"But I want to know!" Katherine cried. "I want to know what you two are up to."

Inga's voice turned cold. "Katherine! You're an extremely attractive young woman with a good education, a job you like, and, my stepson tells me, affectionate adoptive parents. That should content you. And even if it doesn't," she said, her voice colder than ever, "you're not going to learn anything from me."

She hung up.

Hand shaking, Katherine replaced the phone in its cradle. If Inga Dietrich thought she was going to get out of it that easily, she was mistaken. No use, though, to phone the German woman again. She would merely hang up.

I'll go there, Katherine thought. She would wait two hours or more, long enough that the German woman would be at least somewhat off guard, and then go to her apartment. Once they stood face to face, Carl's stepmother wouldn't find it so easy to evade questioning.

In her own apartment, Inga walked up and down the living room. How well had she handled the Derwith girl? Not well, surely. But she had been too shocked to think clearly, or to do anything except try to sound unruffled.

So there was, or at least had been, a map, another map. One drawn long ago by the man Gorman had called the wop kid? Undoubtedly. And Gorman was still hoping to find that map, or some other sort of information, that would lead him to that freight car. That was why he had followed the girl today and robbed her of her handbag. Oh, not Gorman personally. Some goon he had hired.

Carl. She would call Carl. Maybe the time had come when he would be willing to cooperate with her, willing to help her keep Gorman's greedy paws from what lay buried in a mountainside four thousand miles away.

As she moved toward the phone she reflected, as she often had, that if Carl had turned out to be a different sort of man she would have confided in him years ago, and sought his cooperation. But as it was, she thought bitterly, she was forty-eight now, and living in a two-by-four apartment with no income except from an occasional TV job and interest on her savings. And Carl, with his twenty-five thousand a year salary, was not much better off.

But this was no time to work herself up into anger against Carl. She sat down on the sofa, lifted the telephone, and dialed his apartment number. No answer. After several rings she hung up, dialed his TV station, and asked the switchboard operator if Carl Dietrich was still there. After a few seconds she heard his voice.

"Working quite late, aren't you?" she asked.

"I had some details to clean up."

A heavy note in his voice. He was troubled over something, probably the Derwith girl. When men were unhappy, she reflected, some turned to the bottle, others to work.

She said, "Were you busy all afternoon, too? Or were you out purse snatching?"

After a moment he said, "Please, Inga. I'm in no mood for jokes."

"It isn't a joke. Katherine Derwith called me. Someone mugged her this afternoon and took her handbag. She thinks it was you."

"Mugged her! Is she hurt? Did he—"

"Carl! Don't get excited. She's not hurt. Just angry, furiously angry."

"Hang up, Inga, so I can—"

"No, don't call her! At least not now. First you'd better hear the rest of it."

Swiftly she told him of her conversation with Katherine. "Don't you see? Some man Gorman hired must have followed her down there. After she got the key from the old woman—whoever *that* was —he mugged her and took her purse."

After a long moment Carl said, "I guess you're right. Gorman must have seen her ad in the paper last November. Somehow he found out she was the one who put it in. Maybe he's had someone watching her ever since."

"Probably. But however it happened, don't you think that it's high time you and I cooperated?"

Carl was silent for perhaps half a minute. Then he said, "Cooperated in what? Inga, are you trying to tell me after all these years that you have the information Gorman wants? Did my father tell you just where—"

"Right now I'm not trying to tell you anything," she said sharply, "except that I think you ought to see me, so that we can talk this over, and figure out what to do. If not for your own sake, you ought to do it for Katherine's. Don't you realize that as long as Gorman thinks he has a chance, as long as he thinks she may lead him to some sort of information, he'll have some goon watching her? Anything might happen to her."

She let that sink in. Then: "And you ought to listen to me for my sake, Carl. I hate to remind you of it, but it wasn't easy, raising a small boy in a strange country, a child that wasn't even my own."

"I know that," he said heavily. "I'll have dinner someplace, and then come to your apartment."

"Could you make it later this evening? I have my weekly exercise class from seven-thirty to eight-thirty, and it's all the way over on the West Side." Best to try to keep in shape, she thought grimly. If Carl refused to help her, she was going to need those TV jobs. And even if he did agree to cooperate, it might take them some time to figure out a way of cashing in on what his father had hidden.

"Suppose I come to your apartment at ten?"

"Ten would be fine."

After she hung up, Inga still sat on the sofa for a while. Maybe, years ago, she should have turned to some man, one of her lovers, perhaps, and planned with him how best to penetrate the pile of rock and earth choking the entrance to that mine on that remote mountainside. But she had feared that the man might turn out to be inept, or cowardly, or even treacherous. She feared to find herself deported, perhaps even facing the War Crimes Commission. Besides, here was Wilhelm Dietrich's son growing up into what promised to be a taller, stronger, handsomer version of his father—

How could she have known, she thought wryly, that it would be only in appearance that he would have the slightest resemblance to his father?

She got up and went into the bedroom to get dressed.

Half an hour later, seated on a bench beside one of the paths that connected Knickerbocker Town's various buildings, Johnny Wade saw that good-looking kraut emerge from her apartment house and head for a gate in the tall chain link fence that surrounded the entire Knickerbocker complex. He glanced at his watch. Seven o'clock, right on the dot. Every week at this time she left her place at seven, and stayed out about two hours. That was a kraut for you. Methodical all the way.

Well, he might as well get the tape out of her phone, so he could play it for Gorman when he called him at seven-thirty. The little man got up from the bench. Avoiding puddles left by the rain that had ceased only about an hour before, he strolled toward the building's entrance.

17

It was past nine when Katherine entered one of the openings in the high chain link fence surrounding Knickerbocker Town and moved along a wide path to Inga's building. In the foyer with its many rows of push buttons she found Inga's name above the button for apartment 2-H. She did not ring. Instead she waited, confident that, since the building must house at least two hundred people, someone would come along soon.

Footsteps outside. Moving to the inner door, she began to fumble, as if looking for a key, in her handbag. Like the one which she had carried that afternoon, it was of brown leather, but more worn than the bag her tall assailant had taken. A middle-aged couple came into the foyer. "Allow me," the man said, and unlocked the door. Katherine rode up in the elevator with the couple to the second floor and then got out.

She rang the bell of 2-H, waited, rang again. There was a light on inside the apartment. The circular metal shield on the other side of the door, the one that covered the little peep hole, was not in place, and thus light filtered through the thick glass. She rang again. No answer. Without much hope, she reached down for the door knob. It turned under her hand.

She opened the door, took a few steps into the lamp-lit living room, and then halted. "Mrs. Dietrich? Inga?"

Her heart gave a lurch. A few feet away on the beige carpet was a red, moist-looking stain, and beyond that another, and another—

"Inga! Where are you?"

This time there was a kind of answer, an almost inaudible moan.

Stomach knotted, and with tremors of fear running down her legs, Katherine walked along the hall to the bedroom.

The lamp on the nightstand had been knocked over but was still lit. The phone wires had been ripped from the wall and left to dangle from the nightstand's surface. Fully dressed and wearing a green coat, Inga lay slantwise on the bed. With sick horror Katherine saw that the woman had been beaten until she was almost unrecognizable. One eye was completely closed and the other almost so. Her lips were split and bleeding, and her lower jaw, hanging open, seemed out of line with her upper one. Katherine gave a sickened little cry.

Carl. Could Carl have done this?

Her gaze flew back to the useless phone. She managed to say, "I'll go call an ambulance."

"Wait!" Inga's voice was low, almost unintelligible. "Come here."

Katherine approached the bed. "No use," Inga said. "He broke my neck."

With that cold nausea still in the pit of her stomach, Katherine saw that the blond head lay at an unnatural angle. Her lips felt wooden as she said, "All the more reason why I should—"

"No! No use. No time." With visible effort she lifted her left hand and pointed a scarlet-nailed finger at the dressing table. "Bring me—lipsticks—"

Katherine looked at the caddy on the dressing table. It held half a dozen lipsticks. "Which one?"

"Bring—here."

Katherine picked up the caddy, turned back to the bed. The red-nailed finger touched a lipstick in a green lacquer case. Her hand fell back to the bed. "You take it." A flare of hatred in the one blue eye not entirely closed. "Don't let Gorman—"

Katherine wondered, who is Gorman? She bent over the woman. "The man who did this to you. Was his name Gorman?"

Dullness in the almost closed blue eye now, as if that flare of rage had consumed the last of her vitality. "No. But—"

She stopped speaking.

She's dead, Katherine thought.

Hands cold and awkward, Katherine put the green lipstick into her shoulder bag. "I'll find a phone now." Her voice was loud in the room's utter silence. "I'll get an ambulance and the police."

She turned. The light of the upset lamp gleamed on something she had not noticed when she entered the room. A pair of scissors lay just inside the threshold, their long blades covered with blood.

She thought confusedly, as she hurried down the short hall to the living room, Inga's blood? No, surely her assailant's. He'd managed to pull out the scissors, pick up something to staunch partially the flow of blood, then get out of the apartment.

Out in the corridor she turned to her right, jabbed the bell of the next apartment. When there was no response she hammered on the door with her fist. "Help me, please! There's a woman badly hurt. I must telephone." Still no response. She moved to the next apartment, rang and hammered.

Surely not everyone on this floor could be away from home. Surely the occupants of at least one apartment must have heard her by now. But they were afraid. Afraid that if they opened their door someone lurking nearby would rush in, someone who would shoot them, stab them—

There was a public phone on the corner. Better to use that.

She looked at the elevator. The indicator above the door pointed to number eleven. The stairs would be quicker. She ran toward a door with a glowing red exit sign above it. Evidently Inga's attacker too had headed for the stairs, because there were more damp-looking stains on the dark brown hall carpet. She jerked the stair door open.

A dark sedan stood at the curb near a Twenty-second Street opening in the chain link fence. In the front passenger seat the tall man known as Shorty clutched with gloved hands a small yellow satin pillow close to that bleeding wound, just under his rib cage.

"Man, you've got to get me to a doctor."

Seated behind the wheel, Gorman said impatiently, "I told you! You'll be all right as long as you hold that pillow to the wound. And we'll wait only five minutes more. If the police don't come by then, we can be fairly sure she's dead. Otherwise, stubborn bitch that she is, she'd have managed to get to a phone somehow."

He threw the tall man a look of rage and contempt. Bungling fool! He'd been supposed to hurt her just enough, scare her enough, that she'd *talk*. Instead he'd lost his temper and hit her so hard with a karate chop to the neck that, according to his own admission, he had thought he heard something "bust inside."

"Are you sure she didn't say anything?"

Shorty moaned. "Man, I told you. She wouldn't talk. Just kept fighting. Biting, kicking, trying to knee me. And even after I hit her that good one and heard something crack in her neck, she managed to pick up those scissors and—" He broke off. "You've got to get me to a doctor! You can't let me bleed to death!"

"Just a minute or two longer," Gorman soothed. "Then I'll take you straight to an emergency hospital."

Up ahead, from a gateway into Knickerbocker Town, a girl had emerged onto the sidewalk, a tall girl, red hair shining under a street lamp. Gorman remembered Katherine Derwith's description of herself on that tape from Carl Dietrich's phone. "I'm five-feet-seven, and my hair is red—"

He gripped Shorty's arm so abruptly that the wounded man gave a little yelp of pain. "Is that the girl you've been shadowing, the one whose purse you took with that damned useless key in it?"

"Yeah, yeah, it's her. But listen, you've got to get me sewed up, you've got to."

Gorman didn't bother to reply. The Derwith girl must have come here to see Inga. Undoubtedly the stupid hulk beside him hadn't thought to relock the door when he left, and so the girl had gotten inside. Now she was on her way to that call box on the corner. Had she found Inga dead? Or alive—and talking?

Gorman hesitated no longer. He switched on the ignition and propelled the car forward, so abruptly that again the injured man cried out.

Afterward Katherine could never say what made her turn. Perhaps subconsciously she had noticed that although she could hear an approaching car she could not see the beam of its headlights shooting past her along the street, and had wondered why. Anyway, she looked back, and saw the car's dark shape leap the curb and angle toward her, ready to smash her like an insect between its grill and the chain link fence.

Some instinct for self-preservation kept her from flattening herself against the fence. Instead she darted to her left and kept going, in the direction from which she had come.

Behind her she heard a scrape of metal against metal, then the bump of wheels off the curb, then the dwindling away sound of the engine. She turned in at the gate in the fence and ran along one of the cement paths. Every inch of her flesh seemed to be imagining what she had escaped, those tons of metal smashing her to a bloody pulp—

The pounding in her head was very loud now, and a metal band seemed to be tightening around her chest. There was a bench just ahead. She stumbled toward it, sank down onto the plank seat. Soon, just as soon as she could get her breath and fight down the sickness in the pit of her stomach, she would get up from here, lest whoever had tried to kill her would come back to look for her. She would go into the nearest building, Inga's building. And this time she would not call for help. She would scream "Fire!" as loudly as she could. That would bring them pouring out from behind their locked doors, their safety chains.

Through the pound of blood in her ears she heard another sound. Footsteps along the cement walk. Her head swiveled around. A tall man, standing between her and the nearest standard lamp, his face in shadow. The pulse in her throat gave a painful leap. She shot to her feet and started running toward Inga's apartment building.

Footsteps pursuing her. "Katherine!" Hands caught her, swung her around. She opened her mouth to scream. He clapped his hand over her lips. "Katherine! It's all right!"

Carl holding her. Carl, who might have dragged her into that dark, musty-smelling place this afternoon, who tonight might have gone to his stepmother's apartment—

"Katherine, will you listen to me? Will you promise not to scream if I take my hand away from your mouth?"

Suddenly she realized how illogical her thinking had been. If Carl had killed Inga and then fled, the last place he would be was here, only yards from the entrance to her apartment house.

Then it dropped away from her entirely, that mixture of fear and rage she had been feeling toward him for more than twenty-four hours. He could not have been the one who had followed her to the warehouse district that afternoon, any more than he could have been the one who had administered that terrible beating to Inga. He was a liar, yes. He had lied to her from the beginning. But he was no assaulter of women.

"Will you promise not to scream?"

She nodded. He took his hand away. "Katherine, what is it?"

She said, from a dry throat, "It's Inga. I went up to her apartment. I found her—terribly beaten. Oh, Carl! I think she's dead."

He gripped her arm. "Come on."

They went into the foyer of Inga's building. Carl took out a key ring, and with the longer of two keys unlocked the outer door. The elevator was on the ground floor. They took it to the second. As they moved toward Inga's door he said in an odd, harsh voice, "Oh, God! I remember when she gave me these keys. She said it was so I could get in if ever she was unable to come to the door—"

In Inga's living room he said, "Wait here," and went down the hall. She stood there, still fighting down that sickness in the pit of her stomach, and trying not to think of Inga lying there with that terrible vacancy in that one not-quite-closed blue eye.

Carl came back to her. "She's dead." His face looked several years older. "Now tell me about this."

Trying to speak as coherently as she could, she told him of the angry suspicion that had brought her to Inga's apartment, only to find the woman half unconscious. She told him of the lipstick, and of her flight toward the corner call box, and the car that had tried to smash her into the chain link fence.

When she stopped speaking he said, "Better give me that lipstick." His face was whiter than ever now, and his voice had a constricted sound, as if the muscles in his throat had tightened up. Silently she held the lipstick out to him, and he dropped it into his coat pocket.

He asked, "What did you touch in this apartment, besides the lipstick and the lipstick caddy and the doorknobs?"

"Why—why nothing."

"You're sure?"

She nodded. "You're worried about my fingerprints, aren't you? But why—"

"I'll explain later," he said, and turned away.

She waited in the silent room until he came back from the bedroom, his handkerchief in his hand. He polished the doorknob and then grasped it, with the handkerchief between his palm and the metal. "I'll put you in a taxi, and then I'll call the police."

"But I don't understand. Why shouldn't I tell the police about finding her—"

"Not yet, not until you and I have had a chance to talk. I'll come to your apartment after I've seen the police. But just go home now. Please, Katherine. Trust me."

She looked into the face that seemed to have grown so much older in the last half hour, and into the gray eyes that now, more than ever, had that lonely, inward-turning look. "All right. I'll trust you."

"It may be quite late by the time I've finished with the police. If you'd rather I came to your apartment tomorrow morning—"

"No, come tonight. I'll be awake, no matter how late it is."

18

At this hour there was still quite a lot of traffic moving in both directions across the Brooklyn Bridge. Gorman drove with extreme caution, keeping well back from the car ahead of him and glancing frequently into the rearview mirror, lest he be involved in even the most minor of accidents. Shorty sprawled in the corner of the seat, head hanging forward. He had made no sound for at least ten minutes. If he wasn't dead now, Gorman thought, he certainly would be soon. On the Brooklyn side of the bridge a curve sent Shorty leaning leftward, and Gorman had to take his hand off the wheel long enough to push him back into place.

It might have been quicker, Gorman had realized, to take Shorty over to the New Jersey meadows. But then he'd have had to pass a toll collector. Besides, the Brazilian lived in Freeport, Long Island. Gorman would drive far out beyond the Suffolk County line and leave Shorty in a certain patch of woods well off the highway, where it probably would be days before anyone found him. Then he'd drive back to the Brazilian's and get him to help clean up the car. Gorman also would borrow a suit of clothes, since undoubtedly he would find bloodstains on his own. True, the Brazilian was thinner than Gorman, but he was wider in the shoulders and taller, so that the clothes should fit all right. He would arrange, too, for the Brazilian to tell the police that Gorman had spent the evening in his company, if it became necessary for Gorman to have an alibi.

If everything went smoothly, Gorman should be back in his Manhattan apartment by daylight.

He saw the sign for the Brooklyn-Queens Expressway, which would lead him to the Long Island Expressway. Watching the limp figure from the corner of his eye lest it fall forward again, he angled toward the right.

19

It was past two o'clock when Carl finally appeared at Katherine's apartment. "I'm sorry it's so late," he said, as he came into the foyer. "You look very tired."

"So do you." Lines she'd never seen before bracketed his mouth. Repressing the questions that crowded her mind, she said, "Would you like a drink?"

"God, yes."

"Bourbon all right?"

He nodded. "With plain water." He sank onto one end of the sofa.

When she returned from the kitchen with drinks for both of them, she handed him his glass and then sat down at the sofa's opposite end. She said, "Did you have—any trouble with the police? I mean, did they seem to have any idea that it might have been you—"

"Who did that to Inga? Of course not. Whoever killed her has a scissor wound in him and blood all over him."

"What did you tell the police?"

"Just that I came to see my stepmother around ten o'clock. When she didn't answer my ring, I used my own keys to get into the building and into her apartment. I found her—the way she was."

"You said nothing about me?"

"No."

"Or the lipstick?"

"No. Look, Katherine. If, after you've heard the whole thing, you still want to go to the police, I won't try to stop you. But listen to me first."

She said quietly, "All right."

"It begins with my father. I learned when I was very young that he had been an S.S. officer. But it wasn't until I was nine years old—"

He described his shock that night when, awakened by voices, he had heard his stepmother and a strange man—a fat man who said his name was Gorman—talk about a buried freight car, and a half-dozen Italian soldiers buried along with it.

"When he'd gone, Inga told me what my father had done. She also told me that she didn't know where the freight car was buried. That was a lie. I often suspected it was, but I didn't know for sure until a few hours ago."

While Katherine listened, appalled and sickened, he went on. "Most of the time while I was growing up I managed not to think about what Inga had told me. Otherwise I probably couldn't have gotten through high school and college and found a job. Soon after I took my first job, I fell in love with Naomi. I knew I had no right to marry her—or anyone, I suppose—without telling her about my father. But all I did tell her was that he had been in the German army in the war. She didn't even know he'd been S.S. until Inga—" He stopped speaking.

"Until Inga what?"

"One night she showed Naomi a snapshot of my father in his S.S. uniform."

"But *why?*"

"I'm not sure. Inga was drunk that night and in a rotten mood, but that doesn't seem any real justification." He paused, swirling amber liquid around in his glass. "I was fond of Inga, and grateful for all she'd done for me. But always I felt that there were facets of her character which she kept hidden."

They were both silent for a moment. Then Katherine said, "All this about your father. I can't see how it could have anything to do with me, but it does, doesn't it? It's the reason you answered my ad."

He nodded. "You see, I haven't yet told you all I overheard that night when I was nine. This man Gorman spoke of a baby girl left in a warehouse, and of some young Italian, the baby's father, who'd witnessed the burying of that freight car—"

"Young Italian?" Katherine leaned forward, her face pale with tension. "What was his name?"

"Russo. And I'm almost certain the first name was Michael. Anyway, it began with M. This Gorman and a couple of other men—men he'd hired, probably—strong-armed this young Italian, but they heard the police coming, and they had to let him go. After that, apparently, he managed to get out of town."

"Out of town! *Where* out of town?"

"Katherine, I have no idea. I can understand how anxious you are to talk about your father. But first hadn't you better listen to the rest of what I have to tell you?"

She said, past the racing pulse in the hollow of her throat, "All right. Go ahead."

"When I saw your ad in the paper, I knew it almost certainly concerned the baby left in a warehouse by that young Italian. I had to get in touch with you to learn how much you knew, if anything. I had to for Ellen's sake. My daughter must never know that her grandfather was a Nazi, let alone that—that he buried six men alive. Can you understand that, Katherine? And can you forgive me for deceiving you?"

"Yes," Katherine said slowly, "I can, especially now that I know Ellen." She was silent for a moment, and then said, "But about tonight. Do you think it was Gorman who—"

"I'm sure it was. Oh, I don't think he killed Inga with his own hands. I think he hired someone to beat information out of her."

"Information about where it was that your father—"

Carl nodded.

"But I don't understand. Why didn't he hire someone to do that a long time ago?"

"Because it wasn't until a few hours ago that he could feel quite sure that she knew where the freight car was. Early this evening—or rather, yesterday evening—I talked to her on the phone. I asked her if she knew, and although she didn't admit it right out, I got the impression that she did know. And if I got that impression, Gorman must have too. And so he moved fast."

"But I still don't understand. How could he know about what you and Inga—"

"Her phone was bugged." Pain in his voice now. "When I looked down at Inga tonight, I knew he must somehow have known what she and I talked about a few hours earlier. So after I put you in a taxi I went back up there and took the phone apart. I found it, one of those miniaturized taping devices. I took out the tape and then went to that phone box, the one you'd been heading for, and called the police."

"Was it just her phone—"

"No, mine too. After I'd talked to the police I went back to my apartment. I figured it was probably because of a bug in my phone that he knew, last November, that I'd gotten in touch with you about your ad. I found the bug. Then I came here."

Her advertisement. She leaned forward. "Can we talk about my father now? Do you think he could have come back here to New York?"

Carl said gently, "That isn't likely, is it, when he knew a man like Gorman wanted to get his hands on him?"

"He might have come back a long time later, after he'd changed a lot, enough so that he could feel that even if Gorman did happen to see him, he wouldn't recognize him—"

"But Katherine." Carl's voice was still gentle. "Why should he have come back? Why should he run even that slight risk?"

After a moment Katherine said, "Because of me. He may have come back to learn what had become of me. Maybe he's been right here in the city for years, keeping track of me."

"That's a nice idea," Carl said in that same tone. "But even if it were so, you might have a hard time finding *him*. I don't suppose there are as many Russos in New York as there are Cohens or Smiths, but I'll bet that there are plenty, and that a lot of them were christened Michael."

She accepted that in silence. Then she asked, "Did you mention Gorman to the police?"

"Yes, but I doubt that anything will come of it. You can be sure Gorman will come up with an alibi. As for the man who actually gave Inga that beating, he'll probably stay in hiding somewhere until his wound has healed. Either that, or he's already bled to death. In that case, it may be that Gorman has had the body dumped somewhere."

She shuddered, again seeing in her mind's eye those bloodied scissors. "Did you tell the police why you thought they should question Gorman?"

"No. I just said he was someone she seemed to fear."

"You made no mention of the freight car? No, of course you wouldn't have. Naomi and Ellen would know about it then, and that's what you've been trying to avoid all these years."

He nodded and then said, "Yes, but one thing is different now."

She looked at him expectantly.

"Now I know where the freight car is."

Her breath caught. "The lipstick?"

"Yes. There was about a half-inch of lipstick inside it. Underneath that was a tiny rolled-up map. Inga must have drawn it from information my father had given her, because the handwriting on it was hers. It showed the profile of a mountain with a line which had been labeled 'railroad track' emerging from a defile. A spur led to the right to what must be the site of the buried freight car. It's marked with an X.

"On one side of the defile," he added, "she'd drawn something that must be an unusual rock formation. She'd labeled it the Stone Maiden."

I know, Katherine thought, but did not say it aloud. She didn't want to talk right then about the bag lady, and the old locker key, and those hours when she had been bitterly sure that it was Carl who had taken it from her.

"What did you do with the map?"

"I burned it."

"Burned it!"

"But not before I'd memorized it. You see, as soon as Inga's funeral is over, I'm going there."

"To Italy?"

"Yes. I'm going to make sure that there is, or at least was, a railroad spur leading to a place where a freight car and engine could be buried. And once I'm sure of it, I'm going to notify the Italian government, *anonymously*, so that whatever is in the car can be restored to the rightful owners, which I imagine in the case of most of it is the Italian government. I can't bring those Italian soldiers my father killed back to life, but I can at least do this much."

She said, after a moment, "But how can you find it? Even with the map, you don't know where it is. Over the centuries lots of mines of all sorts must have been dug in those mountains. And probably there is more than one Stone Maiden, just the way in the American West there are all those rock formations called Rainbow Bridge or Indian Chief or—"

"But I do know where it is, more or less. Down at the bottom of the map she had written, 'Approximately thirty miles northwest of San Simone.'"

"The skiing San Simone? The one that's so fashionable?"

"It must be. But it's only in recent years that it has become a well-known resort. Back during the war it probably was no more than a collection of stone huts clustered around a church."

She said, after a long moment, "If you're going, I'm going with you."

"Katherine, no!"

"Don't you see? This concerns me as well as you, because it concerned my father as well as yours. Mine saw it—saw it happen, and yet apparently never reported it. Maybe he kept silent because he was afraid, not just for himself but for others too, his parents, say, and later on my—my mother, whoever she was, and me. But he did keep silent. So you're not the only one who feels a—a sort of moral obligation to set things right, at least as much as they can be set right."

He was silent for several seconds. Then he said, "I intend to take every precaution against being followed. Just the same, it could be dangerous."

I know it could, she thought, and that's one reason I want to go with you. I want to help you all I can. Aloud she said, "I don't see how it could be dangerous, not if we keep from being followed. Anyway, I'm going with you. I can go on my own, if I have to. You've told me where it is, remember?"

He smiled faintly. "Quite a bargainer, aren't you? All right, we'll go together. But between now and the time we leave I don't think you should stay in this apartment."

"You think that Gorman might—" Her words trailed off.

His voice was grim. "Oh, I don't think that he'll risk having another woman beaten up. Not this soon. But it's best not to take a chance. As soon as you've had a few hours' sleep, go to your parents' place in Bellmont. I'll keep in touch with you there."

"All right." But she wouldn't go immediately. There was something she intended to do first.

"One thing more," he said. He went into the kitchen, came back with a screwdriver, and lifted the phone from its cradle. He turned the base over, unscrewed its metal plate, and looked inside at the phone's mechanism. "Clean," he said. "I thought maybe your phone too was bugged, but it isn't." He looked at his watch. "Almost five! Good thing today's Saturday and we don't have to go to work." He stood up, and so did she. "Lock the door after me, and bolt it too. And then get to bed."

They stood silent for a moment. She felt exhausted from lack of sleep, and numbed by the shocks she'd received in the past thirty hours or so. She ached for him to reach out and hold her comfortingly close, if only for a few seconds.

Instead he extended his hand and lightly touched her cheek with a crooked forefinger. "Get to sleep," he said, and turned away.

Tired as she was, she did not, after she had locked and bolted the door behind him, go immediately to bed. Instead she lifted the Manhattan phone book from its shelf under the end table and turned to the R's.

As Carl had predicted, there were lots of Russos in the book. Quite a few of them had listed themselves as Michael, and even more as M. Russo. And this was only one borough. There might be even more Russos in Brooklyn and Queens. Just the same, as soon as she woke up she would start calling.

She put the phone book back on the shelf, snapped off the lamp. Through the gray dawn light already filling the apartment she walked into the bedroom.

20

Despite her exhaustion she awoke before ten, evidently too keyed up to get as much sleep as she needed. A few minutes later, still in her robe, and with a cup of coffee beside her, she began to call the Michael Russos listed in the Manhattan phone book.

At the first number a woman responded. Katherine could hear the voices of very young children in the background. Probably, she realized, this was not the residence of the right Michael Russo. Say her father had been in his early twenties at the time of her own birth. Then he must be fifty or past now. Nevertheless she asked, "Mrs. Michael Russo?"

"Yes." The woman sounded suspicious.

"I'm trying to locate a Michael Russo my mother knew a long time ago in Italy. I told her that when I got to New York—"

"You've got the wrong Russos. My husband's only twenty-seven, so how could he have known your mother a long time ago?"

Katherine said swiftly, "But perhaps his father—"

"His father's name is Pietro," the woman said, and hung up.

The next two numbers did not answer. At the one after that, a man in an accent-laden voice creaking with age said that yes, he was Michael Russo.

"Would you mind telling me what part of Italy you're from?"

"Siciliano! I come-a here when-a Hoover was *presidente*—"

"I'm afraid you're not the gentleman I'm looking for," Katherine said, but that did her no good. The Sicilian was so starved for someone to talk to that several minutes passed before she could bring herself to say goodbye and hang up.

Several more numbers did not answer. Then two women in a row, both middle-aged to judge by their voices, told her that their husbands could not be the Michael Russo her mother knew because they had been born in New York and never gone to Europe.

That brought her to the M. Russos. The first did not answer. When she dialed the second one, a voice breathed, "Hel-lo," with such seductiveness that Katherine was sure she had made accidental contact with a call girl.

"I'm trying to locate a Michael Russo who—"

"No Michael Russo here, honey," the voice said in a brisker tone. "The M is for Marilyn, and that's me."

At the next number a man answered. Katherine said, "I'm trying to locate a Michael Russo who used to—"

"Mike ain't here, lady." The young voice had a Puerto Rican accent. "Mike's the super here, all right, but he had to go to the hospital this morning. I'm Ernesto Ramirez, his helper."

A premonition tightened Katherine's nerves. "Could you tell me something about him, so that I'll know if he's the one my mother asked me to locate?"

"Sure, lady."

"About how old is he?"

"Pretty old. Fifty, fifty-two, something like that."

"Do you know what part of Italy he's from?"

"Someplace up north, in the mountains. Mike says people there don't look like most Italians. He sure don't. And he says his wife's people were from northern Italy too, and she was a real redhead."

Katherine could feel the beating of her heart. "His wife's dead?"

"Since a long time ago, lady."

"Does he have any children?"

"He told me once he had a daughter, but when I asked him how come she never came to see him, he clammed up. And he hasn't mentioned her since."

"Could you—could you tell me what's wrong with him?"

Sadness in the young voice now. "The Big C, lady. He expected to stay out of the hospital a few weeks more. But this morning he looked bad, real bad, and finally he let me call his doctor and the doc sent an ambulance."

"What hospital?"

"Callendar Memorial. They got visiting hours, eleven in the morning until four. You going to see him, lady?"

"Yes."

"I'm glad. Mike don't seem to have any friends except me, and some guy named Salvatore who's a doorman over on the East Side. And Mike's a real nice guy. I guess I'll get his job now, and I want it, but I sure hate getting it this way."

"Thank you. Goodbye," Katherine said, and hung up.

She sat there for a moment feeling a blend of emotion, sorrow for the parent she had never known, and thankfulness that she had located him now, rather than weeks or months from now. Then she went into the bedroom and began to dress.

The uniformed guard on the hospital's first floor had thumbed through a card index, muttering, "Russo, Russo," and then handed her a card labeled "Visitor's Permit." In one corner were the stamped words, "Room 1109, Bed A." Now she moved along the eleventh floor corridor, dimly aware of a man mopping the linoleum, of a man in hospital whites pushing a bottle-laden cart, and of pale faces turning hopefully toward her as she passed open doorways. In which bed, she wondered, would her father be lying? Would Bed A be the one closest to the door or to the far wall?

She need not have worried about knowing which of the room's patients was Mike Russo. As soon as she stepped through the room's doorway and saw the man lying, with closed eyes, in the nearest bed, she knew he was her father. High cheekbones like hers, a wide mouth like hers. But he was thinner than she was, so that his body was almost indiscernible beneath the white bedspread.

Heart twisting, she lifted an aluminum and canvas chair, placed it close to the bed, and sat down.

His eyes opened, eyes of the same shade of gray as her own. They held a drugged expression. He smiled and said, looking pleased but not surprised, "Hello, Sophia."

Sophia? Could it be that after all he was not Mike Russo?

He went on, "I guess I better call you Katherine. You don't even know that your mother and I named you Sophia, do you?"

Unable to speak, she shook her head.

The drugged look was clearing from his eyes. He said, "Hey! I never meant you to know— Hey! How come you're here?"

"Please, Father." She took his thin, hot hand and carried it to her cheek. "Don't worry about it. Let's just be glad we've found—" Her voice broke.

"Hey, now! You're crying. Somebody told you I'm going to die, huh? No need to cry about that girl. Everybody has to die."

He disengaged his hand and pointed to the box of paper tissues on the white metal stand beside his bed. As she wiped her cheeks he said, "Right now, having you here, I'm getting a better break than I ever expected." He paused, and then said, "One thing I always wished I could tell you, somehow. I wanted you to know that I didn't *want* to stop being your father."

"I know. I think I've always known it, somehow."

"And you've been happy? Growing up in that nice house in Westchester, and going to college, and now with that newspaper job?"

For how many years, she wondered, had he been watching her? "Yes, I've always been happy."

"But you don't get married, Daughter. You had this rich young guy, must've been crazy about you, and you didn't marry him."

He meant Gil. Strange, this was the first time in weeks she'd even thought of Gil.

"No, but I'll be all right." She managed to laugh. "I'm not exactly a hag, yet."

"A hag, Sophia? Why, you're beautiful. You look just like your mama."

She leaned toward him. "How—how long ago was it?"

"She died when you were less than an hour old. She was sweet and good, your mama. Nice family, too. I've worried. I've worried that *you've* worried what kind of people you come from. All good people, both Maria's and mine. Garibaldi, with his own hands, gave your great-great-grandpa a medal."

The confusion was coming back into his eyes. "Sophia, did you say how come you knew about me? Nothing bad has happened, has it? I mean, it was years and years ago. That man who had his goons beat me up. Has he—"

"No! No, Father. Everything's fine. Please, please just be glad that—"

"I'm sorry, but you'll have to excuse us. It's time for Mr. Russo's injection."

Katherine turned, looked at the middle-aged nurse, and got to her feet. Mike Russo said, infinite pride in his voice, "This is my daughter." Then, to Katherine: "You'll come to see me again?"

"Of course. I—I can't right away. I have to go up to my—to the Derwiths for a few days."

He nodded. "Your other papa and mama. Must be nice people."

"Yes," she said from a tight throat. "And after that I have to take a—a short trip. But I'll phone you tomorrow and the next day and the next. And as soon as I'm back from my trip, I'll come here."

"Please, Miss Russo," the nurse said.

"I'm sorry. I'm going right now." She bent and kissed her father's thin cheek. "I'll phone you tomorrow, just about this time."

She left the room and then, pressed against the wall to keep out of the way of the corridor traffic, she waited until the nurse emerged from Room 1109.

"Nurse, can you tell me how my father is?"

The nurse's eyes, sharp but not unkind behind shell-rimmed glasses, searched Katherine's face. "I think you know how he is."

"Yes. But how long—"

"Who can say? He's scheduled for chemotherapy, starting day after tomorrow. If it works, he may have months ahead of him, even years. If it doesn't—" She left the sentence hanging there.

"Thank you," Katherine said, and turned away.

It was dusk when Carl Dietrich stopped his car, rented for the day, in front of the modest green frame house his ex-wife and his daughter occupied in a small Rockland County town. Even though snow had not fallen recently in New York City, a thin coat of white covered the dead lawn bisected by a cement path. Carl went up onto the small porch and rang the bell.

Naomi, in blue jeans and a brown turtleneck, opened the door. Her face in its frame of dark curls looked as rosy and almost as young as when he first met her. She led him into the living room, where a card table held a stack of leaflets and a stack of stamped and addressed envelopes. "I'm mailing out literature for the League of Women Voters," she said. To supplement her child support payments, Naomi worked in a local dress shop. In time left over from her job and from caring for her daughter and her house, she worked for various community projects. As always, Carl felt very proud of her.

"Won't you sit down for a moment, Carl?" When they were both seated on the sofa she said in a low, appalled voice, "I've seen the papers."

He nodded. The story about Inga had been on page three of the *Times*. The *News* had banner-lined it on the front page: "Blond Model-Actress Found Beaten to Death." Carl had searched both papers, and later on the *Post*, for mention of recent stab victims, whether dead or alive. There was none. But then, he reflected, with a yearly homicide rate running into the hundreds, and men and women with stab wounds turning up by the thousands in hospital emergency rooms, it was not surprising that whoever Inga had stabbed with those scissors had escaped the notice of the press. Unless the victim was a "blond model-actress," or a rich person, or a celebrity of some sort, violence simply wasn't news.

Naomi went on, "The paper said you found her."

"Yes."

"The police aren't giving you any—trouble, are they?"

"Of course not. They know I didn't do it. Unless the guy was stupid enough not to wear gloves, they'll probably never find the one who did do it."

She shivered. "I hid the newspapers from Ellen. I suppose she'll hear about it sooner or later, but I felt I couldn't cope with her shock and my own too, right now. I mean, I wasn't fond of Inga, especially after that night she— But just the same, I'm terribly sorry." She paused. "You won't say anything about it to Ellen, will you?"

"Of course not. And I want to thank you for allowing me to take her out to dinner tonight."

"Carl, you know that you can see Ellen at any time. But was there some special reason—"

"In a way. I'm going to Europe in a few days, and I wanted to see her first."

"Are you going on business for the TV station?"

"Well, no."

After a moment Naomi said, "Ellen told me about that Miss Derwith. Ellen likes her a lot." The implied question was plain: are you taking Katherine Derwith to Europe with you?

He said, "Yes, she's very nice."

"Carl, are you going to marry her?"

He made his voice light. "Marry her? I'd have to ask her first. She might say no."

"I don't think she would."

He thought, but that's because you still don't know everything about Wilhelm Dietrich. Katherine does know about those six murdered men.

Naomi went on, "Carl, don't think I'd be—resentful of any happiness you might find. I'm not small-minded."

"I know. You're about the least small-minded person I ever met." He smiled at her, remembering what their world had been like when they loved each other, and realizing now that for both of them that world was dead.

"I told Ellen I wanted to talk to you for a few minutes alone, but I'll call her now." She crossed the room to the foot of the stairs. "Ellen."

Red tam-o'-shanter on her dark curls, ends of red scarf flying behind her, Ellen hurtled down the stairs and into her father's arms.

"All right, young lady. What will be your dining pleasure?"

"The Cheeseburger Rancho! Please, Daddy. I know it's not very —intime, but the food is really neat."

Over their daughter's head, Carl shot his ex-wife a look of resigned dismay. "The Cheeseburger Rancho it is."

Half an hour later, in a booth built to resemble a small corral, and with a coiled lariat on the wall beside them and a lantern illuminating the rough wooden table, Ellen laid down her half-eaten cheeseburger and asked the question her mother had not put into words. "Daddy, is Katherine going to Europe with you?"

"Yes."

"I wish I could go too. I would be absolutely ecstatic."

"You have to stay in school now, Ellen. But maybe you can go soon." Before she could ask, "With you and Katherine?" he said, "Incidentally, have you been studying anything especially interesting in school?"

"Well, in social studies we've been reading Roots. And we have interesting discussions about it. What makes them so interesting is that there are both black and white kids in our class."

"And so?"

"The black kids talk about how they feel about their ancestors, and the white kids talk about how they feel about their ancestors."

Carl was aware his heartbeat had quickened. "And what do you think they should feel?"

"I see it this way, Daddy. Suppose one of my ancestors was one of the really bad people in *Roots,* like the ones who cut off Kunta Kinte's toes. I'd feel sorry, but I wouldn't feel it made *me* bad."

She thrust aside her now-empty plate and, one elbow on the table, cupped her chin in her hand. "Don't you see? It works the other way around, too. I'm glad you're a good person, but your being a good person doesn't make me one. No matter how good or bad the people before him were, each new person in the world has a chance to try to be good. That's what I said in class, and Miss Entwhistle—she's the teacher—said she agreed with me."

Bless you, he thought, and bless Miss Entwhistle. He was still determined that, if he could, he would protect her against ever knowing what a monster her grandfather was. But even if she did find out someday, perhaps it would not utterly crush her.

"Another cheeseburger?" he asked. "No? Then how about some dessert?"

21

The big plane flew eastward under a full moon. It flooded the sky with radiance, so that only the major stars were visible. Now that the cabin's lights had been dimmed for the night, Katherine, from her window seat, had a good view of the clouds below, a billowing silver sea that hid the real sea. She turned to look at Carl. He was sleeping, face turned toward her, cheek pressed against the headrest.

Even while he slept there were lines of strain on his face. That was understandable. In the past four days he had arranged for Inga's funeral. To hold the press and the morbidly curious at bay, the ceremony had been kept completely private, with only Carl, four of her neighbors, and a few of her TV colleagues present.

He had also talked several more times with the police, who as yet had made only negative findings. They had established that neither a man found stabbed to death in the Bronx that night, nor any of the still-living stab victims treated at the city's many hospitals could have been Inga Dietrich's murderer. As for Gorman, they had found nothing to link him with Inga's death. True, Gorman had said, he had known Inga, the wife of a fellow officer, in Berlin, and he had seen her a couple of times in New York, but for a good many years now he'd had no contact whatever with her. As for the night of Inga's death, he had been miles away, at the home of a friend on Long Island. The friend had confirmed that story.

For Katherine, too, the last few days had been stress-filled. Lying was always a strain, and to protect them from worry, she had lied to Ed and Clara Derwith. She had decided to take her vacation now rather than next summer, she told them. She would spend a few days with them, and then fly to Italy for a few days' skiing in the Dolomites.

"And Gil?" Clara Derwith asked. "I know Gil likes to ski. Perhaps if you asked him—"

"I don't think he would want to come along, Mother. And anyway, I won't ask him. That's definitely over. Besides, I'm going there with Carl Dietrich."

Clara said, after a brief, disappointed silence, "The man who works for a TV station? Does this mean it's—serious?"

She tried to keep ruefulness out of her voice. "If you mean, has he asked me to marry him, the answer is no. And I have no idea that he ever will."

Did all parents, Katherine wondered, feel such anxiety over daughters who reached their late twenties still unmarried? Or was it only the happy couples who, so to speak, started looking through the Yellow Pages for wedding caterers as soon as their girl children reached their teens? Certainly Ed and Clara Derwith had been happy. And to judge from the tone of his voice when he said, "Maria," her real father and mother had been happy during their brief time together.

Each afternoon while she was with her foster parents Katherine left the house and called Mike Russo from a nearby drugstore. During the first phone conversation he said, "You didn't tell those nice people that you've seen your real papa, have you?" His voice, thick and a little slow, told her that he must have been given sedation recently.

"No, Father. I've never wanted to hurt them by letting them know how very much I needed to learn who my real parents were."

"That's right, Sophia. Better not to hurt them. And anyway, some awfully bad things happened way back there, things I don't want them or you to know about." Confused anxiety came into his voice. "Or *did* I tell you about it?"

"No, Father. And since you don't want me to know, I won't ask."

After a brief silence he said, "Sophia, I can't remember. Did you tell me how you found me?"

"No. It's a long story. Perhaps I'll tell you when you're stronger. Right now I'd better say goodbye for now. They told me at the switchboard that you weren't to talk for more than five minutes."

She left the drugstore and, through quiet streets made even

quieter by falling snow, walked back to the house where she had grown up.

That evening Carl Dietrich had phoned her. "Can you talk?"

"Yes. My parents are playing bridge next door."

"I've booked two seats on Wednesday night's seven-thirty plane to Milan. They're under the name of Mr. and Mrs. James Stirling."

"But Carl! We can't go under false names. Our passports—"

"I know that. Now listen, Katherine. I'm going to wait until the very last minute—six-thirty, say—to cancel those reservations. Of course, they don't have to hold reservations open that long, but they probably will on a Wednesday night, because not many people fly midweek, especially in winter. Now here is how we'll work it. We'll meet in the Biltmore lounge at five-thirty Wednesday afternoon. We'll both carry hand luggage so that we won't have to spend time checking suitcases. When we get to Kennedy, I'll go to one of the phones inside the terminal and cancel that Mr. and Mrs. Stirling reservation. That way we will be almost sure that there are at least two seats left. We'll go immediately to the airline's ticket counter and buy tickets under our own names. We'll walk to the departure lounge. By that time it should be seven or a little past, almost flight time. We ought to be the last people to enter the departure lounge. If we're not, if someone shows up there after we do—"

He paused. Katherine said, "If someone shows up at the last minute like that, we'll know there's a good chance he has been following us."

"Exactly."

His plan had gone smoothly. They had met at the Biltmore and ridden in a taxi to Kennedy, through rush-hour traffic so thick that, Katherine felt, even the most skilled driver would have trouble trailing them. At Kennedy Carl had made his call, canceling the Stirling reservations, to a no-doubt-irritated clerk. Then they had gone to the ticket counter, bought their tickets, and, carrying bags small enough to fit under the plane's seats, walked to the departure lounge. About two minutes passed. Then a pleasant feminine voice said over the loudspeaker, "The New York to Milan flight is now boarding. First class passengers will hand their boarding passes to the attendant at Gate A, economy class passengers to the attendant at Gate B."

Just to make sure, they had waited a few more minutes, and then followed the last of the passengers moving through Gate B.

Now, as she looked at Carl, the huge plane banked slightly. Reflected moonlight shot off the plane's starboard wing into his sleeping face. He frowned and muttered something. Quickly and noiselessly she lowered the window shade. Then she looked back at his gaunt face, still dimly visible in the glow of the cabin's night lights. Tenderness for him flooded her heart. She thought of what it must have been like for him, growing up with the knowledge that his father was a mass murderer, and then striving to keep his wife and daughter from that knowledge, and now trying to make what restitution he could for Wilhelm Dietrich's crime.

But she must not, for her own protection, let her feelings run away with her. It might be that, after the pain of his divorce, Carl had steeled himself against love so thoroughly that he was no longer capable of it. Think of something else, she told herself.

She looked at the back of the seat ahead, an empty one, and thought of Mike Russo. It was foolish of her, she knew, to hope that he would live much longer. Just be grateful, as she knew he was grateful, that they had found each other, even if only for a little while.

The plane would be landing soon. She turned in the seat so that she faced the window, put her cheek against the backrest, and willed herself to go to sleep.

22

The small bus with its racked skis and ski poles on the roof, and its load of skiers—Italian, American, German, English, Japanese—inside, moved up the narrow Alpine road through the late afternoon light. By leaning close to the window Katherine could see lofty white peaks, some wreathed with clouds. But there was no snow at all on this tortuous road, and very little on the pine-forested mountainside sloping steeply upward on the right and, on the left, falling steeply away to a dark thread of river. Around her and Carl the other passengers were complaining about the lack of snow. "Not just here," an American-accented voice said, "but everywhere—Innsbruck, Vermont, Squaw Valley—"

Another American voice said, "So what? They're expecting snow tomorrow. And besides, San Simone has snow machines."

"Snow tomorrow?" the first voice said. "I'll believe it when I see it. And snow machines somehow just aren't the same."

For Katherine the colorfully clad skiers were another of the myriad impressions that had swarmed in on her since that morning. First the Milan airport, with its loudspeakers blaring information in several languages. Then the twenty-four-mile trip by bus and taxi to the Milan railroad station, where Katherine, seeing men in embroidered Turkish caps, women in black chadors, and whole swarthy-skinned families surrounded by paper bundles and crates of squawking chickens, realized that Milan was indeed the gateway to the Middle East. They had taken the train to Bolzano, with Katherine, suddenly overcome by fatigue, sleeping most of the way. And now this last stage of their journey.

The bus turned a curve. Ahead, in a fold in the mountainside, lay a village that Katherine recognized from photographs as San Simone, one of the newer ski resorts in the Italian Alps. As the bus moved across a paved square to stop before a building with the words, "Autobus Terminal" written in Italian, German, and English across its façade, she saw that every structure on the square had been built in the centuries-old Alpine style, with steeply pitched roofs, windows framed in red or green or blue shutters, and wooden balconies which, in warm weather, no doubt held hanging pots of bright flowers. But only the church at the opposite side of the square looked authentically ancient. With its onion-shaped steeple, it was also a reminder that in previous centuries these mountains had been under the sway of the Austro-Hungarian Empire.

Carl was taking their hand luggage down from the rack. As they filed past the driver Carl asked, "Which is the San Simone Inn?"

"That four-story building across the square, two doors from the church."

As they moved along the sidewalk that ran around each side of the square, the gas street lamps bloomed in the deepening dusk, and the bell in the onion-shaped steeple began to ring for vespers. The sidewalk was thronged with young men and women, most of them in ski clothes. Their voices, speaking in half-a-dozen different languages, mingled with the ringing church bells. Katherine was aware of shop windows displaying hand-knit sweaters, *après ski* jumpsuits, Angelo handbags, and a Russian lynx coat.

The hotel combined rustic simplicity with modern comfort. A wooden-railed second-floor balcony ran along three sides of the room. Boars' heads projected from the walls. Interior shutters, brightly painted with flower designs, were folded back from the front windows. But beside the registration desk were the grilled doors, covered with gold leaf, of an elevator, and through an archway at one side of the lobby she could see white-clothed tables, each with a bouquet of fresh flowers.

Carl said to the blond young man behind the desk, "I made reservations for Katherine Derwith and Carl Dietrich."

"Oh, yes. You phoned from Milan this morning." The clerk spoke English with that indefinable accent of a European who speaks several languages. "Your rooms are on the top floor, across the hall from each other. I am sorry that it was not possible to give you adjoining rooms."

Carl's voice was curt. "I did not ask for adjoining rooms."

Discreetly the clerk made no reply to that. Instead he turned the register around for their signatures, asked for their passports, and then struck the small bell on his desk. The porter, a hefty blond woman who looked fully capable of carrying the suitcases they did not have, rode up in the elevator with them, unlocked the door of a fourth floor room, and swung it back. "For you, signora." She handed Katherine a key and then unlocked the door of the room opposite.

When the woman had gone, Carl asked from his doorway, "Dinner in about forty-five minutes?"

"All right."

"I'll knock on your door."

The bathroom, with its glass-enclosed tub, heated towel rack, and bath towels about as large as a single-sized bedspread, was downright sybaritic. She showered, went back into the bedroom, and put on the green velour jumpsuit she had folded into her canvas tote bag, feeling that it would be neither too plain nor too dressy for dinner in a ski resort. She pulled the jumpsuit's zipper up to a few inches below its collar. Then she crossed the room, illuminated only by its bedside lamp, and looked out the window.

Below her the square, bathed in the glow of gaslight, was like a stage setting. The door of a bar or café across the street opened, and five or six laughing people came out. Before the door closed behind them Katherine heard a snatch of "Santa Lucia," played on an accordion. The old Italian folk song made the square seem even more like a set for some light opera. Beyond the little village she could see a snow-covered run, illuminated with a double row of torches for after-dark skiing. A night wind, fragrant with the scent of pines, cold with the breath of icy peaks, sent the torch flames streaming now this way, now that.

Longing tightened her throat. How wonderful it would be if they had come here, not for the reason they had come, but for some quite different reason.

She pushed the thought aside. Crossing to the dressing table, she turned on the strip of fluorescent light above the mirror and applied lipstick and eyeliner. She was brushing her hair when Carl knocked on the door.

In the dining room they found that the menu, like the local architecture, was more German than Italian. But it proved to be both good and plentiful, as befitted meals for hungry skiers. While they were finishing their wiener-schnitzel, Carl said, "Before dinner I went to the car rental place here. The proprietor said that a few miles outside of town there is a road running to the northwest, but it's so little used and narrow and rough that we'd better rent a four-wheel drive."

"Did he know anything about that rock formation, or an old railroad line?"

"No. He's from Milan. He's worked here only a few months. All he knows is that people don't drive that road. At least he doesn't know of anyone who has since he's been here."

"Why don't people drive it?"

Carl shrugged. "Maybe because the road's so bad it would tear an ordinary car to pieces. Or maybe because, as he said, there's nothing in that direction to interest people. If you want to go to another ski resort, or make some of the famous rock climbs, or photograph the most dramatic scenery, you take the much better road that runs to the southeast."

They had a chocolate torte for dessert. By that time they could hear accordion music from the other dining room—a smaller and more informal room, Katherine judged from the glimpse she had caught of it—on the opposite side of the lobby. Carl asked, "Would you like to have coffee and perhaps brandy or something over there?"

Glad not to have to return to her room and her own thoughts, Katherine nodded.

The smaller dining room had booths with bare tables, more bare tables in the center of the floor, and a stone fireplace that held blazing logs almost five feet long. Two middle-aged men in sweaters and lederhosen sat on stools before the fireplace, one with an accordion, the other with a zither lying across his bare knees. Most of the tables near the fire were full, and every few minutes a new group of people came into the room.

Carl and Katherine sat in a booth and drank coffee. After that, because the waitress reported that the bar at the far end of the room was temporarily out of brandy, they drank wine. It was thin red Italian wine and not very good. But the atmosphere was festive, and the polkas and love songs the two musicians played spirited and languorous by turn. Katherine heard laughter and singing. She saw, all over the room, eyes meeting, and hands and lips. She felt an aching envy of other visitors to this fairy-tale village, people who had come to San Simone with lovers, or would acquire them here, while she and Carl sat like polite strangers, exchanging a remark now and then, but most of the time not even looking at each other.

The accordion and the zither began "The Third Man Theme," music that spoke of lost love, and mystery, and sadness. Katherine felt a stinging sensation behind her eyes and realized, with horror, that in another moment she would be crying. She said, "Could we go now? I feel very tired."

They stopped by the desk to get their keys and then rode to the fourth floor. He unlocked her door, reached inside to turn on the overhead light, handed her the key. "Good night," she said, and walked into the room.

"Wait."

She turned to find him standing in the doorway. "Yes?"

"Why did you want to leave all of a sudden?"

She could still hear, very faintly, the accordion and zither music. She started to repeat that she felt tired and then, with a flare of bitter rebellion, decided not to. "What do you care about why I wanted to leave?" she asked. "What do you care about anything I feel?"

"You think I don't?" He took a step into the room. "Don't you know that ever since the day I met you I've wondered what you thought, what you felt?"

"Felt about—what?"

"About me. Wilhelm Dietrich's son. Colonel Wilhelm Dietrich, whose killings weren't always in the line of duty."

"Oh, Carl!"

It was all she said, but evidently it was enough to make him understand, because he moved toward her and put his arms around her. For several seconds they stood in a silent embrace. Then he took her face between his hands and kissed her lips, her closed eyes. Again his arms embraced her, and her arms went around his neck, one hand cupping the back of his head to press his mouth even closer against her own.

After a while he reached back and touched the light switch. Now the room was illuminated only by the dim glow of the bedside lamp she had left burning. The fingers of his right hand grasped the metal tag of her jumpsuit zipper, pulled downward. As he pushed the lightweight green velour from her shoulders he said, "God! All evening! You'll never know how much, all evening, I've wanted to pull down that zipper." He kissed her bare shoulders, then lifted her and carried her across the room.

Much later, as she lay in bed with her cheek against his bare chest, she said, "I guess this was also a reason that I wanted to come to Italy with you. Did you know that?"

They'd turned out the lamp by then. Moonlight flooded through the windows, moonlight as bright as that which had fallen, the night before, on the sea of clouds beneath the plane.

"No. I only know now that a hope of holding you like this must have been one of the reasons I let you come with me."

For a moment she thought he was going to mention the other reason they were here. He did not, and she was glad. Tomorrow would be time enough to talk of that. For now she did not want to think of that Stone Maiden waiting for them up there somewhere among the wilderness of wild crags and deep valleys to the north and west. Above all, she did not want to think of what had happened up there more than thirty-five years ago.

She lifted her head to kiss his lips. His arms went around her, holding her tight against him.

23

When she awoke in the morning, Carl was gone. He'd left a note though, written on the hotel's stationery and propped against the bedside lamp's base: "Could you be able to leave the hotel by eight? Anyway, I'll come to your room then."

It was already seven-thirty by the little traveling clock she had placed on the bedside stand. She phoned down to the desk to have orange juice and coffee and croissants brought to her room, and then swung out of bed. As she crossed to the bathroom she saw through the open window that the morning was gray, with more than a hint of long-absent snow in the air.

By the time she finished her quick shower her breakfast had arrived. Feeling unusually hungry as well as giddily, almost young-girlishly happy, she ate the last crumb of the croissants and drained the last drop of coffee out of the pot into her cup. Then, swiftly, she began to dress in the clothes she'd worn when she left New York—heavy brown turtleneck sweater topped by a brown wool blazer, wool skirt of brown and white plaid, heavy ribbed pantyhose, knee-high fleece-lined boots. She added to that a knitted white wool cap and then a garment she had bought shortly before she met Carl at the Biltmore for the taxi ride to Kennedy. It was a poncho of white mohair, styled like those worn by Andean sheep-herders, long enough in front and back to reach to her knees, and on the sides to reach her wrists. Those layers of clothing, plus white knitted wool mittens, ought to keep her warm enough.

Carl knocked on the door and then, at her bidding, came in. For a moment they just looked at each other. On his lips was the same sort of smile, almost foolishly happy, that she knew must be on her own. Then he took her in his arms and kissed her.

"All set?" She nodded. "I've parked the four-wheeler out front. Before we leave, though, I want to talk to the man at the desk."

The desk clerk on duty now was a short man, sallow-skinned and impeccably dressed, of late middle age. Carl asked, "What can you tell me of the country about—oh, about thirty miles northwest of here?"

"Northwest, sir? Very little. When I was a small boy I went on a hunting trip there with an uncle, but I've not been there since."

"Didn't there used to be a rail line—"

"Yes, I believe so. One of the spurs off the line running north from Verona. But it ceased operation for lack of business long ago, sometime between the two world wars." The man paused and then asked, "Do you mind my asking, sir, why you are interested?"

"Because we plan to drive in that direction today. The man at the car rental place said that there was a road running northwest off the highway that passes San Simone."

The desk clerk looked horrified. "But such a road, sir! No one goes that way except an occasional hunter, and so the government doesn't bother to keep it up. Climbers and skiers and photographers find the country southeast of here much more to their liking. In fact, I gather that the road would never have been laid out except for some iron pyrite mines in those mountains. But they were exhausted long, long ago, shortly after the turn of the century, I'd say."

"We'll be all right," Carl said.

"I hope so, sir. It wouldn't do to get lost or have a motor breakdown back in a wilderness like that, especially not today. There is going to be snow, you know. They are not predicting a heavy fall, but still—" He broke off, looking past them toward the lobby's front windows. "In fact, it's snowing now."

"We'll be all right," Carl repeated.

He and Katherine went out to the car, an unlovely tan vehicle slung so high that Carl had to boost her onto the front seat. As he started the car, Katherine said, "Pessimistic type, that clerk."

"You can't blame people up here for feeling like that. Tourists must be always breaking their legs or even their necks scrambling around on rock faces, or skiing slopes too difficult for them. And then the local patrols have to go out and find them and carry them in."

Through the light snowfall they drove across the square and past the bus station, and then turned onto the road in the direction opposite to the one from which the bus had brought them the previous evening. They passed the ski slopes she had seen from the hotel window the night before. A line of brightly clad men and women stood at the foot of the ski lift, waiting to ride upward in the dangling chairs. Other skiers moved down the mountainside, some cautiously, checking their descent with their ski poles every few yards, others swooping with swallowlike grace from side to side. This morning, seated beside Carl, she looked at them without envy. She wouldn't have changed places with any of those girls over there, no matter how lovely or young or rich.

He said, "The man at the car rental place told me that the road we want branches off to the left, about three miles beyond the village." A few moments later he said, "That must be it, up ahead."

They turned off onto a road that was like a narrow tunnel through the pines. The road's surface—gravelly, potholed, fissured— as yet showed only a light dusting of the snow that filtered down through the dark green branches. They hit a jarring pothole. "Sorry," Carl said, and then added, "But it won't be any worse than uncomfortable. This car's slung high enough that we could drive over a small boulder, and the four-wheel drive ought to take us through anything short of quicksand."

The snowfall was heavier now, sifting down through the trees to cover the road more thickly, so that fissures and potholes became a spine-jarring surprise. Twice Carl had to get out to move large fallen branches from across the road. In spots undergrowth had encroached, so that branches scraped along the car's metal and snatched at Katherine's white poncho.

Soon the snow was falling so heavily that Carl turned on the headlights. For Katherine the journey was taking on a dreamlike quality. The dark pines arching over them. The steady sound of the engine. The way the headlights' beams gave the illusion that the snow, instead of falling straight down, was being sprayed toward them by invisible twin nozzles. The snow under the wheels, an ever-thickening carpet, now cushioned most of the road's irregularities.

And then she heard it, or at least thought she did—the hum of another engine. She put her hand on his arm. When his face swung toward her she said, "I think I hear another car."

In the few seconds that their eyes held she was sure she could read his thoughts. On this almost never-used road, especially in weather like this, there could be only one person following them—Gorman, or someone acting upon his instructions. And yet, remaining in the departure lounge at Kennedy until all the other passengers had gone into the boarding tunnel, they had seen no one who could have followed them onto the plane. They had not seen Gorman at the Milan airport or the railroad station or in the train to Bolzano. And on the bus from Bolzano to San Simone, filled with chattering young people in casual but expensive clothes, there almost certainly had been no one who could have been an emissary of Gorman's.

Carl stopped the car, turned off the ignition. For a few seconds Katherine thought she could hear, through the "pings" of their own cooling motor, through the sough of wind through the pines, the sound of a following car. Then she could no longer detect it.

"Hear anything?" Carl asked.

"Not now. But for a moment there—"

"Sound is tricky in high mountains, what with all the echoes. Snow distorts sound too. Maybe all you heard was the wind." His voice quickened. "Or maybe it was that. Listen!"

From somewhere—she would have found it impossible to say just where—came a droning sound. As she listened, it faded to nothingness. Then the drone came again, only to fade.

"A plane up there somewhere," Carl said. "Now you hear it, now you don't. Hope his instruments are okay, flying in weather like this." He paused. "Is that what you heard before?"

"I'm not sure. It didn't sound exactly— But then, I suppose it must have been."

He nodded. They drove on through that unreal world of headlamps tunneling between the walls of pine, and snow that seemed to fly straight at them along the twin paths of yellowish light. She lost all track of time. Had they been driving two hours? More?

Carl looked at the mileage meter. "We ought to see it soon."

"See what?"

"The old railroad embankment. According to the notes on that map, this road should turn soon and parallel the embankment for about half a mile. After that the road just peters out."

Katherine did not have to ask what map he meant. She knew it was the one he had memorized and then destroyed, the one that for no telling how many years had been rolled up inside a lipstick on Inga Dietrich's dressing table.

Up ahead the road curved. They followed it. Abruptly, there was no longer a wall of thick-trunked pines on their right. Instead, the trees were younger and smaller. "There!" he said. Looking through the young trees, she saw that the snow-covered earth sloped upward to a kind of terrace. He drove on for a hundred yards or so, until the headlights showed them only a tangle of rocks and undergrowth ahead.

He stopped, switched off the lights and the ignition. His voice was tense. "Think you can walk about a mile through the snow? Or would you rather wait here for me?"

She was silent for a moment, feeling both excitement and fear. She knew that part of the fear came from the strangeness of their surroundings—the steady, silent fall of snow, and the sounds the wind made, not just a sough through the pines, but a more distant keening through high crags and peaks they could not see. Too, she felt a lingering uneasiness over that other sound, one that she might or might not have heard, and, if she did hear it, might or might not have been a small plane flying through the gray smother.

"I'll come with you," she said.

They got out and climbed up the embankment through the young trees. At the top Katherine stumbled over something, and would have fallen if he hadn't caught her arm. He scraped snow aside with the edge of his boot sole, revealing rusted metal. "So the old tracks are still here. That means the ties are too."

But the snow was so thick underfoot now that they could not feel the ties as, heads bent against the falling snow, they moved down the ancient railroad bed. Soon that dreamlike sense of isolation again descended upon her. She and the man beside her seemed to move in a little pocket of visibility scooped out of the falling snow, a pocket that moved along with them. She could never see more than three feet ahead through the gray-white curtain, and she knew that if she turned she would be able to see no farther than that behind her. The only sounds were the squeak of their footsteps and the keen of wind through high peaks hidden from them by the undulating curtains of snow.

Perhaps thirty yards behind then, Gorman was glad that Dietrich had the girl with him. That meant the long-legged bastard had to shorten his stride, which in turn meant that Gorman could fit his own booted feet into the tracks the tall man left. And it would be important that, when Dietrich and the girl returned this way, they would see no sign that they had been followed. He didn't want to have to kill them too soon, certainly not where searchers, finding their bodies, also might have their attention drawn to the site of that old mine. Instead he wanted to wait until they had returned to their car. By the time their bodies were discovered, he would at least be back in Milan, and more likely back in New York. And the search party would have no way of guessing the reason for their deaths.

Head bent against the stinging snow, gaze fixed on his booted feet, he smiled. It had been easy, easier than he expected. He had been sure that Dietrich, if he had learned of the freight car's location, would go to northern Italy within the next few days. Gorman had decided not to run the risk of sending someone who, like Shorty, might turn out to be a blunderer. And so he himself had gone to Kennedy each evening. Seated near the Alitalia desk, and shielding his face with a newspaper, he had kept an eye out for Dietrich until it was time for the Milan plane's departure.

On the fourth night his vigil had paid off. He'd seen Dietrich and the girl hurry up to the ticket clerk, hurry off toward the departure lounge with their economy-class ticket envelopes in their hands. He'd laid his paper aside, picked up the flight bag he'd carried with him to the airport each evening, and approached the desk. "A ticket to Milan, please."

"On *tonight's* plane?"

"Yes." As the clerk stared at him with mingled incredulity and annoyance, Gorman added, "A first class ticket, please."

"Very well, sir." A note of deference in the clerk's voice. "I'll try. But the plane leaves in a very few minutes. The other passengers must be aboard by now. Any luggage?"

Gorman held up his flight bag.

The clerk's fingers flew, punching a computer, filling out a ticket for Phillip Heligman—the name on the passport in Gorman's breast pocket—ripping off carbons, stuffing the ticket in an envelope, swiftly counting the bank notes Gorman handed him. "Have a good flight, Mr. Heligman. And hurry."

Gorman strolled down the ramp to the departure lounge. He still had five minutes. As he had anticipated, the lounge was now empty of passengers. He showed his ticket to a startled attendant and then walked through the first class tunnel onto the plane. The pretty dark-haired stewardess looked not only surprised but pleased to see him. A moment later he saw why. Business was bad. There were only two other first class passengers, a white-haired man and his white-haired, sable-clad wife.

Safe behind the heavy curtains that shielded first-class passengers from the gaze of the hoi polloi, he slept most of the way across the Atlantic. In the morning, after the plane had taxied to its assigned spot at the Milan airport, and after the white-haired couple had begun to move toward the exit, Gorman picked up his flight bag from the seat beside him. He started to get up and then, with a gasp, sank back onto the seat.

"Mr. Heligman!" Pretty face anxious, the stewardess bent over him. "Are you all right?"

"Can't—get my breath—"

"Just sit there! I'll get the airport doctor, just as soon as I've—"

She hurried away. He heard her saying goodbye in a carefully calm voice to his fellow first class passengers. After that he heard her speaking in low, hurried tones to someone else. Then she was back beside him. One of the other stewardesses will notify the doctor. I'll wait with you until he comes."

Gorman protested in a feeble-sounding voice, but she remained in the seat across the aisle, an encouraging smile on her face, until the doctor entered the plane. Then she accepted Gorman's murmured thanks and left. The doctor, a thin, dark-haired young man who spoke English with only a trace of an accent, asked a few questions, and then listened through his stethoscope. "Your heartbeats are regular, Mr. Heligman, but quite fast."

No wonder, Gorman thought. He was scared. Scared that they wouldn't let him stay on this plane until after Carl Dietrich and the girl had cleared immigration and left the airport.

"Fatigue or excitement may have caused your dizzy spell," the doctor went on. "Or perhaps, as you Americans say, we wined and dined you too well last night."

Gorman said, in that feeble-sounding voice, "Maybe so."

"I'll leave you now. But if I were you I would just rest here until the men come aboard to service the plane. That shouldn't be for some time."

It was more than half an hour before the cleaning crew came aboard. Gorman walked off the plane and through a series of corridors to the immigration desk. He presented his passport, one of the many lost and stolen passports which a friend of the Brazilian supplied, for varying sums, to an exclusive clientele. He gave "pleasure" as his reason for visiting Milan and then moved out to the area beyond the immigration desk. Through the big front windows he could see that only empty buses stood out on the tarmac, awaiting the next load of arriving passengers. That almost certainly meant that Dietrich and the girl were already aboard a Milan-bound bus.

He looked around him. As he had expected, over there was a counter with a sign on it that said, in several languages, "Car Rentals." He strolled over. Just to make sure that Dietrich and the girl had taken a bus or taxi into Milan, he asked, "Did you just rent a car to a tall man, about thirty-five? He has a red-haired young woman with him."

The clerk, a dark, fortyish man with hornrims, said morosely, "I did not. I've rented only one car so far today, and that was to a couple of women."

"Business that bad, eh? Well, I'll make it a little better. Do you rent cars with four-wheel drives?"

"Why, yes. Some people prefer them if they plan to drive in the high mountains." His surprised tone seemed to say that Gorman had not struck him as the mountaineering type. He picked up the phone. "I'll have one brought around."

While he waited for the car Gorman filled out the necessary forms, bought a road map from the car rental clerk, and then moved to a rack which displayed resort folders and bus and railroad timetables. The road map told him that he could drive to San Simone—that village whose name a drunken Wilhelm Dietrich had let slip long, long ago in a Berlin café—by driving from Milan to Bolzano and then north to the skiing resort. The railroad timetable told him that Dietrich and the girl could travel by train from Milan to Bolzano, and then by connecting bus to San Simone. Of course, there was a chance that they would rent a car in Milan, but Gorman felt almost certain that they would choose public transportation, the much cheaper form of travel, to get them as far as San Simone.

In Milan Gorman went to a gun shop where, his Brazilian friend had assured him, the proprietor for a steep price would overlook his lack of a gun permit. Gorman bought a thirty-eight revolver and the ammunition for it. After that, in a sporting-goods store, he bought a fleece-lined duffel coat, heavy brown wool trousers, wool stockings, hiking boots, and a canvas carryall to hold his purchases. Then he drove toward Bolzano. He knew that by now Dietrich and the girl were probably two or three hours ahead of him, but that was the way he wanted it.

In Bolzano he phoned ahead to the Hotel Alpine, after consulting the San Simone folder to make sure that the Alpine was the more expensive of the resort's two hostelries. He made a reservation and then drove on. It was well after dark when he reached San Simone and left his car in the public car park beside the bus station. His hotel, the parking attendant told him, was on the left-hand side of the square. Walking fast through the sidewalk crowd of young people, praying that he wouldn't have the bad luck to run into those two, he went to the hotel. Its lobby was a model of casual elegance —highly polished teakwood floor with oriental rugs scattered over it, and sofas and armchairs of dark brown leather.

At the desk he said, "My name is Heligman. I have a reservation."

"Oh, yes, sir." The clerk spun the register around.

Pen poised above the page, Gorman asked, "Did a Mr. Dietrich and a Miss Derwith register here this afternoon?"

"No, sir, but they might be at the San Simone Inn across the square."

So his luck was holding. He signed the register and then asked, "Do you have a room overlooking the square?"

"Several, sir. Most of our guests prefer a view of the mountains."

Gorman surrendered his passport and followed a bellboy to his room. Afraid to push his luck any farther he had dinner sent up. At nine he phoned the desk and asked to be awakened at six-thirty. Then he went to bed.

Already dressed in Alpine garb, he was sitting at his window the next morning when a tan four-wheel drive car stopped in front of the hotel across the street. A tall man got out and went into the hotel. Instantly Gorman stood up, picked up his already packed hand luggage, and left the room. At the desk downstairs he paid his bill and retrieved his passport. Walking very fast, and with his head bent against the first snowflakes spiraling downward, he went to the car park, paid his bill, and got into his rented car. He was sitting there, hunched low behind the wheel, when Dietrich and the girl drove past onto the highway and turned north. He waited about a minute and then followed.

Despite considerable traffic—private cars, a truck carrying two crated and bawling calves, a tourist bus probably headed for Innsbruck—he had little trouble keeping them in sight. After they turned onto that narrow road, little more than two tracks through the pines, his problem was of course different. Now, driving without headlights, he had to keep far enough back that they would gain no inkling that he followed. As the snow fell more thickly, he drove a little faster, afraid that if he stayed too far back he might find their tracks covered. In that case, following whatever map they carried with them or in their heads, they might turn off into some even more obscure track through the trees without his knowing it.

Once, through the sough of wind, he caught the sound of their engine. Instantly he stopped his own car. If he could hear them, then they could hear him. Seconds later the sound of their engine ceased. For a while there was only the sigh of wind. Then he heard the drone of a small plane that some damn fool was flying. With the trickiness he remembered from the months spent in these mountains during the war, the droning ceased, sounded again, faded to silence. Then, hearing that car start up somewhere in the gray-white smother ahead, he smiled. Even if they had heard his engine, they must have decided that the sound came from that plane. He waited a few seconds, and then moved ahead.

Driving without lights, he almost, but not quite, ran off the track when it swerved to the left. Heart leaping, he saw the steep, thinly treed slope on his right. A railroad embankment. Perhaps the goal was close now. He switched off the engine. The sound of the other car continued for perhaps two minutes. Then it too ceased. He waited. Their engine did not start up. They must have left their car to go the rest of the way on foot.

Very quietly he opened the glove compartment, took out the revolver, dropped it in the pocket of his duffel coat. He got out of his car, leaving the door open lest some tricky wind current carry the sound of its closing to their ears. He moved forward slowly, very slowly, following the car tracks. When the car's dim shape loomed up through the falling snow, he halted, retreated a step or two. No sound. Again he moved forward. With a leap of triumph, he saw that their boot prints ascended the embankment.

He knelt, unscrewed the valve on their right front tire. When they returned they would start to inflate the tire with the hand pump which, along with other emergency equipment, rental agencies in mountainous regions always placed in the trunks of cars. But they would never finish pumping up the tire, because by that time he would have followed them back here, with the gun in his pocket.

He stood up and climbed the embankment.

Now, as he fitted his steps to the tall man's boot prints, he thought, for God's sake, how much farther? It seemed to him that he had been slogging for hours through eerily swirling snow and through cold that made his chest ache. He regretted them now, all those heavy meals the Brazilian liked to ridicule. Even though the old roadbed's upward slope was gradual, he found each step a greater effort. He kept doggedly on, though, now and then hearing their voices, but keeping well back, lest one of them, looking over a shoulder, see a dim shape through the snow.

24

It was Katherine who saw it first. The snow curtain had thinned by then. Perhaps a wind current, tearing it, had made it even thinner. Anyway, she glimpsed the banks of a defile ahead and, on the right bank, a gigantic, looming shape. "Look!" She clutched Carl's arm. Then: "Oh, I can't see it now."

"See what?"

"I think it was the Stone Maiden."

They hurried forward, almost running. Then they halted, seeing her clearly. A rock column rising almost straight up for perhaps fifty feet. Then, above that, a bulge suggestive of a bosom and a thinner column for a neck, topped by a rough round head.

Katherine continued to look up. So she was real, that Stone Maiden who in a way had always been a part of Katherine's life, even though Katherine had never heard of her until a few days ago.

"Come on," Carl said. Beyond the defile, the roadbed began a fairly sharp descent. They had gone only a few yards when Carl caught her arm.

To their left, along the mountainside, stretched a shelf perhaps twenty feet wide. Even though underbrush as well as snow covered it, the straightness of its outer edge showed that it was a man-made terrace, carved out of the mountain. They turned and hurried along it, with the underbrush tearing at their clothes.

They halted. The shelf ended in a pile of rock perhaps eighteen feet high, with the edges and planes of individual boulders visible through their snow covering. Bushes and even a young fir tree, its trunk slanting out over the terrace, grew from between the rocks.

Carl thought, feeling numb, so there it is, the place where my father buried a great fortune, and six living men.

Beside him Katherine was silent too, looking at the pile of rock which marked what had once been a mine opening.

Crouched close to a tree trunk on the slope above what had been the spur's roadbed, Gorman too looked at that pile of jumbled rock, then at the snow-blurred shapes of the motionless man and woman, then back at the rocks.

When he'd followed their footsteps onto the shelf he'd recognized it as the roadbed of an old spur, and knew that the goal must be very close. He should stay well back, he realized, hidden behind a tree or bush on the slope above the shelf, until after they had begun their return trip to their car. But once he was on the slope he could not resist moving forward slowly, silently, until he could see it, that blocked mine opening which, for more than half his life, had obsessed him. It stood only yards away now beyond that tumbled earth and rock barrier, a freight car holding enough wealth to satisfy a half-dozen men.

Heart pounding, he pictured himself following those two back to their car with its deflated tire. After he had killed them he would drive straight back to Milan in his own rented car and take the first plane back to New York. With the Brazilian he would work out the details—when he would return here, which of the Brazilian's associates would be both competent and trustworthy enough to help him blast an opening through that tumbled rock, and how, afterward, he could most profitably dispose of the gold and gems. He would not bother with the paintings and statuary. Let someone else stumble across them sometime after he himself was on the other side of the Atlantic. Art works were too hard to turn into money. For the first time in his life feeling a superiority over the dead man, Gorman thought, Wilhelm was a fool to give pictures and statues room in that freight car.

Were those two going to stand there forever, staring at that pile of rocks? His crouched legs, after that long, laborious hike through the snow, were beginning to feel cramped. He shifted his position.

A clatter, like that of a machine gun, in the pine tree beside him.

Instants later, as the winged creature shot with a high pitched scream out across the terrace and disappeared into the snow, he realized what it must have been—a species of buzzard prevalent year round in these mountains. But by then the damage had been done. Startled, he'd allowed one booted foot to slip. It had struck a bush and set the ice-covered twigs to rattling.

Those two had turned to stare up at him.

What should he do? Shoot them as they stood there, immobile with surprise? That would be easy enough, but what about afterward? He had no shovel to dig graves in the winter-hard earth beneath the snow. True, he could shove their bodies over the edge of the terrace, but the steep slope below was so heavily wooded that they would not fall far. And when the San Simone car rental agent had a search party sent out, as he inevitably would, the bodies must not be found near the mine.

Only one thing to do. March them back to their rented car and, as he had first planned, kill them there.

He got to his feet. His hand went into the pocket of his duffel coat and fastened around the gun. Then, careful not to let his feet slide out from under him, he went the rest of the way down the slope.

They had watched him, still motionless and silent. But now Carl Dietrich said, "Hello, Gorman."

Gorman took the revolver from his pocket. "Back to your car, both of you." He motioned to his right with the gun. "Walk ahead of me. Move."

"Come on, Katherine." Dietrich took her arm. Gorman saw that her face was stiff with shock, her skin almost as white as her knitted cap, and her eyes enormous.

"Move," Gorman said again.

They turned, walked back toward the defile. He followed, careful to stay about five feet behind them, close enough to see them clearly, but not so close that he would not have time to fire if Dietrich whirled around and grabbed for the gun.

Suddenly he saw Dietrich's arm shoot out and knock the girl sideways onto the snow. Shouting, "Run, Katherine, run!" Dietrich crouched low, whirled. Gorman fired as the younger man dove at his knees.

Dazed, and with the wind knocked out of her, Katherine lay there for a moment, aware of snow burning her cheek. Then she managed to get to her feet. After a moment she found that she could make out the figures of the two men. They stood locked in a struggle which had carried them three or four yards away from her.

She saw tiny spurts of flame through the swirling snow, heard three shots.

Then, between herself and the struggling men, she saw a patch of darkness on the snow. Even though in this dim light it looked more brown than red, she knew it was blood.

Carl's blood. He must have been hit by that first shot, the one Gorman fired as Carl dove at him. Maybe even as he fought he was bleeding to death—

Involuntarily, she screamed.

Two more shots. Then one of those dimly seen men dropped to the snow. The other bent briefly, straightened, and moved toward her. While her heart hammered in her throat he took shape through the snow, a bulky man of medium height, gun in the hand that hung at his side.

Carl was dead. Otherwise that monstrous creature would not be coming after her. Despairingly, she turned and ran.

Seconds later, she saw that she had run the wrong way. Ahead of her was the rocky barrier to the mine.

She whirled around, pressed her back against a boulder's sharp edge. He was still coming toward her. Why, she wondered numbly, did he move so slowly? Because he was exhausted? Or because she was an unarmed woman, and he was a man with a gun in his hand, and knew he had all the time in the world?

He was only a couple of yards away now. She wondered why he did not fire. Was it because he could not make out her shape clearly as, in the white poncho, she shrank back against the snow-covered rocks? Or was it because—

Her mind emptied of everything except an incredulous thanksgiving. Another figure, tall in the gray-whiteness, moved toward the stocky man.

At the last instant Gorman must have heard something, or sensed something, because he whirled around, grappled with the oncoming man. For several seconds, unable to move, she heard their panting breaths, saw their booted feet, as they struggled, carry them toward the shelf's edge.

And then she could not see them at all.

After a paralyzed moment or two she walked shakily to the edge of the terrace. There was a wide swath in the snow which covered the steep, almost vertical slope. After a few yards the path made by their rolling bodies was no longer visible, but she could see, through the falling snow, the darkness of pines.

Carl down there someplace, already dead, or bleeding to death.

On legs that felt wooden she began a stumbling descent of that swath in the snow. Then she halted, breath stopped, stomach contracting. A dark figure, half crouched, climbed toward her through the spiraling snowflakes. She stood rooted, unable now even to scream.

"It's all right," he called. "It's all right."

Carl's voice. Relief made her so weak for a moment that she feared she would fall. Then she found she could move toward him. "Oh, darling! How badly are you hurt?"

"Katherine, I'm all *right*."

"But you're not!" They were climbing the steep slope now. "There's blood on your sleeve."

"A bullet grazed my shoulder when I turned and tackled him. It bled some, but it feels as if it's stopped now."

"He shot you only once? I thought I heard—"

"You did, but those shots went wild. He had the gun, but I had my finger over his on the trigger, and I kept it there until he was out of bullets."

They had reached the terrace now. Katherine faced him. "But I saw you go down!"

"I slipped, that's all. Before I could get up he bent over and slugged me with the gun butt."

"I thought you were—"

"Maybe I would have been, if he'd had much strength left. But he hadn't. A man that age, and out of condition. It's a wonder he was able to do as much as he did."

"What—what's happened to him?"

"He's dead. A deep gash in the back of his skull. His head must have hit a sharp rock as we were rolling down the slope."

She shuddered, thinking of how it could just as well have been Carl's head. Then she said, "It can't be the way we planned, can it? Now we can't notify the authorities anonymously about the mine. We'll have to tell them how Gorman died. I mean, people knew we were coming up here today, so when they find his body, even if we haven't told them—"

"I know."

"Unless you explain the whole thing, they may think you—you murdered him."

"That's right."

"And even if you don't tell them about the mine, they'll notice it once they start looking around up here. And if they investigate, they'll guess that what's inside has some connection with you."

"No."

"What do you mean, no?"

"They won't have to guess. I'll tell them."

"Everything?"

"Everything. Who placed the car in the mine, and what he did—later."

She said, her heart aching for him, "Oh, Carl. The one thing you didn't want was for Ellen to know that her grandfather—"

"That can't be helped now. Better she know that I told the truth about my father, rather than made the police drag it out of me."

After a long moment she said, "Carl, I have a feeling that despite her—earlier difficulties, Ellen has become stronger than you realize. I don't think this will crush her."

"I think you're right." He added, smiling, "After all, if she feels that kids descended from the men who went after Kunta Kinte shouldn't blame themselves for it—"

"What on earth are you talking about?"

"Something she said the last time I saw her. I'll tell you about it later."

Her gaze went past him through the thinning snow curtain to the Stone Maiden. What hour of the day, and what sort of day, had it been when the seventeen-year-old who was to become her father had looked across a narrow valley and seen that gigantic figure, sculptured by millions of years of wind and snow and rain? And where had he been standing that day, that monstrous man, father of an infant son—

She thrust the speculations aside. No point in thinking about the sad and violent and unalterable past. What mattered was that out of that past had come the man beside her, and herself, and a chance to mold whatever sort of future they wished.

He touched her arm. "Let's start back."

Heads bent against the still-falling snow, they walked along the terrace toward the defile.